AF591186

MISSING

MISSING

By

James McEwan

Published 1 June 2019
Revised July 2020
Alibrasphere

Copyright © James McEwan 2019

James McEwan has asserted his right in accordance with the Copyright, Design and Patents Act 1988 to be identified as the author of this work.

All rights reserved. No part of this publication may be reproduced or transmitted in any form by any means, electronically or mechanically, including photocopying, recording or any information storage or retrieval system, without either prior permission in writing from the author or by licence permitting restricted copying. In United Kingdom such licences are issued by the Copyright Licensing Agency, 90 Tottenham Court Road, London W1P 0LP

All characters and locations in this book are fictitious and any resemblance to actual persons, living or dead, and places is purely coincidental.

British Library Catalogue–in–Publication Data.
A CIP catalogue record for this book is available from the British Library.

Paperback ISBN 13: 978-1-913202-00-2

eBook ISBN-13: 978-1-913202-20-0

Books by James McEwan

The Listener Anthology of Short Stories
ISBN 978-1-508938-97-2

The Case of the Mahjong Dragon
Russell Holmes Stories
ISBN 978-1-515133-25-4

Short Stories and Flash Fiction blog
at

jplmcewan.wordpress.com

Contents

§

Between my finger and my thumb,
The squat pen rests; snug as a gun.

From, *Digging* by Seamus Heaney

Chapter One

Laura checked her map; she was definitely at the right place.

'Yes,' she said, and a euphoric wave of satisfaction washed through her. 'Yes!'

The intermittent rain showers had eased to a drizzle, and she squinted through the haze. Nettles grew along the ditches and up against the tall hawthorn hedges that bordered Springwater Lane. It appeared as a long tunnel shrouded in a veil of mist. She punched the air. It was not far to go and less than a fifteen-minute walk to Russet House; her birth place.

Spot beams, diffused by the rain, swept like searchlights from further down the road, and they flickered and flashed as the vehicle turned through the zigzag of bends.

Laura switched off her torch and closed the map case. She slipped them into her trouser pocket where their dampness was cold against her thigh. With a pull on the straps, she adjusted the rucksack on her back and strode up the lane away from the junction. Far enough to avoid being seen from the road and the possibility of being offered a lift.

§

Scott was tired and tearful. His daily vigil with Mary in the hospital had worn away his energy, leaving him deflated and drained of hope. A good night's sleep in his own bed was what he craved and when Dr Jamal gave his wife a strong sedative, he grasped the opportunity to go home.

The journey was slow in the evening traffic. He kept yawning, so he turned the car blower to cold and put the radio on loud to force himself to stay awake and concentrate on his driving. At last, he steered his car into the lane towards his house.

The headlights lit up a figure standing off centre; he swerved. There was a clunk, and something slid along the near side of his vehicle. He braked to a stop, switched on his four-way indicators; rushed out of the car and stepped into a rut in the grassed verge. His shoes filled with water. He dashed around the car, slipped on the mud, and landed on his back. He took a moment to catch his breath while the drizzle washed over his face. He could just lie there, but it was wet and miserable.

Water soaked through his woollen suit, and the cold prompted him to move. He rolled onto his knees and looked up. He struggled among the vegetation and crawled onto the solid surface and got to his feet. Lit by the rhythmic on-off orange glow of the car's lights, he rubbed at the nettle stings pulsating on his hands and wrists. He saw a stranger on the road, and the oval hood of a weatherproof jacket obscured the face. Water dripped from the draw cords.

'Are you okay?' said Scott. 'I hit you. Are you hurt?'

'Yes, I mean no,' she said. 'Your mirror hit my bag.'

Scott walked along the car to inspect the damage. The mirror was intact, and in the semi-darkness he could not see if there were any scratch marks along the vehicle's body.

'Are you sure you're okay?' Scott called as the woman walked away. 'Hang on a minute.' He ran over to her and grabbed her shoulder.

She turned and whacked off his hand.

'What do you want?' she shouted.

'Sorry.' He stepped back and lifted his arms in a gesture of surrender. Hell, the nettle stings irritated him. 'Do you need a lift?'

She retrieved a rolled-up sleeping mat from the middle of the lane and re-attached it to her rucksack. She lifted it onto her back and pulled the straps tight.

'I'm okay, honest.' She pushed past him.

'It's two miles to the farm and in this rain—'

'I'm going to the B and B.' She interrupted and walked on, adjusting her hood further down over her face. 'I can walk,' she shouted.

He returned to his car and drove alongside with the passenger window lowered.

'Come on, get in,' he called out to her. 'It's pouring.'

She ignored him, increased her pace, and splashed through a rut on the verge.

'Look, I'm trying to help you,' he said. 'It's about a mile further on.'

She hesitated and stopped walking. 'I know.'

'I own the B and B. Come on, get in.'

A gust of wind whipped rain against her face.

'Okay.' She opened the car rear door, threw in her backpack, and got into the front passenger's seat.

'Where have you come from?' He shivered as the dampness in his jacket penetrated through into his shirt.

'I'm on holiday.' She lowered her hood, water splashed onto her knees. She kept a hand on the door handle and ignored the seat belt.

'It isn't far. Look at the rain,' he said and pulled a cloth from the door pocket. 'The farm is much further, and the lane becomes a muddy track after the house.'

He wiped away the condensation from the inside of the windscreen and switched the wipers to a higher speed.

'Name's Scott, like I said I own the B and B.' He turned on the heater blowers. 'I wasn't expecting anyone tonight.'

'The Wheatsheaf had double booked.'

'You walked from the village?'

She stared at him. 'It's not a problem, is it?'

He shook his head and saw her glare; he shuddered.

'No, it's not a problem.' He returned to wiping the condensation from the windscreen. 'I have three rooms. They are all available.' The humidity in the car increased as warm moisture rose from his trousers.

'Will you be staying long?'

'Not sure.'

'So, what brings you to Kirkindale?'

'How much is the room?' She undid the top zip on her Gor-Tex jacket. 'Can I pay with my debit card?'

'Yes, I take most cards or cash if you like.'

He steered off the lane into a driveway where the gravel crunched under the car's wheels. On the approach to the house the security lights switched on, illuminating a blanket of red ivy that clung to the walls and with rogue branches dangling over the porch.

He pointed to the porcelain sign by the door.

'Orchard View,' he said and turned off the engine. There was a moment of silence and no one moved.

'Rain has stopped,' he stated, then sneezed.

'Thank you for the lift,' she said, and got out. She retrieved her rucksack from the back seat and carried it to the front door. She pressed the bell button. A series of chimes echoed inside the hallway.

Scott took two full plastic bags out from the boot of the car, then locked it. He walked up to the house door and inserted a key.

'No one's home,' he said, and pushed it open. His shoes squelched on the parquet floor as he walked to the kitchen. He looked back towards her; she seemed hesitant to enter the hallway. 'Well, don't just stand there, come in.'

In the kitchen, he put the bags on the table, took off his wet jacket and hung it on the back of a chair, removed his shoes and soaked socks, then returned to the hall.

'How long will you be staying?'

'Just a few days, not long.' She lowered her rucksack onto the floor.

Scott closed the main door and locked it. The chain rattled as he slotted it into place. He then shut the inner door to the porch and bolted it top and bottom. He turned and glanced at the woman who stared down at him. He stepped back off the icy floor onto the doormat.

Perhaps it was the thick soles of her walking boots that made her appear taller than his five feet eight in his bare feet. He stepped forward and grabbed hold of her rucksack.

'This way.' He went up the stairs. 'It's en-suite, and with some magnificent views across the valley.'

She followed him into the room and undid her jacket and waterproof trousers. She slipped them off and took them to the bathroom, where she shook off the water and then hung them over the shower rail.

Scott waited and watched as she raked her fingers through her light-brown hair. It was nice to have company. How many lonely nights have it been? She appeared to be about twenty or even a late teenager, slim, strong, and athletic. A two-inch scar beneath her right eye disrupted the fresh complexion of her face, and a glance from her grey-green eyes prompted a flash of recognition. Who? Did he know her? He shivered momentarily followed by a burst of rapid sneezing.

'You need to be careful,' she said and nodded. 'The flu could kill you.'

'Yes, well. There is a buzzer next to the kitchen door if you need anything.' He sneezed and placed her rucksack by the only chair in the room. 'My wife is in hospital, so I'll be leaving early tomorrow. Please, can you help yourself to some breakfast?' He sneezed and left the room before she answered, and on his way down the stairs he avoided standing on the patches of mud. Hell! Mary would have made guests take their boots off in the hall. He wasn't thinking.

Back in the kitchen, he opened his Think-Pad and checked his files. Yes, he had printed the information sheet—Closed; not accepting bookings until further notice. Tomorrow, he would call the Black Swan and remind them not to send their overflow guests to him, although he had done so already when Mary had collapsed, and the ambulance rushed her to hospital.

The woman mentioned she had booked into the Wheatsheaf Inn. How strange, it has been closed for years. Why did she get it wrong? But how could he possibly have turned this girl away on such a wild, wet evening? She was pretty.

He switched to his accounts page to add a name. Tomorrow he would get her name and address with payment details. He yawned, and a shiver rippled down his back. He craved a hot shower and then sleep. Yes, sleep at last.

§

When Scott left the room, Laura locked the door and jammed the chair against the handle. She sat on the bed, removed her walking boots and pulled off her woollen socks. She rubbed her feet, checking for dry and chapped skin. A blister had burst on her left toe and stained her sock with blood.

That afternoon, she had walked ten miles following country paths, avoiding people where she could and thankful of the occasional bursts of rain that had deterred casual walkers. During a heavy down-pour she had jogged into a barn by the corner of a woodland track and watched as a rider on a horse galloped across the field. An elderly woman dismounted and came into the barn, leading her stallion.

‘Don’t blame you, such awful weather,’ the woman had said. ‘Not a brilliant day for walking or riding. Going far?’

‘To Russet House.’ It was the first time she had mentioned her plans to anyone and had regretted being so forward and impulsive as gossip in small communities can be omniscient. However, this woman may be a useful source of information. Regardless, if she wanted to keep her intentions private, she should say nothing.

‘I haven’t heard that name for a while, Russet House.’ The woman had led the stallion to a feeder at the back of the barn and tied the reins to a post. The horse immediately had chewed on some hay. ‘It’s a Bed and Breakfast nowadays, but she couldn’t remember what they called it, Orchard something or another.’

Laura had asked her to confirm the location on the map.

The woman had pointed to the house shown along Springwater Lane. ‘Yes, that’s the place, a popular stop off for the Dale walkers. Well, so I am told.’

The woman spoke about the house belonging to Springfield Farm when they grew a variety of apples, the Russets. She sat down on a straw bale and had mentioned how they couldn’t get apple pickers anymore, since it was too much like hard work for some people. Her tone had become sombre as she lamented on about Old Charlie, who farms beef cattle and lives alone. His wife had passed away in a terrible tragedy. She laughed when she had remarked that the old misery-guts lives like a hermit.

She had asked the woman if she knew the new owners of Russet House. Immediately, she regretted her impulsive curiosity and of being drawn into the woman's confidence.

The woman replied that she was not sure, but thought it was Mary Dawson, Old Charlie's daughter.

Laura had gasped at the mention of the name and then coughed to clear her throat; she had to wipe her nose with a tissue.

The black clouds had drifted down the valley taking the rain away, and the sky had brightened. The woman had got up and grabbed the horse's reins and led it out of the barn. She mounted and had trotted the horse off down the track towards Kirkindale. In what seemed like an afterthought, she had turned in her saddle and gave a slight wave. Impulsively, Laura had waved back.

Laura stood up from the bed and stretched her arms and legs to ease the numbness from her shoulders and calf muscles. Out of the rucksack, she hauled her sleeping bag and shook it open before draping it over the chair to air.

After a hot shower, she dressed in her grey towelling tracksuit which smelled of soiled socks, but it was dry and comfortable. Tomorrow, she planned to organise a laundry day to freshen up her clothes since they reeked of the musty odours of the woods.

She switched off the light and gazed out through the bedroom window. The rain had stopped, and stars dotted the sky. Down in the valley, she could see the dim flicker of streetlamps from the village. The fields were in darkness and she strained to see if there was an orchard on the right. She couldn't make out any trees, perhaps she had just imagined them on the drive to the house. On the left, chestnut trees dominated the garden, those she recognised from her dreams. Once a swing hung from a branch, would it still be there? Probably not.

The garden had been her favourite place in the warm afternoons, chasing a dog around the lawn. She remembered a dog. Was it her mum's? Someone used to push her on the swing. Sometimes it was her mum and at other times it was a girl.

How long ago was it? Almost fifteen years, but the place and time were blurs in her mind, a hazy jumble of confused memories. She was three years old when she had listened to the strangers talking in the kitchen. Her mother was missing, and someone had placed her into care. She had hidden her teddy, because if they couldn't find it then they couldn't send her away, not without Numpty. She was wrong.

She had screamed and cried as a policewoman coerced her off the swing. She had run away shouting for Numpty and screaming for her mum. Where was she? Mum! Something she had not understood was going on.

The policewoman caught her, and someone took her away to live with Aunt Gertrude, who she had never met before. Was she really family? Why? No one had explained why.

As she reached and closed the curtains, a loose floorboard squeaked beneath her right foot. It made her jump. Yes! The squeaking and rattling; as a child she would be in bed and listen to the noises from the house. It came alive in the dark when everyone was asleep.

She scrambled the carpet back from the wall and fetched her Bowie knife to ease out the only nail on the short plank. In the space between the joists she reached in and felt around, searching for a furry bundle. She bit on her top lip in concentration. Where had she hidden Numpty?

She had been sitting on the swing, humming "Round and Round the Garden", feeling smug that no one would find her teddy. A policewoman had torn her stockings on one leg from her ankle to her knee and had reached for Laura's hand. She had not wanted to leave the swing, and she had screamed.

She replaced the floorboard, rolled back the carpet, and sat with her back against the wall. For a moment, she tried to force a recollection of her time in Russet House. There was a gloomy place where no one had looked, then screaming, running and being caught.

Round and round the garden,
where's my teddy bear?
One step, two steps.
You'll never find it there.

Her empty belly moaned and prompted her to fill the kettle and make a hot a drink.

She got into bed and pulled the duvet around her shoulders and over her legs. Echoes of grumbling reverberated from her stomach as the warm chocolate settled. It was a reminder of her meal of porridge cooked on a gas stove as the dawn had crept up the valley over the woodland and hills. What she would love now was some hot beef broth or else roast chicken with mash and broccoli. However, her hunger pangs would have to wait until the morning as going down to the kitchen might entail an inevitable series of questions.

She opened her diary and took out three envelopes. The first contained a copy of her birth certificate.

Her parents;

Mother–Irene Sarah Dawson, nee Stewart. Housewife.
Father–William David Dawson. Farmer.
Address; Russet House, Springwater Lane, Kirkindale.

She leaned back on her pillows and closed her eyes. She imagined Mum's face with her gentle smiles and the way she pushed back her hair when she laughed. Mum would read bedtime stories in a soft lyrical voice that sent her to sleep.

She was sure this room was her bedroom as a child, but it didn't have a toilet then. However, her mish-mash memories of blank faces and shadows would not materialise as recognisable people. Perhaps her neurotic curiosity was constructing a past that did not exist.

When they met would she recognise her mum? Most likely not, but she would. How could she not know her own mother? She had no recollection of her father. What did he look like?

This was home at last, and her eyes watered, and tears dripped onto her diary. All she ever wanted was to discover the truth about her mother. Russet House should have been her childhood base, the fields, the woods, the farm, the village, and friends. Did she have any brothers or sisters?

In the second envelope was a reply from Mrs Wilcox, the librarian in Kirkindale, who wrote about going to school and growing up with her mother. In her letter, she also mentioned that she remembered Laura as a child and was looking forward to seeing her. This was evidence of her past and of someone who knew her mother.

The third envelope contained a card with a typed warning.

STAY AWAY
YOU DO NOT BELONG HERE
YOUR MOTHER IS DEAD

She put her diary and envelopes onto the side table and fetched a bottle of lavender flower essence from her rucksack. She sprinkled a few drops over the pillow. The aroma made her feel calm and the sweet smell eased her anxiety and thoughts of what she might discover. She snuggled beneath the duvet. The comfort was enchanting, warm, dry and so peaceful. In the background, the rustling from the branches of the chestnut trees was rhythmic, soothing, and familiar.

For days she had the company of the creaking from old oak trees and the squawking of night creatures with the wind flapping her tent while camping in the woods. She had become accustomed to the nightly orchestra of nature. Once, a fox sniffed around her shelter and left behind a rancid odour, a smell now embedded in her sensory memory.

Finding her parents was essential for her peace of mind, an important part of who she was, and a vital thread to her identity. It did not matter if she discovered some painful truths, but she wanted answers. Why was she taken into care? Her foster mother claimed legislation restricted her from enquiring into Laura's past. This reluctance to help was frustrating and difficult for her to accept. Her adolescent years swung between depression and periods of determined euphoria, thinking about her mother and father. Could she not accept the situation and get on with her own life?

Walking the Dales alone and feeling free from perceived civilisation, in a self -imposed isolation, she was searching for a spiritual connection that may help her decide. It was a time to be alone with nature and contemplate her future, to make her own decision, and now she had; to find out the history of her parents and learn the truth.

She took deep breaths to induce a state of hypnotic relaxation. It always helped her towards sleep and subdued her fears.

Frequently a haunting image would appear in her dreams and scream: "*You skinny snivelling little bitch*".

Chapter Two

Laura sat alone when she travelled on the school bus. She stared out of the window. Her birth surname was Dawson and out there; somewhere, someone knows what has happened to her parents, but where and who? Could she accept and understand why she was a foster child? Would she ever discover the truth? Until she knew these answers; no matter how illogical it seemed, how could she shake off her self-loathing and lack of self-worth unless she understood her identity? Without a past, she remained a nobody.

Mrs Fletcher, her teacher, had announced their class project was a study of their personal history. They should draw a family tree showing their relatives and create a record book with pictures and details of their lives. They would learn the relevance of their family background and the origins of their present identity. They were to compare how the past events influenced changes and the decisions their family made at unique points of their lives.

Laura bit on her tongue and in the class-break went into the toilets and cried.

When she told Jenny, her foster sister, about the project, she had held her hand and told her not to worry; she was a McLean now. Besides, it was only a learning exercise. She would help; Laura could copy her relatives, maybe just change the names, no one needs to know. She could borrow photographs and places, or pretend they were sisters and create an elaborate family tree.

That was not the point. She was a foster child, not an orphan, not a refugee, not someone whose family ended in tragedy, not even adopted. Her parents abandoned her. There was no family history to tell; she existed out of thin air, but that could not be true. Yes, she would tell people that her parents were dead. The result of a tragic accident, and they would feel sorry for her. She did not understand what had happened to them, and Mrs McLean never answered her questions. What was the secret no one would tell her?

Mrs Gertrude McLean, her foster mother, had explained how her biological family were too poor to take care of her. She found that hard to believe as there were many underprivileged children at the school whose parents were badly off. Were her parents destitute or maybe homeless tramps? She didn't care. She had begged Mrs McLean to tell her the truth. All discussions about the past were dusted away with gentle answers, such as they live too far away, and kind remarks that they were lovely people who couldn't cope and had passed away peacefully.

'One day you might meet them.' Mrs McLean had said when she wanted to stop Laura's persistent and probing questions. What did she mean, "one day"? So they weren't dead.

She would imagine running down the street and throwing herself into her mother's arms or being swept up into the air by her father. They would hug her, laughing and crying with joy, and tell her how much they missed their baby. That day was still to come.

She had hazy memories of a house and frequent nightmares of a woman who chased her along a narrow track where nettles stung her hands and face. She would jolt awake, kick off the bedclothes and rub at her face. She remembered a swing in an enormous garden and a teddy bear, Numpty. Were these just silly dreams, or an exaggerated recollection of her childhood before she came to stay with Mrs McLean?

For the school project, and with approval from Mrs Fletcher, she became Jenny McLean's fourteen-year-old sister. She now had actual people to research: uncles, aunts, and great grandfathers. Many of them had been in the army in WW2, one was a bus driver and there was an aunt who lived in New Zealand. She had a variety of pictures of the McLean families to use for her project scrap book.

At night, she laid in bed and speculated about her own lost family. Would her father have been a soldier who died somewhere, did her mother die of a broken heart when he had not returned home?

On the day of the class presentations a boy, David Manse, from the back of the class called out.

'You're a fake, a liar, and a scabby mongrel bastard,' he shouted and laughed.

How could he dare? She had burst into tears in front of everyone, and the class giggled with muted embarrassment. Her temper roared and in a fit of sheer indignation she attacked David with a chair. In the affray, she sent desks and books spiralling around the classroom resulting in the boy's nose gushing blood and Mrs Fletcher's shin being bruised.

The next day, Mrs McLean sat with her as the headmaster, behind his oak desk, lambasted on about understanding self-restraint. He spoke about how she must conduct herself within the rules of acceptable behaviour in school. Also, he had consulted various teachers about her demeanour in their classes. Together, they had decided that she would benefit from a few sessions with the visiting psychiatric nurse. He looked over the top of his glasses when he told her how he was sympathetic of her family situation and that in time her feelings would heal.

She was not clear what demeanour they had discussed.

The headmaster suggested that her mother; he nodded towards Mrs McLean, should also come and speak with the nurse.

He did not understand the situation as he kept calling her Jennifer. As an incentive, he decided she may wish to improve her attitude, otherwise he would remove her from the school cultural trip to Berlin.

She bunched her fists as she left the headmaster's office and had David Manse been in the corridor, she may have thumped him again. Her angry agony and shame of being a nobody pierced like hot needles through her heart.

Regardless of the outburst, she received the highest marks for her project folder and Mrs McLean and Jenny were proud. Some consolation as she still felt a fraud, a person with no history. A mongrel. A nobody.

§

A few months later her passport arrived along with the return of her birth certificate, which she had never seen. Mr McLean had kept it locked away in his writing desk until he required it for the passport application.

Here was a piece of paper recording the birth of Laura Dawson. For the first time she learned the names of her mother and father, where they had lived, and where she had been born. Why didn't Mrs McLean tell her this before? Was she hiding something?

Laura took the birth certificate as a starting point to search for the family who had abandoned her. She would visit the National Archives to find her parents' record of marriage, death notices if any and search out all those relatives. She must have relatives, surely everyone has a family tree that goes back in time, there must be records. She would search boxes in people's attics to find their photograph collections and treasures of mementos, paper clippings from local newspapers, education certificates, baptism records and so much more.

She intended to discover the whereabouts of her parents. She would tell them she loved them and ask them why they gave her up. Would she forgive them? She would discover her history and her place in the family tree. There must be relatives, perhaps brothers and sisters.

She would create a book about the life of Laura Dawson for her sons and daughters and their generations to come. She would ensure everyone has an important place in her family history and know the origins of their identity. She would be someone that could hold her head up and say, 'Yes, I know who I am. I am somebody, and this is my identity.'

On the journeys home from school, she would stare through the bus window and she would think about her mother. Sometimes, a face would momentarily appear as a reflection in the glass. When this happened, she closed her eyes and wiped away the tears.

Once, she got up and pushed past the other pupils getting off the bus. Someone had whispered and called her a poor sad orphan. She walked home sobbing. The only person who could make her feel better was herself. If she was alone in the world, was that such a terrible thing? But the voice in her head kept asking, where are you Mum? Out there, somewhere, someone knows, but where and who?

Chapter Three

A clatter and loud music woke Laura. She pulled the duvet up under her chin, and she strained to listen for movements in the house. Someone turned the radio off, and moments later a car door slammed. The gravel in the driveway crunched as a vehicle drove away towards the lane.

Scott had said he was leaving early. Laura checked her watch on the side table. It was six-thirty in the morning, and it would not be daylight until after seven.

She felt comfortable in bed, and she could just lie there for the entire day, or at least for another hour. She stretched her legs to ease the stiffness from walking for days.

She sat up. What had happened during the night? She had a strange dreamlike experience. Someone persistently called her name, and she had looked out of the window. The dim light from a gibbous moon fluctuated in intensity through the sweeping veil of clouds, and she had watched a fox scavenge around the garden. It sniffed and scrapped among the flower beds. She had put her hand against the cold glass and whispered, 'Tell me, where is Mum?' At that moment, the animal turned and looked towards her, and they stared at each other. She shivered and crouched onto her knees by the window ledge. Her mother is close, is that what the eyes said, is she here? The fox crept away like a shadow, merging and fading through the hedge.

It was just a dream, like many others. Even when nodding off on the return bus from school she would often sense her mother watching her. She imagined finding her in the park, walking a Scottie terrier, or meeting a homeless beggar who knew where she was. By putting a few coins in the cups of street sleepers, it comforted her to think she was helping her mum, who was out there somewhere in a state of hopeless anxiety. She would imagine finding Mum among the homeless and would coerce her to come home and get better.

She got up and filled the kettle, then remembered she was free to make her own breakfast. Her woollen jumper was on the bed, she pulled it over her head and slipped her feet into her plimsolls.

The kitchen was a spacious modern extension to the old house; it had wide windows and a view over the garden. On the table was a scribbled note stood against an empty orange juice carton. She deciphered the writing as an apology for the lack of essentials, like fresh milk and bread. There were instructions for her to complete an information form in the dining room. She slipped the note into her pocket.

In the fridge, she found two eggs, and some milk past its use-by date, which she sniffed and decided was okay. There was a container of beans with a layer of blue mould. On the middle shelf were: stale cheese, butter, margarine, and a leftover meal of chicken curry. She opened the freezer and took out a packet of bacon and some sliced bread. Looking around in the cupboards she found: tins of beans, mixed herbs, salt and pepper and a container of unopened muesli. On a top shelf, there was a range of medications, and she lifted out a packet to read the label; Abstral Fentanyl tablets.

She enjoyed the pleasure of cooking in a kitchen instead of squatting by a camping stove with her back to the wind. Her stomach moaned in anticipation as the tang of frying bacon floated around her. She heated the beans and fried the eggs, over-easy. Together with buttered toast and dripping yolks, her meal stirred up the pleasures of the Sunday cooked breakfast Mrs McLean lavished on the family.

Behind the tea and coffee containers, she found a jar of marmalade and spread it thickly over the toast. This was a rare indulgence. Usually Mrs McLean only allowed her to have marmalade as a Sunday treat.

Through a side door was the utility room. Piles of plastic bags stuffed with nightdresses lay on top of a large dryer and two washing machines. She smiled at the opportunity of getting all her clothes cleaned and refreshed. Surely the owner wouldn't mind. If he doesn't return until late, like last night, he would not need to know.

Back in her room, she slipped the note from the kitchen into her diary. She undressed and wrapped herself in the large dressing gown from the en-suite bathroom. She raked through all her clothes from her rucksack, checked the pockets and shook off the leaves, twigs and woodland dirt, and then carried them to the laundry room. Later, she intended to air her ground sheet and tent in the garden if the weather stayed dry.

The dining room had a table and eight chairs. There was a sideboard with bottles of wine in a rack, and on a tray were napkins and a Ketchup bottle. The polished oak floor had a layer of dust and the Lincoln green curtains were tied back. An overhang of ivy partially blocked the view out of the window to the front driveway. She looked around the room and couldn't find the information forms.

The fireplace was set with decorative logs piled in the grate. On the mantelpiece were figurines of flamenco dancers, possibly souvenirs from holidays in Spain. Above hung a large landscape painting showing a panoramic view of the Kirkindale Valley. She admired the natural colours; the azure sky with shades of drifting clouds, the fine detail of the leaves and blossom of the apple trees, and in a distant field two dogs herded a flock of sheep. In the bottom corner of the canvas, she read the scrolled signature of the artist: I Stewart.

Her eyes watered with delight; her mother was an artist. Why did she ever think she would be a homeless beggar? The romantic idea of saving her mother from a life of destitution was a fairy tale. Her mother was an artist. The woman who read and sang to her with a soft voice, occasionally sweeping back her hair as it fell forward, was an artist. She sat down on a chair and forced herself to think. Did she draw and paint with her mother? The signature was, I Stewart. Does this mean she stopped painting once she married and had a child? Was it her fault her mother stopped painting?

She stared at the picture; in art class she had no patience, and the class scoffed at her attempts of drawing. She did not have her mother's talent to paint a scenic representation of the countryside in such fine detail. The woman, who painted this landscape, would never have abandoned a child, would she? Her soft sobbing interrupted the silence, and she looked around; loneliness had crept into the room and engulfed the moment. She reached for a napkin from the side table.

She got up from the chair and left the dining room. The only free access around the house was to the bedrooms upstairs, the kitchen and the dining room. There was a locked door off the hallway.

In the kitchen, she opened the French windows that led onto a flagstone patio, and she followed a path to the bottom of the garden where she gazed into the mist. If there had been orchards in the fields, as she had remembered as a child, the trees were gone and replaced by a wide expanse of grass. Further up the hill, she saw the outline shapes of farm buildings which were half-obscured by the semi-transparent blanket of fog. This haze crept over the ground and moved downwards into the valley. A gossamer spiral of smoke drifted skyward from the farmhouse. In the distance, she heard sporadic whistling and shouting from someone herding animals with a dog.

She followed the path beside the edge of the flower bed and distinctly smelled the spoor of a fox. Two large chestnut trees with their tops hidden in the low haze, dominated the other side of the garden. She noticed the knurling of the bark on a large overhanging branch where the swing had been attached. She placed her hands on a trunk; if the trees could talk, what would they say? Further back, a thicket of rhododendrons lined the curved access drive and concealed the house from the lane.

The snorting and grunting of cattle somewhere in the mist became louder; they were heading towards the garden. A lone bullock ran up the slope of the field and the others appeared behind as they walked through the mist. She stood by the trees and watched as the animals came up against the garden's fence.

'Away, get away,' a voice called.

A collie dog darted forward to coax and steer the cattle towards the farm.

A man, in a tweed coat and carrying a thick stick, followed on. When he saw her, he stopped and stood staring towards her.

'Hi there, Mary. You're at home,' he called. The echo of his voice reverberated along the walls of the house. He took off his flat cap and wiped his brow before walking up to the fence.

'How are you?' he said and leaned on a post. 'So, when did you get back?'

'I'm not Mary,' said Laura and walked towards him.

'No. You're not Mary! It can't be, no, no. Get away from me,' he shouted and put his cap back on. 'You can't be, no, no.' He turned, slipped in the wet grass, and fell.

'Oh, hell!' he said and got up. He hurried after the cattle heading towards the farm.

'Wait!' she shouted. Her gown flapped open as she ran to the bottom of the garden.

'Hello, please come back,' she called. Her gown hung loosely. She saw him stride away. 'Hello, hello, please come back,' she shouted. She pulled her dressing gown together and tied the belt tight around her waist. She watched the man fading into obscurity through the mist. She shivered. The humidity had formed droplets on her hair, and a claustrophobic loneliness tightened in her chest. The surrounding cloud of haze thickened and rushed in to engulf the house and garden.

The man had mistaken her initially for Mary, and then as someone else. Did he know her mother? Was he Old Charlie, the farmer that the woman in the barn had mentioned?

Back in the kitchen, she sipped black coffee and felt elated by the reaction of the farmer. He had recognised something about her, but did the sight of a woman dressed in a white robe under the trees shock or embarrass him?

She would visit the farm and find this man, but first she planned to walk to Kirkindale. Where she intended to meet Mrs Wilcox, the librarian who had replied positively to her letters.

Chapter Four

She found two keys in the utility room and one of them fitted the lock to the outside door leading into the garden. She took the other and tried it on the door off the hall into the private area of the house. It didn't fit.

In the garden, Laura shook out her backpacking tent, groundsheet and sleeping mat, then she hung them over the washing line. The fog had cleared, and the morning sun warmed the back of her neck.

Mrs Gertrude McLean, her foster mother who she had refused to call mum, would always encourage thoughtfulness and self-sufficiency. It was out of habit and feeling positively useful that she completed a few household chores while her laundry washed and dried. She vacuumed and dusted the dining room, washed the kitchen floor, cleaned out the fridge and disposed of all the stale food. She emptied the plastic bags of the nightdresses into the washing machine. The light underwear items in the bags, at least a month's worth; she washed by hand and hung them out in the garden in the fresh breeze.

She sat in the kitchen sipping black coffee while she studied her map on the table. It showed a footpath leading from the back of Russet House to the river. She preferred to call it Russet House and not the B and B name of Orchard View. The path led the way to the River Marrs and continued along its bank into the village. She checked the map scale and decided this was a shorter route than walking along the lane and major road into Kirkindale. After last night's weather, the river path might be muddy in places, although taking this path would avoid being offered a lift from inquisitive strangers on the road.

The warm sun and a light breeze dried the nightdresses, so she collected them in and left them folded in the kitchen. The tent and ground sheet needed longer to air, and she left them hanging out.

In her room, she packed her waterproofs into a small-pack, filled a bottle with water and put it into a side pouch. She slipped the letter from the librarian into her pocket.

She locked the French doors in the kitchen and left the house through the utility room door. At first, she considered hiding the key under a potted plant, but after a moment of hesitation placed it in her purse instead.

The entrance to the path from the garden was through a dilapidated wooden gate overgrown with brambles. The path to the river, between the unkempt hawthorn hedges, was blocked with rambling dog rose and nettles. Instead, she climbed over the fence into the field and jogged all the way to a stone wall by the river. As she clambered over a stile, a wooden step gave way and she fell onto her knees. She stood and followed the winding track through the yellow gorse into a gully where a grassed area sloped to the river's edge. She gave a small gasp and smiled.

The wide pool that spread out from the base of the waterfall reminded her of art classes and how she would giggle at the oil paintings by Vecchio. The lecherous art teacher would make everyone blush as he described the brush strokes and skin tones of the voluptuous bathing nymphs. She could just imagine swimming naked in this secluded place and perhaps singing along with the Goddess Aphrodite.

Sitting on the grass, she closed her eyes and turned her face towards the sun. The flowing gurgle of water seemed therapeutic for a moment until a loud plop and splash disturbed the ambience. She looked around. Concentric rings spread across the water's surface. Perhaps a fish had taken a fly. There were dragonflies hovering above the bull reeds and occasionally one would swoop low across the open water and back again.

A boulder stood further back in the open area. Had she been here before? Her mind raced–*Round and round the rugged rock the ragged rascal ran.* Yes! Mum used to chase her around the enormous boulder when they came here on picnics. She remembered they paddled in the water and threw skip stones. They had screamed as they swatted at wasps. She remembered digging in the watery sand, eating banana sandwiches, and playing hide and seek among the reeds.

She found a flat stone and sent it skimming across the water. Three skips and then it sunk. She tried again, and this time the stone managed five skips before it sank into the water. Determined to reach the other side of the pool, she tried once more. She sent the next stone flipping over the water and it bounced much higher and landed on the far bank. She laughed. A returned stone came splashing and skimming across the pool towards her. She glanced towards the far bank, searching for someone, but there was no further sound. She waited and watched for movement on the far side of the pool as ridges of water raced across the surface and dissipated on the soft sand by her feet.

'Hello!' she shouted. 'Hello!' Her voice echoed from the gorge above the falls. She stood and looked around, then squatted down and listened for any sign of who may have thrown the stone. Further down the river, a team of ducks splashed over the water and took flight. They came gliding towards her and turned away abruptly as they detected her presence and flapped furiously. They rose higher in the air and flew across the field.

Whoever had thrown the stone had gone off along the far side and through the woods. Perhaps her stone throwing had disturbed someone's peaceful solitude or a couple in their privacy. She smiled, this would be an ideal spot for the artist Vecchio to paint his nymphs cavorting beneath the waterfall.

From the pool a high fence blocked the way along the riverbank, and she had to retreat to the wall and climb over the broken stile. Further up the field she found an opening through the brambles and followed a zigzag path among the gorse back to the river. Tangled strands of sheep's wool hung on the barbs of the vegetation and a few rabbits rushed around as she approached, their white tails flashing a warning of her presence. She stumbled on along the tracks, brushing aside the nettles with a stick until the path opened out on a raised embankment by the river's edge.

She walked on. As she came closer to the village, the rough footpath became improved with shale and gravel. At one point she passed a man, a cap over his face, lying among the long grass beside his three fishing rods set on supports. He seemed oblivious of her approach and of a rod tip twitching, its line connected to a red float that bobbed and dashed frantically about in the water.

'Fish, fish!' she shouted.

She looked back over her shoulder as she strode away and saw the man reeling in the catch. She chuckled and carried on at a brisk pace.

Nearer to the village, cherry trees lined both sides of the path. There was a solitary wooden bench with a brass plaque. She stopped and spoke the words: 'May they rest in peace.'

The path and the river passed under a road bridge. The footway led up a series of steps onto a pavement separated from the water's edge by a wall with railings. From here on, sandstone embankments on both sides narrowed the river. It opened out at a weir where sluice gates channelled the water towards a rotted, disused water wheel.

On the opposite side of the river, a group of children were dropping small sticks into the water. They were shouting with encouragement at their floating racers as they watched them slip and fall over the dam. Nearby, a swan swam and circled as if waiting for an invitation to join the children for an opportune meal of breadcrumbs.

Further along, the pavement ended at a tall building, its walls dripped wet and green algae clung to the bricks. Clumps of rosebay willowherb and nettles grew from the decay around windowsills and from within the rusted guttering. A slippery stone staircase diverted the way up along the side of the dank structure onto the village road.

She checked her map for the location of the library building. It was on the main street opposite the Kirkindale Parish Church.

Chapter Five

Laura pushed open the inner door of the library and walked towards the information desk.

The teenage girl behind the counter looked at Laura, then turned away. Her long black hair bounced in the air as she rushed with a bundle of books to a trolley where she sorted them into different piles. She glanced back over her shoulder.

'I won't be a moment,' the girl called.

The smell of coconut shampoo from the girl's hair was like the cheap brand Laura had once bought in Boots. She was fourteen at the time and had a Saturday job on a market stall. She sold imitation jewellery and designer bling for Mrs Jacky. A lovely lady who liked the way she chatted and charmed the customers and as an extra reward would give her a bonus of free bangles or earrings.

'Sorry,' the girl said when she returned to the counter. 'I am busy, Mrs Wilcox doesn't like me standing idle and all that, or gossiping. I mean, can you see the crowds?'

'Is Mrs Wilcox here today?' said Laura. She pulled the letter from its envelope.

'Ah, yes, she's upstairs. You're that girl, aren't you? She's been talking about you all week.'

'Upstairs?' Laura said and headed towards the entrance hall.

A telephone rang.

The girl nodded. 'Yes, Area Librarian, it's on the door,' she said and hurried to the desk behind the counter. She fumbled with the telephone handset before she spoke.

The stairway led to a carpeted landing where a leather sofa stood against the balustrade. Nearby, a few magazines lay on an occasional table. Opposite, a door stood ajar and a woman in the office looked up from her reading. For a moment, she stared hard at Laura. She leapt up from her chair behind the desk and hurried out into the hallway.

'Yes,' she said and grabbed hold of Laura's hand. 'I'll admit I didn't know if it was true, but you have the Dawson look.' She led the way into her office. 'Please, come over here.'

'Mrs Wilcox,' said Laura. 'Are you Mrs Wilcox?'

The woman had a cheerful smile, a clear complexion, and she had gold-rimmed glasses attached to a long, braided cord draped over her shoulders. She wore a dull grey skirt and matching jacket with a light blue blouse. She had a floral silk scarf wrapped around her neck.

'Oh, sorry. Oh yes, dear.' She pointed to the chairs by the window. 'I've just made tea. Would you like some?'

'Please, just milk, no sugar.'

They sat with their backs to the daylight. Laura sipped her tea, it was a refreshing change from the black coffee she had earlier in the morning. Later, she would go shopping and milk was on her list.

She placed Mrs Wilcox's letter down on the table by her saucer.

'Thank you for writing. That was—'

'You have your father's eyes.' Mrs Wilcox stared at her as if examining every detail for recognition. 'You are as I imagined.'

Laura shifted in her seat and sat back. She looked out of the window.

'You wrote in your letter, you went to school with my mother.'

'I've always wondered where you were, but I knew one day, yes, one day.'

'Why? It was not until I wrote, and you replied.'

'Yes, Miss McLean, can I call you Laura,' said Mrs Wilcox, and she took a sip of tea. 'Why did you change your name?'

'Laura is fine, McLean is my foster family's name.' She smiled. 'Did you know my mother well?'

'Oh yes. We were all shocked when she ran away.'

Laura glanced up, expecting her to give an explanation, but Mrs Wilcox continued to stare back. Laura sat forward, and she sensed an emptiness in the woman's eyes.

Mrs Wilcox looked away, and she added more sugar to her cup. 'Well, that is not true. No one believes she ran away.' She stirred her tea, and the spoon rattled in the porcelain cup.

'Do you know where she is?'

'No, I wish I did. We thought Irene went off with the travellers.'

A memory flashed in Laura's mind; images of people in an orchard. She saw them laughing in the warm bright day as she sat on someone's knee and sucked an overripe sweet plum. She saw women filling baskets with apples and men loading them onto a trailer attached to a grey tractor. Its exhaust fumes made people cough, and they shouted for the driver to turn the engine off. The faces in the crowd misted over as if in a hazy dream.

Laura put down her teacup. 'Do you think she is still with the gypsies?'

'Who knows? The travellers were hard workers and an exciting bunch. No, they kept their own to their own.'

'What about my father?'

'Yes, Billy.' Mrs Wilcox reached and touched Laura's hand. 'He was handsome, a wonderful man.' She returned to stirring her tea. 'It's a pity you never met him, he was adorable.'

'Where is he?'

'I'm sorry Laura.' Mrs Wilcox glanced at the wall clock. 'Could you come back tomorrow?' She got up and went to her desk. She took a small bottle from her handbag and put two pills into her mouth. She flicked through a diary. 'I have a meeting. You understand, I was not expecting you today. Tomorrow, I'll get George to help you. He doesn't work afternoons.'

Laura finished her tea.

'You mentioned in your letter, you wanted to research your family history.'

'Yes, I said in the letter and—'

'I'll have more time tomorrow,' interrupted Mrs Wilcox. 'I have photographs to show you and we can look through them together.' She came back to the window. 'George will help you tomorrow. He is good with local history and the archives.'

'Thank you.'

'Sorry dear, but I need to go. Where are you staying?'

'Russet House at the B and B.'

'No!' shouted Mrs Wilcox. 'You can't stay there.' She grasped her face. She lowered her voice. 'Sorry, no you mustn't, if Charlie finds you, oh dear. It would be better if you came to stay with me at Oakwood Farm.'

'Charlie?'

'I have a room for you at the farm, you must come and stay.'

'What if Charlie finds me?' Laura stood.

'Your mother, Irene and Charlie didn't get along.'

'Surely,' said Laura, 'he will know something—'

'No!' she said, 'Come to Oakwood, I've already prepared your room.' She walked to the door. 'You will be safe with us. Best to stay away from Springfield Farm. No, no, or if you like there is the Black Swan. Their rooms are comfortable.'

'Or perhaps at the Wheatsheaf?' said Laura, and she picked up the letter and followed Mrs Wilcox out to the landing.

'The Wheatsheaf? No dear, that has been closed for years. Come and live with me. We can talk about Billy, your father.'

'And Mum.'

'Your mother. Yes, Irene. Now you've returned to Kirkindale, you must live with me at the farm.'

'I'm not sure about staying since I start Uni in September.'

'University! Oh, I never thought. Ah, yes in the holidays you will come back.'

'I expect I could.'

'Good. Well, I must get on,' she said. 'Tomorrow, George will get the records and newspaper articles you need.' She grabbed both of Laura's arms. 'I am so pleased you've come home.'

'Oh, there is also this.' Laura fumbled in her side pocket and pulled the warning note from its envelope.

Mrs Wilcox shook her head as she read the warning. 'No, no, it's not true!'

'Who would send—'

'Old Charlie. I told you it's best to stay away from Springfield Farm.' She returned the note to Laura. 'Tomorrow, we can speak more then.' She walked back into the office and slammed the door shut.

Laura made her way down the stairs and out of the library on to the street.

The Wheatsheaf Inn was marked on her map in Kirkindale, and she had originally planned to stay there until she found the location of Russet House. Scott at the B and B must have known it was closed. Did it matter?

§

In the supermarket, Laura packed the groceries into her bag: milk, bread, a complete chicken, potatoes, and broccoli. She was tempted to buy much more but restricted herself to some sliced ham, cheese, tea bags and a small apple pie.

She would return along the river path to the B and B, although she preferred to think of it as Russet House. Mrs Wilcox wanted her to leave the place and move to Oakwood Farm. She said she had a room ready. Mrs Wilcox never mentioned this in her letter, or she must have glanced over the suggestion. Did she miss the invitation to stay at Oakwood Farm?

When she arrived at Russet House, she experienced images of her childhood emerging as hazy memories. The chestnut trees reminded her of a swing and the garden of sunny days playing with daisy chains or eating ice cream as she sat on a rug. The wooden gate at the end of the overgrown track was important, but she was not sure why. The familiar groaning sounds from the house and the rustle of the branches from the trees were comforting and a reminder of singing lullabies when she laid in bed. In her mind she knew she had hidden her teddy somewhere around Russet House, but where? She would stay.

Along the walkway, a boy was sitting on the wooden bench. In the light breeze, cherry blossom fluttered from the trees and swirled on the ground around his feet.

'I saw you,' he said to her as she came towards him.

He was thin, perhaps malnourished, and his head seemed small for his body. His arms had outgrown his shabby school blazer, and he wore tatty, scuffed shoes.

'Was it you at the waterfall?' said Laura. She moved upwind from him, to avoid his unpleasant body odour.

'Why did you run away?' she said and stared at him.

'None of anyone's business. Anyhow, nobody be allowed there.'

'Yes, I see. Because it's dangerous.'

'It's not dangerous, that be daft.'

'So, why were you there?'

'I like it, and none of your business, and anyway it be the drowning place for witches.' He got up and walked away.

'Bye then,' she called after him.

He stopped and turned. 'If you be a witch, you be drowned and throttled like them all.' He ran off towards the weir.

Laura pulled the straps of her small-pack tight over her shoulders and set off at a determined pace. The thought of roast chicken for dinner prompted her stomach to rumble.

Mrs Wilcox had pictures to show her and suggested she reads the archives with George to discover her family background. She was looking forward to seeing the photographs and her search through the library records.

She was interested in reading through the newspaper archives to discover what happened in 1979. The year they sent her into care. Perhaps she might pick up a clue to her parents' whereabouts. They could not possibly disappear, someone must know where they are, or if they were dead. She didn't want to believe her mother was dead, but it was a niggling doubt that would upset her and make her cry.

She carried on her journey and jogged along the path by the river.

'Hoy, you! Do you want one?' The man called to her.

She saw him coming down the path. The angler had his tackle bag strapped over his shoulder and he waved his dismantled rods in the air to emphasise his presence. What now? He came closer.

She had not noticed the eye patch earlier when she saw him asleep in the grass.

'Look, a nice trout. A nice one for you.' He held up a fresh fish by its gills. 'Have it for tea.'

'It's okay, no thank you.'

'Here, you made my luck.' He smiled, displaying a mouthful of broken teeth. 'You woke me from my dandy dreaming.' He pushed the fish towards her. 'Take it and I won't tell.'

'Tell?' She could smell the tang of pipe tobacco smoke from his clothes.

'You be trespassing on Springfield land. He doesn't like that.'

'It's not gutted or cleaned.'

He put down his bag, pulled out a thin knife. He smiled as he saw her take a few steps back. He took the fish to the water's edge, slit the belly open and washed the entrails away. He held it up. 'It'll be nice with crispy onions.' He washed the knife in the water and dried it on his dark corduroy trousers.

'I am sure you—'

'Take it! Or I'll tell.' He lifted his eye patch to show an empty socket. 'Best not upset him at Springfield Farm.'

Chapter Six

Laura climbed over the fence into the garden of Russet House. She noticed her tent had blown away from the washing line and lay on a flower bed. She picked it up and shook off the dried leaves, and she threw it over the wash line. She double knotted one of its cords to stop it from falling off and then saw the long slash in the canvas down one side. The wind had blown the tent onto the fence and ripped on the barbed wire. She examined the tear. It was a clean cut done with a sharp blade. This was not accidental, it was deliberate. She turned the tent over and read, GO HOME; someone had sprayed the letters on in white paint.

Was whoever did this still here? She glanced around the garden and peered into the rhododendrons behind the chestnut trees. She checked the front of the house; the front door and garage were closed. There did not appear to be a break in.

She entered the house by the utility door and locked it. She shivered in the chilled interior of the kitchen, and the squeaking of her boots against the parquet echoed through from the hallway. She stood still for a moment. What if someone was already in the house? She waited behind the kitchen door until the silence confirmed there was no one moving in the house.

She searched in the kitchen and in the hallway for the heater thermostat and concluded it was in the private area. The boiler was in the kitchen and she undid the control flap and switched on the override; the gas burner fired up.

There was a radio on the window ledge, and she trawled for a station. Ah, those fun days cooking and baking with Mrs McLean and Jenny listening to Madonna on the radio. They would sing along at the top of their voices while stirring pancake mix or chopping vegetables for soup. However, this evening she was in the mood for some background music and settled on Radio Three with Tchaikovsky's highlights from the ballet, *Sleeping Beauty*.

It was lonely in the kitchen and she missed the company, but knew that at any moment, Scott might return. What would he say? It might look like she had moved in. Maybe she will.

She cooked the chicken for dinner and sat in the kitchen to eat her first substantial meal for a week. There was enough roast chicken left for Scott, and she wrapped the carcass in aluminium foil.

After her meal, she left the radio on in the kitchen while she moved around the house without switching on the lights. She looked out through the windows into the garden and the driveway. If someone was watching the house; were they hid among the thickets? There was nobody lurking in the garden or down the drive that she could see. It was getting dark, and the wind stirred the branches of the trees and bushes, and their movements formed shadows that danced around the lawn.

On the landing by her bedroom door, she noticed a hatch in the ceiling. The attic! She stood on a chair; pushed the cover to one side and climbed up into the loft. It was dark. She chuckled. She dropped back down to fetch her torch. Back in the attic, she switched on the torch and its light was weak. She added new batteries to her mental shopping list.

There was a wooden floor fitted over the joists. She saw a jumble of suitcases, cardboard boxes, piles of books, jigsaw puzzles and paintings stacked in a tea crate. How did that get through the hatch? She swung the torch light towards two wooden easels on a table and a box crammed full of paint tubes with palette boards rammed in. Under the table were leather-bound photographic albums stacked in piles. Next to them was a shoebox full of letters, and on its side was a picture of red slippers. She knelt and pushed it away and picked up an album.

A light flashed further along the attic through a skylight window in the roof. The driveway gravel crunched, and the sound of a vehicle prompted her to grab an album. She lowered herself out of the attic onto the chair and reached to close the hatch. The house front door opened and banged shut. She took the chair back into her bedroom and stuffed the dusty album into her rucksack.

In the bathroom mirror, she noticed cobwebs in her hair and dust over her trousers and shoes. She cleaned herself up. Would Scott come up to speak to her? It might be better if she went downstairs to talk to him and discuss her length of stay.

In the kitchen, Scott had switched the radio off and was eating a sandwich. He looked up as Laura appeared in the doorway. There was an excited voice coming from the speaker on his mobile telephone. He picked it up.

'Sorry Anne, got to go, speak later,' he said and switched the call off. He nodded towards Laura. 'Hello, please come in.' He smiled. He layered slices of chicken onto a bread slice. He pointed a kitchen knife towards her.

She took a step back.

'This is delicious,' he said through a mouthful of food. 'I'm famished.' He continued to cut slices from the chicken carcass and layer them onto the bread. 'I think you've earned a free night.'

'Do you mind if I make tea?'

'Please go ahead, but I don't think there is any—'

'I bought some.'

'Milk,' he said.

'I am thinking of staying until Saturday.'

'Four nights.' He waved a chicken leg in the air. 'I'll only charge for three.'

'How's Mary?' Laura dropped two tea bags into the pot and added boiled water.

'She is better,' he said and put his sandwich on a plate. He stared at her. 'Do you know my wife?'

She poured tea into the cups. 'Milk?' She fetched it from the fridge.

'How do you know Mary?'

'I don't.' She sat down and faced him across the table. 'This morning I was in the garden, someone called me Mary.'

'Someone?'

'A farmer was herding cows in the field.'

'Ah, Old Charlie,' he said and took a bite of food. 'His eyesight is not so good these days.' He sipped his tea and stared at her. 'Usually the walkers along the Dale Way only stop the one night.'

'I'm meeting a friend in the village,' she said. She walked around the kitchen.

'Where does your friend live?'

Damn. She noted the curious tone in his voice. She will need to be careful what she says from now on.

'Sorry, but I am exhausted.' She finished her tea.

He got up and fetched his ThinkPad. 'What's your name?'

'My name?'

'For the guest list, I have to keep records, name and address, please.'

'I thought the B and B was closed. Your wife—'

'Mary, she is Mary,' he shouted. Then in a lowered voice said, 'Sorry, I've had a hard day.'

'Someone slashed my tent this afternoon.' She sat at the table.

'Your tent?'

'I left it hanging in the garden to air and when I came back, someone had damaged it.'

'Sorry to hear that.' He poured himself another tea. He smiled. 'Maybe we'll forget the records. I am not really here to look after the place or make your breakfast and all that.' He closed the computer lid. 'Perhaps we could come to some other arrangement, Laura.' He grinned.

'No! I can pay,' she said and met his stare. 'You know my name already.'

'Yes, Miss Laura Dawson, or is it McLean?'

'I don't want any arrangements.'

'You haven't heard me yet.'

'What kind of arrangement?' She pushed her chair back and glanced at the door.

'I need to be back at the hospital tonight, as if being there every day isn't enough.'

She watched as his face relaxed, and he laughed.

'No, I see what you mean, no.' He pointed at the chicken. 'I would like you to look after the place for the next few days. You know get food in.'

'In exchange for the room.'

'It's only until Saturday.' He glanced at his fingernails. 'You said, just a few days.'

'Sounds like a deal.' She shook his hand and then cleared the plates and cups from the table. 'One thing though.'

'Yes.'

'The heating thermostat needs resetting.'

'I thought it was warm in here tonight. It's in the dining-room.' He picked up his jacket and computer. 'See you tomorrow evening then.'

Laura stood by the dining-room window and watched Scott get into his car. He sat and spoke on his mobile phone for a few minutes before he drove off.

Back in her room, she flipped through the album. It contained group pictures of people of various ages in front of a wooden barn. They were all smiling. In some photographs there were baskets full of apples and Shire horses shackled to carts in the background. The men wore flat caps and collarless shirts, and the women, with their hair tied back, wore long dark dresses. They were the apple pickers collecting the harvest, and from their clothes the period may have been the 1920s. There were pictures of dirty-faced children wearing oversized clothes, they stood beneath the apple trees. A family sat next to a smouldering fire in front of a caravan and appeared to be the gypsies who came to harvest the fruit.

Another photograph showed a group by the river; the women and children were sat on woollen rugs. There were wicker baskets and plated sandwiches and cakes. They wore light fabrics with flower patterns and all the girls were composed by size and they were smiling. A younger boy had his back to the camera.

Laura inspected the rear of all the photographs, looking for names and perhaps a date, or a sign of where these pictures were taken. If she could find out the details of these people, she might discover if they were her distant relatives.

A dog barked. Her bedroom light was the only one on in the house, so she kept away from the window. She should have closed the curtains earlier. She crept down the stairs. The dog barked outside the front door and someone shouted at the dog to come away.

In the dining room, she peered through the window and saw a man in the driveway. The security lights illuminated him before he walked out of range and the lights automatically switched off. He sauntered on towards the road. A cloud shifted and in the subdued moonlight she saw he carried a stick in the crook of his arm. Or was it a shotgun? For a moment, the dog trotted alongside him and then dashed away in front. Although she couldn't be certain she suspected this was the man, Old Charlie, who had been herding cattle in the field.

Impulsively, she rushed to the front door to call to him. Perhaps invite him in and ask him about her mother. Damn, there wasn't a key in the lock. Maybe it would not be such a good idea to go chasing after someone in the dark. What was he doing at this time of night snooping around? Was he after a fox?

Back up the stairs, she pulled the chair onto the landing and once more climbed into the attic. The light from her torch was useless for viewing photographs. Besides, the shadows caused by her flashlight among the pockets of darkness and the creaking of the house unsettled her.

She took four trips to bring the albums from the attic to the bedroom. She cleaned off the accumulated dust with a damp cloth and counted twelve folders. She pushed them under the bed. She also brought down a flat cardboard box and in a brief rummage saw it contained a wedding dress wrapped in white tissue paper. Perhaps it was her mother's? In the box, underneath the dress, were a few cuttings from a Gazette newspaper. She closed the box and slid it under the bed.

She checked the front door was still locked and then the French windows in the kitchen and the outer door of the utility room; they were all secure.

It had been an interesting day, and tomorrow she wanted an early start at the library. She took a shower, made a hot chocolate, and sat up in bed.

At last, she was among people who knew her mother. They will know why her mum ran away.

She flicked through her notebook and stopped at the page with the scored-out bucket list, one of many. One started with, "I will marry prince charming". In their bedroom, she and Jenny would fantasise and giggle over their plans of weddings as they sang along with Madonna's *Who's That Girl.*

Her prince charming was a boy at school, Johnny Blake. His family owned a transport business and were rich. She had asked Johnny for a dance at the school disco. He told her sorry, but spotty faced tramps were not his style. The prat!

It was when Madonna and Sean Penn broke up and so in a wild hysterical moment of emotional purging; she ripped all their posters from her bedroom wall. Jenny had been in hysterics, laughing.

She turned to a page in her notebook where she had listed her dreams and goals. She read these items every morning and evening to boost her focus and confidence. It was a routine the school psychologist had taught her, a method of meditation where she would visualise her goals and their outcome. She relaxed back in her bed and took slow, deep controlled breaths. This technique had helped her to deal with her anxieties and feelings of abandonment by her mother. Initially, she had been reluctant to try the exercises, and it took persistence before she experienced the benefits. The method worked, her self-esteem improved, and she had developed a positive determination to be somebody. She was not a nobody.

'I will discover where you are. I will find you, Mum.' She spoke the words and visualised her joy when being in her mother's arms and telling her all about her life with the McLean's.

'I will find you Mum wherever you are.'

Chapter Seven

In the library, a group of women sat around a table and they stopped talking when Laura walked in. They stared at her as she approached the counter.

'Hello,' the girl said. 'I'm sorry but Mrs Wilcox is not here today.' She fiddled with a plastic badge and attempted to attach it onto her blouse.

'Mrs Wilcox said, George would help me in the archives,' said Laura.

'George!' said the girl. Her name tag came loose and landed face up on the counter, showing the etched lettering: Miss Anne Ferguson. 'Oh yes, he is in. I'll show you.' She picked up the badge and looked at it. 'The pin's come loose, I'll fix it later.' She pushed it under her watch strap. 'He's down in the dungeon, well basement really. This way.'

Laura followed her to the hallway and down two flights of a stone stairway. She pulled her jacket collar up under her chin as they reached a door.

Anne gave two hefty knocks on the solid oak panel and turned to Laura. 'He's deaf as a post.' She pushed the door open. 'George,' she shouted and looked at Laura. 'Come on, he'll be here somewhere.'

They walked between the rows of steel shelves loaded with cardboard boxes.

'George, you have a visitor.'

A chair scraped against the floor, and at the far end of the room a man stepped out from behind a bookcase.

'Over here,' he said and waved.

Anne led the way to where George was sitting next to his desk. He looked at them and took a long drink from a glass cup. 'A quick coffee to get my engine running,' he said and pointed to a chair.

Laura sat.

'George, this is our visitor Mrs Wilcox spoke about,' said Anne. She leaned her bottom onto the edge of his desk. 'What are you looking for?' She directed her question at Laura.

'Anne, off you go,' said George, and he patted her elbow. 'Don't you have a readers' circle coming in?'

'They're already here.' She walked off towards the door and looked back at Laura. 'If you need anything, I mean anything, let me know.'

The door closed with a bang.

The sound echoed around the basement, and Laura gasped; she looked at George.

'It catches in the draught.' He shrugged. 'I've ordered dampers.'

George was in his late sixties with a lightly tanned complexion. He had a small Vandyke beard and wore gold-framed glasses with round bi-focal lenses, which accentuated a professional impression. His white hair was neatly trimmed above his ears and around the sides of his head. He wore a checked cotton shirt that smelled of starch, and his beige woollen tie was knotted and tucked under his paisley patterned waistcoat. A tweed jacket hung on a hanger balanced on the bookcase behind him.

'Good morning, Miss McLean.' He grinned. 'Or should I call you Miss Dawson?'

'Please, I'm Laura.' She held her hand out, but he ignored her offer of a handshake.

'Mrs Wilcox said I—'

'Yes, Diane told me about your family history project.' He interrupted.

'Diane?'

'Diane Wilcox. Now, where would you like to start?'

'I can't remember anything about my father or much about my mother.'

'The Dawson family has been around for a while,' he said and got up. 'Come on, follow me.' He walked from behind his desk, then stopped. 'Sorry, how impolite. Would you like a coffee before we start with the records?'

'No, thank you. I'm fine.'

She followed him into a room which was brightly lit with a row of fluorescent strip lights. There was a wide, long table in the centre. Two microfiche machines sat on desks against one wall, and on the other side were stacks of large wooden folders laid flat on steel shelves.

'I suggest we start with the Kirkindale Gazette from about twenty years ago.' He lifted a folder from the shelf and placed it on the table. 'Be careful turning the pages, some are delicate. We had a problem with creeping damp a few years back. However, we rescued these before there was any serious damage.' He went over to a cupboard and brought out a leather-bound book. 'This is one of the old parish records. Here you'll find details about marriages, births, and deaths. Mind you, they go back a long way and won't cover the records concerning your parents.'

Laura stood at the table and opened the newspaper folder, dated 1976. The Weekly Gazette was a broadsheet paper, and she folded each large page over using both hands. She took care not to rip the tattered edges.

There were articles about the Sunday Fayre, sheep sales, and one about a prize-winning Charolais bull.

'I'll get the land records and some maps, although they are old copies and no longer the current official documents. You'd need to go to the Land Registry for those.' He left the room whistling *Auld Lang Syne.* It sounded slow and out of tune.

She glanced through the report from the local agricultural show with its pictures of the owners and their winning animals. Best animal of the year had gone to William Dawson of Springfield Farm for his Charolais bull. Laura pulled over a chair and sat to read the article. There was a black-and-white picture of a man who must be her father. He stood shoulder to shoulder next to the animal, and he held its halter with a second rope attached to the bull's nose ring. They were in a steel enclosure with onlookers behind the rails. Most of the spectators were men in flat caps, but two youthful women, both indistinct in the grainy picture, were standing to one side of the group.

This newspaper copy was printed in the same year in which she was born, and she wanted to rip the page out. Instead, she would ask George about making photocopies of all the pictures and sections she wanted to keep.

In the picture, her father was smiling and appeared relaxed next to the bull. What colour were his eyes and his hair? She had the urge to get up and run to Springfield Farm and ask Old Charlie if he knew where her father and mother were? The lady she had met in the barn had said that Old Charlie lives alone. So, where are her parents?

George returned with a folded map and a leather-bound book. 'Have you done much family history research?' he said and placed the items on the table.

'A few years ago, I did a school project,' she said, avoiding eye contact with him.

'Ah, so you understand the basics, that will get you going.' He spread out the map. 'This will show you the layout of the parish, and from the records in the book you can work out a history of the ownership of the farms and the buildings.'

She leaned over the map. 'This is from the 1890s. How does it help?'

'It puts context to the historical detail.' He passed her the heavy book. 'Once you go through the records, you will have a better understanding of the places and perhaps how the family relationships developed.'

'I am not sure if this will help me find my mother.' She shook her head.

'Your mother, ah yes, Diane told me. So sad, her maiden name was Stewart.' He pointed at the book. 'If you look at the map, you will see it associates the name with the village Cotton Mill. Perhaps you can trace all the Stewarts in the records and build your family tree on your mother's side.'

'Ah, Springwater Lane.' She placed her finger on the map. 'Where is Russet House?'

'Russet House?'

'It's where I was born and it's on Springwater Lane.'

'Yes. Place names often change. I will see if I can find a later map, perhaps an Ordnance and Survey from the 1930s.' He stood by the door and looked back. 'Russet House was probably not built until much later. Can I bring you some paper and a pen?'

'No, I've my notebook.' She rummaged in her bag.

'Not one of those new portable computers. We sometimes get Americans with their fancy gadgets and cameras, but you know what?'

'Found it.' She opened up her softback jotter.

'They forget their chargers, adaptors and have the wrong plugs,' he said and walked out of the room.

She carried on reading through the Gazette newspapers and she chuckled when she found the announcement of her birth. There was also a date set for the christening at the Kirkindale Parish Church. She tore a page from her notebook to mark the newspaper page.

In the Gazette a few weeks later, she discovered the article about an inquest describing how a bull had gorged its handler at Springfield Farm. The report concluded that the incident was a tragic accident where William Dawson had gone into the bullpen and the animal had butted and crushed him. He died in hospital.

Why had no one told her about this? She had lived for three years at Russet House and couldn't remember her father. She was newly born before the accident, but surely as she grew older, she must have asked about a daddy? Did she? Why had no one told her about the accident? Perhaps they did, and she was too young to understand. She closed her eyes and searched for memories; nothing came to mind. Her eyes watered. She slapped the table with both hands. She walked around the room; this is not what she had expected to discover, but then again, the truth is what it is. She went back to the table and read the article again. Tear drops dripped from her chin.

George returned with two more maps and some large folders. He placed them on the table. 'This will keep you going for a while.' He unrolled a chart and spread it out. 'This is a blank family tree, if you put your name here.' He marked a large dot at the bottom with a pencil. 'You can then go back and forwards filling in the gaps.' He let go of the sheet which rolled back on itself. He pulled a pack of tissues from his waistcoat pocket. 'Yes, I know,' he said. 'It can be overwhelming. Here, take these, I'll let you be. If you need anything, give me a shout.' He left the room without closing the door.

Laura picked up a tissue, wiped her eyes and blew her nose. She turned over the blank chart and wrote her name next to the dot. That was her whole life so far; a black dot. Above this, she added the names of her parents.

She found an obituary in the Gazette for William Dawson, twenty-six years old, the youngest son of Charles and Sophia Dawson of Springfield Farm. He was a loving husband to Irene and a father to his only daughter, Laura. There was more about the date and place of the funeral, and his sister Mary Dawson had requested donations to Cancer Research instead of flowers.

She searched one of the older maps and found Springfield Farm with a track that lead to the river. A pool was marked next to the waterfall of the River Marrs and a building, annotated the Smithy and Mill, was drawn alongside the river. A wide track, notated Springwater Way, was shown to follow the river down to the village of Kirkindale.

She compared these details to her own map, on which there was no building shown at the waterfall. On her map the footpath from Russet House aligned with the track on the older map which lead to the farm.

She examined an earlier Ordnance and Survey map from the 1960s and found Kirkindale. A track was shown to follow the river from the village to the waterfall where some ruins were marked. A footpath then continued away from the river and ran between the fields, notated as orchards until it ended at Russet Barn on Springwater Lane.

She pushed the maps and the parish books to one side on the table as these were a distraction from her search for her mother. Later, they would be useful in finding details of her great-grandparents as the records covered the periods from the 1890s. Perhaps a discussion with George, about the time when her mother disappeared, would be beneficial and save time.

She went back to looking through the newspapers.

She lifted the folder, 1974, from the shelf and folded over the pages. She found a section in the May issue with black and white photographs of wedded couples. She saw a picture of her parents. She blew her nose into a tissue. There was her mother and as she remembered her.

'Mum,' she said and touched the paper. This showed her mother on her wedding day as a young bright girl who was smiling and looked full of happiness. Her mum who had chased her around the garden and pushed her on the swing. She reached to rip the page out but hesitated. Instead, she tore a sheet from her jotter and marked the place.

She fetched the 1979 folder from the shelf. This was from the same year they took her away from Kirkindale. Turning through the pages she found that the reports, over the weeks and months, were like the many articles from previous years. The pictures were different, but the same fayre happened in May, the market sales were reported weekly and there were many double spreads of the annual agricultural events. Also, there were the similar outraged letters about graffiti, fly tipping, litter, and dog fouling in each weekly issue.

The July and August copies were missing. In the third quarter of the September paper, there was a snippet stating that the police search for the local woman had gone nationwide. No names were mentioned, or reasons given.

'How are you getting on?' George said from the doorway.

'I've got as far as my grandparents and that Mary Dawson is my aunt.'

'What about your mother's side?'

'George would it be possible to make copies from the newspapers?'

'The photocopier is by my desk.'

'Thank you. There appears to be papers missing in this year.' She folded over the sheets to June. 'What do you think?'

'Missing!' He came to the table and nudged her to one side. He rubbed his hand along the gutter of the folder. 'Someone has ripped them out. Sheer vandalism.'

'Would there be any other copies?'

'Not here.' He shook his head, 'Vandalism! There might be copies in the Council Offices in Marston, if you are lucky.'

'Do you know anything about a missing woman?'

'All I know is that someone has been in here and with no respect for local records.'

'No, I mean, do you know what happened in Kirkindale in 1979?'

'How long ago, sixteen or fifteen years ago. No, not really, I was a solicitor in Marston. I've only recently retired here.' He sorted the record books on the table. 'Laura, can you come back tomorrow? I finish at lunchtime.' He pointed towards the clock on the wall. 'I need to lock up.'

'Didn't you read the local news at the time?'

'Would you expect me to know every detail?' He laughed.

'They put me into foster care, something must have happened to my mother. Don't you think it's strange?'

'Strange, about your mother or the vandalism?'

'Both.' She packed her jotter into her bag. 'Can I leave these here?' She waved at the maps and record books. 'For tomorrow.'

'Yes, I remember there was a suspected drowning and a missing woman. But you needn't concern yourself.'

'I wouldn't be here otherwise. Would I?' She stared at him. She looked closely at his face as he examined the torn paper edges in the folder. Surely, he must know more?

'Of course not.' He picked at the ragged fragments of the newspaper in the folds of the gutter. 'I must tell Diane about this.'

'What can you tell me about the missing woman?'

'Diane won't be pleased. Sheer vandalism,' he said. 'Perhaps the damp damaged these copies. Let's go.' He pointed to the door.

Laura followed George out of the basement and said goodbye to him at the top of the stairway. She rushed out of the library.

She squinted her eyes in the sunlight and wandered across the road towards the church. She reached the gateway into the graveyard and stood for a moment between the stone pillars. She touched the ends of the iron hinges set into the stone, and she remembered the gate.

After Sunday school, Mum would wait for her at the end of the graveyard path. The children would run out from the vestry through an archway and between two black wooden doors which had rows of metal rivets. Someone would shut the doors, which squeaked and clanged, as the last person left. She would climb onto the gate and let it swing back and forth until her mother had finished talking to people. Who were those people?

The gate had gone, and water puddled on the flagstones of the steps. The paved path looked uneven, and she took care not to trip as she walked towards the rear of the church. The wooden doors hung lopsided, and she went through the open archway into the courtyard. She remembered there were prickly red roses and white flowers around a green manicured lawn. But it had changed; ragwort and dock weeds grew in the flower beds, and the lawn was littered with sandstone bricks stacked in piles. A scaffold structure lined the outer courtyard wall where men laboured resetting the stonework.

She retreated to the graveyard and meandered among the headstones and stopped occasionally to read the inscriptions. She came across the Dawson family graves and saw her father's memorial granite stone. She sat down on the grass. What was he like?

Further back in the plot was a worn headstone listing William Charles Dawson as seventy-eight years old and his wife Claire Marie Dawson aged seventy-five years. Laura took out her notepad and recorded the names and dates. Had she found her great-grandparents? They both died in the same year, 1975, and before she was born.

A small marble stone recorded the short life of Robert Michael Dawson, beloved son of Charles and Sophia Dawson. It showed his birth and death dates as the same day in 1974. This was two years before she was born. A tear rolled down her face. Her grandmother must have had a still-born child in her later years? Perhaps in her mid-forties or even fifties. Uncle Robert's life was so short. What a tragedy.

She leaned back and let the sun warm her face. She was among family and wished they were still around; if they were, what would they tell her?

Chapter Eight

Scott held Mary's right hand and smiled when she opened her eyes. Her pale face had lost the radiant sheen of the youthful country girl he had met thirteen years ago.

He first met Mary at his veterinary surgery, where she was in tears and afraid for her pregnant mare. A tree had crashed through the roof of the stables and injured the animal's neck and shoulders.

Scott investigated the horse's heavy bruising and examined the health of the unborn foul. He informed Mary of the positive outlook and good news. She had jumped up and hugged him. Her enthusiasm was infectious, and an intense emotional flush had rushed through his veins, he had fallen in love.

He felt ashamed with his thoughts of disappointment as he sat by her hospital bed. It was not entirely her fault that fate was indiscriminate in the choice of its victims.

Mary stared at him and struggled to move around in the bed. In response, he nodded as he adjusted the pillows and helped her sit up.

'How are you today?' He asked the same question whenever he arrived by her bedside.

'Fine, I've been feeding the lambs with Dad.'

'Aye, it's that time of the year.' He patted her hand, avoiding the black bruises left by the intravenous needle. The nurse had transferred it to her left arm earlier in the morning. Around the medical tape holding the needle in place, her skin was bruised and showing a yellow discolouration.

'Well maybe next year,' she said. She chuckled, then coughed and closed her eyes.

Seeing her propped up in the bed with the intravenous tube attached had become a familiar sight. He gritted his teeth and punched the edge of the mattress. This was not how he had envisaged their life together or how it would end. It was so unfair.

Mary moaned and opened her eyes; she grimaced. 'Don't Scott. Doctor Jamal says it's working.'

'Sorry.' He picked up the folder from the end of the bed and read the list of medications being administered. He did this out of habit during each visit, and as always there was no change to the quantity of drugs or their dosage. He replaced the folder on its hook.

He rubbed at the irritation on his upper arm where his annual anthrax booster injection had caused an inflammation.

'Yes,' said Mary.

'Yes.' Scott leaned in closer to her. 'Yes, what?'

'Yes, I'll marry you.' She gave a soft moan and closed her eyes.

Years ago, he had proposed to her during a boat cruise along the river Danube. She had said yes. People had cheered and clapped.

'We are married.' He saw Mary screw up her face. 'We need another holiday, that's it. A break from this place.'

When the consultant had told them it was cancer, Scott arranged a holiday for Mary to soften the pain of the awful news. The tests confirmed the diagnosis was stage four breast cancer, and this revelation infuriated him because he had missed the early signs of Mary's illness. She must have told him, but had he been too busy to listen or notice? Unfortunately, in the week before the holiday trip she had collapsed in the barn where one of the stable boys had found her lying unconscious on the straw.

The previous year, she had insisted they review their wills and Mary had laughed and had said; what's yours is mine and what's mine is mine. She also suggested they celebrate the occasion with a steak dinner at the Black Swan. During the evening, she kept toasting to their good fortune and to a long and happy life. Her exuberant behaviour unsettled him. They had sat at a table on the veranda overlooking the river and later in the evening a deep red sunset appeared like flames across the sky.

Mary held up her hand and looked at him. 'If we are married, where is my ring?'

'They're at home,' he said. 'Your rings and bracelets are in the safe at home.'

'I know,' she said.

'I'll buy you a diamond one, you'll see. A present for getting well and I'll have it engraved with our names.'

Mary laughed. 'You are so full of promises, now let me sleep.' She shuffled lower in the bed and turned her head to one side.

So what should he do now? Perhaps arrange a bedside ceremony to renew their vows to please her. Would she appreciate the gesture, because that was all it would be. They had been married for twelve years and had no children.

'Scott,' she said, 'Scott. Scott, where are you?' She shuffled around on the bed.

'I'm here.' He reached and held her hand.

'I thought you had left.'

'No, I'm still here. Would you like some yoghurt?' He watched as she slumped back and closed her eyes. 'Ah, perhaps not,' he said and shook his head.

He wanted to get back to normal and back to work. His partners at the veterinary practice, Michael and Sarah, had advised him to stop doing farm visits as there was a risk of transferring fungal or other infections to his wife. They pointed out how Mary's immune system would be impaired during the chemotherapy treatment and he should not risk contagion. In reality, he knew his emotional instability was a disruption, and they were being kind to suggest he was better out of the way until Mary improved.

A nurse came into the room. 'Hello, Mr Ferguson.' She checked the drip lines and levels. 'Your wife is doing really well.'

'She is drowsier than yesterday and last night.'

'That's the pain relief. Dr Jamal increased the dosage this morning.' She nodded and smiled at him. 'Don't worry, give her an hour, and she'll be chatting away.' She signed off on the charts in the bedside folder and gave a brief look towards him. She closed the door when she left.

'Don't listen to her,' said Mary. 'I've always had morphine ever since I came in.'

'Can you believe this.' Scott sat forward on his chair. 'We have a guest at Orchard View, she is staying until the weekend.'

'Only one, you're hopeless.' She pointed to the side table. 'I thought we were closed. Can I have some water, please?'

'It's your niece.' He held the plastic tumbler to her lips. 'She was doing the Dale walk. Anne said—'

'Who!' Mary pushed the tumbler away. 'My niece, Scott, who?'

'Laura, she visited Diane Wilcox and is asking for information about her mother.'

'I need to meet her,' she struggled around on the bed. 'Get the pillows!'

He pushed the pillows back on the bed and helped her to get comfortable.

'I want to see her. Yes, she was a beautiful girl,' said Mary. 'Her mother! She should forget all about her.' Mary grabbed at Scott's hand. 'Tell her.'

'Mary, easy now, calm down.'

'There is nothing for her here, and it will break her heart. Tell her Scott, please.'

'Tell her what exactly?'

'No one knows really, but she went missing after the murder.'

'Who—'

'They think Irene murdered my mother,' she shouted.

'You told me. That was years ago.'

'Some think so. I don't. Maybe the murderer had abducted and killed her.'

'You never told me Irene had a daughter.'

'No, they sent her away. I don't want to talk about it.' She leaned back in her pillows. 'Water, please.'

He passed the tumbler over and helped her drink.

'It was after Mum lost baby Robert. The arguments and fighting at the farm.'

'Mary, I'll bring Laura, I am sure she'll want to see you.'

'Then the accident and William's funeral. Awful.'

'I know Mary, it's . . .'

'I moved in with Irene to help with the baby, but I wanted to get away from Dad. He was so unpleasant.'

'I understand. What would you expect after the accident?'

'Accident! William would never have gone into the bull pen alone. Why, oh why.'

'You know Mary, some bulls are easy to handle, but just one wrong move and their temper can be sudden.'

'I was so happy with Irene, she was like a sister and baby Laura was so cute.'

Scott sat down and watched Mary drift into a sleep. He had never met Sophia Dawson and her death had occurred years before he had arrived in Kirkindale and joined the Marston Veterinary Practice.

He studied Mary's face. She looked so peaceful, but it was only a matter of time until she would be gone. He wiped his nose; this cancer has hijacked his life and has slammed his career on hold. His dreams were now nightmares fluctuating between a confusion of hope and evil expectations. When Mary dies the house would be his; he might sell up and move into Marston to be near the practice. Perhaps he would move out of the area altogether.

Mary had the stud at Springfield Farm, but he had no intention of running it on his own. Why doesn't she die and take his pain away? He shuddered in a cold sweat from the shame of his thoughts.

Together, they had fantastic dreams, a future all planned out, but now their ideas were suffocating him in a long black tunnel. Would Mary's survival be the light at the end? Or would Mary's demise be a fresh opportunity? He knew which he preferred.

Mary stirred and lifted her free hand towards him. 'Scott, please you must burn the box in the attic.'

'Mary, what about the attic?'

'Irene, her things. I should have listened to Dad.'

'Why can't we give them to Laura? It will get rid of all that junk.'

'No Scott, please. There is a box with newspapers. Please burn it.' Mary attempted to grab his arm. 'Listen, Irene just disappeared. Burn the papers in the attic.' She took a deep breath. 'Let Laura have what she wants,' she mumbled. 'Let her take the paintings, but not the box.'

'Yes Mary, I'll burn everything.'

'You would love that,' she said, and pointed at him. 'Please, the newspapers in the box will upset Laura. Water.' She coughed.

Scott lifted the tumbler of water to her lips and helped her drink.

'Tomorrow, I'll get the boxes out and burn them.'

'Just one box, Scott,' she said, 'Please, it would be better tonight before she knows.'

'Why would she?'

'What would you do in her place?'

'Perhaps, but—'

'Tonight Scott, tonight.' She shifted around in the bed as he reached and adjusted the pillows. 'I need to sleep. Go before she finds the box.'

'Won't there be copies of newspapers in the library?'

'Knowing Diane, probably not. There were rumours.'

'Mary, what is going on?'

'Promise me, burn the box.' She leaned back and closed her eyes.

During the months in hospital, he had seen how drawn her face had become. Some days, she was strong, coherent, and recovering, on others she was fragile. He stroked the transparent skin on the back of her hand. Will she recover? He tried not to think of any other outcome, but his mind was numb and tired.

He got up and looked out of the window over to the car park. He watched a mother, hand-in-hand with a child, walk to her car. Mary had wanted children, but later, it was always later. Their plan was for two; he wanted girls; she wanted boys and after years of trying; Mary became pregnant, and it overjoyed him. This turned out to be ectopic and the emergency surgery removed both fallopian tubes.

Outside the hospital, the afternoon sky was bright. Swallows perched on the telephone lines, resting after their return journey from their winter migration. A group of magpies were scavenging among the overflow from a park bin and a red setter raced towards them. They took flight and landed in the branches of a cherry tree, dislodging pink blossom like confetti into the breeze.

After their disappointment, Mary declared that breeding Friesian horses was her dedicated ambition. The stud grew, as did Mary's enthusiasm for a full and passionate life, including turning Orchard View into a B and B for ramblers.

Soon, he would be on his own since Mary was dying. A wash of shame rolled down his back; it was not his fault if he was being realistic, and his thoughts raced ahead to the future. He will never forget her. He kicked a chair across the room.

'Mr Ferguson!'

He had not heard the nurse come in to check on her patient. She came over to the window.

'Your wife is doing well, Mr Ferguson.' She reached out and touched his shoulder. 'Look, what a beautiful day. Life goes on.'

Chapter Nine

Laura jogged through the woods; she relaxed in the warm air and concentrated on her footing. She looked ahead on the path and she saw a woman who waved. What did she want, who was she? Laura recognised her mum's kind, smiling face. The woman laughed and dashed through the wood; she zigzagged between the pine trees.

'Wait!' Laura sprinted along the track.

The woman gave out a high-pitched mocking scream; she ran and dodged through the undergrowth.

Laura leapt over a ditch and stumbled into a bramble patch where she scrambled among the prickly shrubs. She pushed on through the thicket onto soft ground which swayed beneath her feet. Her trainers sank in the soaked moss. She turned to escape the suction, but her feet sank deeper into the bog. She pushed hard to free her legs, but without a firm stance to brace against, she sank into the mire. The quagmire clawed up her body until the mud clung around her waist.

The woman reappeared and stood among the bull reeds on the edge of the swamp. She smiled and watched as Laura struggled. She waved and stretched her arms out towards Laura.

'I am here, Laura,' she called. 'What are you waiting for?' She then pointed at a branch over Laura's head. 'Try harder, come on, try harder.'

Laura sank deeper into the black soakaway. She made frantic grabs at the overhanging branch and on the third attempt caught hold and pulled.

'Help me,' she screamed. 'Will you help me?' She dragged herself free and slithered across the slime onto solid ground. She looked towards the reeds. 'Where are you? Is that you?' she shouted.

The woman turned and walked away until she disappeared among the trees.

Laura crawled over the grass to a rowan tree and laid against its protruding roots. She looked up at the small buds formed on the end of the twigs.

'You saved me,' she said to the tree, and hugged its trunk. It must be true that witches are afraid of the rowan. She closed her eyes.

She could smell smoke. Was the grass on fire?

'Where are you?' she shouted.

She coughed and coughed in the smoke.

She sat up in bed and looked around. The duvet was lying on the floor; her pillows were at the foot of her bed, and her pyjama top was torn off her shoulder.

Smoke!

She rushed onto the landing, but the smell was not from within the house. Back in her room, she opened the curtains. There was a bonfire at the foot of the garden and the wind wafted smoke in faint swirls through the open window into her room.

Down the valley, she saw the wide pink sunrise as a faint glow behind the wooded hills. She checked the time on her watch; it was just after five thirty.

She dressed in her tracksuit and made her way into the dining room. She checked out through the window and saw Scott's car parked in the driveway. He came out of the garage with a cardboard box and carried it towards the garden.

Something must have happened to Mary. Perhaps this was his reaction to bad news.

Laura ran into the kitchen and through the French doors onto the garden patio. She waited for him to appear around the corner.

'Good morning,' she said and saw the startled look on his face.

'Oh, you're up, sorry. I didn't mean to wake you.'

Not a hello or a how are you.

In her deep sleep, she had not heard the car arrive in the drive or heard the garage door open.

'It's early for a clear out,' she said.

'Time is not my own these days.' He stared at her for a moment. 'Tea would be nice.'

Laura put the kettle on in the kitchen and fetched two cups. Obedient, she was the obedient housekeeper now. Of course! He wanted her away from the garden. She ran out across the lawn to where Scott was feeding the fire with torn pages. A pile of folders was in the box by his feet.

'My old university notes,' he said. 'Just felt the need to expunge the past.'

'First thing in the morning?' She picked up a shoebox with a picture of red slippers on the sides.

'I'll do that!' He grabbed the box from her and gave her a folder instead.

It was full of scribbled notes, and diagrams of animals annotated with veterinary terms. She ripped a few pages out and threw them on the fire.

'I'll get the tea.' She dropped the folder onto the ground.

'Mary told me about your mother.' He watched her for a reaction.

She stepped closer to him. 'What?'

'She told me your mother was missing.'

'Where has she gone, did Mary say?'

'No.'

'I would like to visit Aunt Mary.'

'Your mother's paintings are in the attic. You can have them all.'

'Yes, I would like that.'

She fetched the cups from the kitchen and stood next to Scott as they drank their tea. They watched the flames as the letters and jotters burned.

'Why are you burning those?'

'When you first arrived, why didn't you tell me who you were?'

'I didn't think it was any of your business,' she said and sipped her tea. 'Those letters could be important.' She pointed at the envelopes, turning brown at the edges. She wanted to dash into the flames and rescue them.

'I don't think they are any of your business.'

'I would like to visit Mary.'

He nodded. 'Yes, she would like that.' He offered her his empty cup. 'She wants to see you. I'll arrange a time and take you into the hospital.'

'I'll make a cooked breakfast.' She grabbed at his cup and returned to the kitchen.

Once in the house, she ran to her room and checked under the bed. The box with the wedding dress was there, as were the photograph albums. She dragged the chair onto the landing and pushed the attic hatch aside. She pulled herself up into the loft. The strip lights fitted to the roof lit up the space and she could feel a strong draught from the far end. There were two more shoe boxes full of letters, and she carried them to the hatch opening.

She looked around the attic and saw the staircase leading into the garage.

She retreated through the hatch to her room and slipped the rescued shoe boxes under her bed.

She heard Scott move around in the loft and she felt like crying. What else was he burning? Should she not stop him, what was she afraid of?

She met him at the garage door.

'Can I have those?' She blocked his way.

He put down the boxes. 'Why? What business is it of yours?'

'They are my mother's personal correspondence.'

'I doubt it.'

'Can I look through them to check? If they are not my mother's papers then you can burn them.'

'Can I? Now go and make the breakfast and be a good girl.'

She rushed forward and grabbed at the boxes.

'Now Laura! What are you doing?'

'Just a quick look.' She backed towards the door. 'Is that a problem?'

'Ah, Laura. I don't know what happened to your mother, but do I care,' he said. 'Take them, but don't tell Mary.' He turned and locked the door to the attic staircase.

'You don't care.'

'Not like that, I care. I mean, take the stuff.' He pointed to the house. 'How about that breakfast?'

'So, you can burn my mother's past when I am out of the way.'

'Those were the last.' He shrugged. 'I'm famished. We can talk about it over coffee and toast.'

In the kitchen, they sat at the table with a breakfast of fried eggs, bacon, beans, and mushrooms.

'You make a mean breakfast,' he said and looked at Laura. He waited. 'I'll let Mary know you want—'

'She is my aunt. Wouldn't she expect me to visit?'

'Laura, Mary is not well. Perhaps tomorrow, I'll speak to her.' He stood up. 'When did you last see her?'

A shock like an electric pulse ran down her spine. She got up and took a plate to the sink. She kept her back to him. Although, she wanted to shout her reply;

when did her aunt want to see her? Instead, she gritted her teeth to check her emotions from her sudden flash of anger.

'I'll see you later.' He picked up his mobile telephone. 'I need to go.' He checked the door to the private area of the house was locked and left.

Laura watched through the dining-room window as Scott locked the garage door. He sat in his car and spoke into his mobile before he tooted the car horn and drove out along the driveway.

She returned to the kitchen and collected the two rescued cardboard boxes. In the dining-room, she emptied the contents onto the table.

The first box contained old bank statements, years of monthly electricity bills and correspondence from a solicitor's office; McCarthy and Sinclair in Marston. These letters related to a dispute between Mr Charles Dawson and Mrs Irene Dawson over the ownership of Russet House. According to the dates on the letters, the issue lasted for over eighteen months before it concluded. Enclosed in the envelope of the final letter were a photocopy of the title deeds and an invoice for three thousand pounds which was stamped; paid.

She felt elated and her stomach churned at this revelation. So, her mother owned Russet House after the death of her father, and perhaps she still does. She intended to ask George at the library on how to discover the ownership of a property. Or she could ask Mary?

She put this letter and the attachments to one side and scooped the remaining papers back into the box. They could be burned.

The second carton contained: a selection of knitting patterns, a folder of collected recipes, old copies of *The Artist Magazine*, and at the bottom of the box was a large fawn envelope containing school photographs.

She placed the pictures on the table in order of school years, starting with those from the Kirkindale primary, and finished with those from Marston Grammar.

A group photograph of the final year students from the school was in colour, along with a list of names. She found Irene Stewart; she was a beautiful girl with a wide smile. She recognised this expression, and she remembered what they sang at bedtime; *The Owl and the Pussy Cat*. Her eyes watered.

Someone had blackened two faces in the photograph and scribbled out their names. She looked through more pictures and in each one someone had obscured a face or else drawn over it with a moustache and glasses. She replaced them all in the envelope along with the solicitor's letter. These she would keep.

She gathered up the rest of the items and carried them to the garden, where she stirred up the ashes of the fire and added the contents of the boxes piece by piece. She watched the fire flare as the knitting patterns fluttered and the magazines crumpled in the heat. Their ink added a range of colours to the flames before the paper disintegrating to a powdered white ash. A moment of regret flashed through her mind as it seemed she was incinerating mementos of her mother's past existence. The past had gone, and it was one that Laura would never know.

She gritted her teeth as a surge of anger shuddered down her spine. Should she continue looking for her mother or accept her life as Laura McLean? If she did, would she ever be free from her obsessive and hopeless need for answers?

She picked up the last box and emptied its contents onto the bonfire, kicking those items that slipped out of the middle of the fire back into the rising flames.

Her mother had abandoned her; the ultimate betrayal from any mother to her child. Surely, maternal instinct is the strongest bond between a mother and her child. So why did she leave her? She lifted her arms in the air and gave a long cathartic scream.

She climbed through the hatch into the attic. The lighting was still on and she noted that Scott had left the paintings, the oil paints and the suitcases untouched. She walked towards the draught of air coming from the far end of the roof space. The narrow staircase led down to the closed door leading into the garage. It was locked, but only from the outside. She turned the catch and pushed the door open; she walked into the spacious garage.

There was sufficient room for two cars. A lawnmower and garden tools stood in the far corner. A short corridor at the back of the building led to a glass door giving access to the house. It was also locked. She rattled the door and then remembered there was a second set of keys in the utility room.

She retraced her way through the loft and collected the keys.

She returned and tried them in the lock of the glass door; it opened. She hesitated and then locked the door again. There wasn't enough time to search through the house, besides what would she find that belonged to her mother. They had stored all of her possessions in the attic.

She had arranged to meet George and continue her search through the archives for details of her family history. There were many questions she wanted to discuss with him, particularly ones which might help her discover her mother's family.

What has happened to her mother's parents; her grandparents? Did her mother have any siblings? Perhaps she is living with them, but where?

Chapter Ten

Mrs Diane Wilcox stood at the top of the library steps and waited by the open door. She watched Laura walk across the road.

'Good morning, Laura,' she called and moved aside to let her through. 'I expect George will be in the archives already. He's an early bird.'

'Hello,' said Laura. 'I wonder if you have time—'

'Yes,' she interrupted. 'In fact, I've some photos to show you, come on up. George can wait.'

They climbed the stairs to the landing where Mrs Wilcox searched through her handbag for the office keys.

'Come in,' she said and dropped her bag onto the desk. 'I'll put the kettle on.' She strode to the adjoining kitchenette. 'A quick coffee to start the day, would you like one,' she called from through the doorway.

'No, I'm fine. Thanks.' Laura sat at the table by the window.

Mrs Wilcox carried her cup to the table, then returned to her desk. She took a small bottle from her bag, slipped out two pills and swallowed them. She opened a bottom draw of the desk and removed two patchwork covered photograph albums. She carried them to the window seats.

Laura stared at the tattered material and loose threads, then looked up and smiled.

'Yes, I know,' said Mrs Wilcox. 'My mother insisted we covered everything. School books with brown paper or with wallpaper cut-offs.' She laughed. 'I made these in needle work. I think the entire class did the same.' She sat and opened the first album.

'These are my school photos.' She turned over the pages and pointed. 'Yes, look, there is your mother next to . . . I'm not sure who the teacher was. What a memory.' She picked up her cup and sipped some coffee. 'My, my, we look so young, but then again we were. Look, that's me.'

Laura had seen a copy of these pictures at Russet House. She nodded, holding back her curiosity and not sure what to say as Mrs Wilcox went through each of the photographs, and pointing out Irene and herself. Mrs Wilcox was the young Diane Clarke, and the person blacked out in the photographs she had rescued from the attic.

Laura pointed at a boy in the colour picture. 'Who is that?' It was the second person marked out in her copies at Russet House.

Mrs Wilcox reached over and held Laura's hand.

'You have beautiful fingers.' She touched each as if counting them.

Laura eased her hand free. 'Thank you,' she said. 'Who is this boy?'

'That is—'

Someone knocked on the door, and she stopped talking. George walked in.

'Hang on a minute,' she said to Laura. 'Yes, George, what is it?'

'Sorry, I was wondering if Miss Dawson was coming in today.' He looked towards Laura. 'Ah yes, sorry to disturb you.'

'No, George, it's fine,' she said and turned to Laura. 'I need to get on. We can look at these later. During lunch, perhaps.' She went to her desk.

'Diane, what about the local history presentation?' George said and shrugged. 'Is it going ahead?'

'Let's check.' She thumbed through her diary.

Meanwhile, Laura flipped over the pages in the album and found a picture of a tree trunk with "Diane–Loves–Billy" carved into its bark. The next picture showed a teenage Diane with her arms around Billy and kissing his cheek. Billy, the young William Dawson. On the next page, knitted baby booties tied with blue bow ribbons were in a polythene envelope. The words "Ryan, 1st May 1969" were handwritten underneath.

'Yes George, tomorrow first thing,' Mrs Wilcox said and returned to the window seat for her coffee cup. 'Laura, you wanted to ask me something.'

'Yes, I—'

'Not now,' she interrupted. 'I'll see you at lunchtime. Yes, let's talk then?'

'Okay yes,' said Laura, and she stood. 'About twelve?' She closed the album. Her heart rate had increased. How should she ask about the inscription carved in the tree? Were the young Diane and Billy teenage lovers, or was she being presumptuous?

She followed George out of the office and down the stairs.

On the way to the basement, her mind raced with a frenzy of irrational thoughts, none of which she could pin in a logical series. How should she frame her questions to Mrs Wilcox in the afternoon?

Laura entered the basement room into a pleasant aroma of percolating Arabic coffee, which smelled like a mixture of cinnamon and chocolate.

'Coffee is ready, you must have one.' George poured out two cups from the glass jug and added milk. He looked up at Laura. 'You take milk?'

She nodded. 'One sugar.'

'Please take a seat. We can't have drinks in the research room.'

She sat. 'George, how would I find out who owns Russet House or maybe it's called Orchard View?'

'From the parish records?'

'No, I mean today, the current owners.'

'The Land Registry should have the updated details.'

'What do you mean, should?'

'Yes, I worked with McCarthy and Sinclair in Marston before retiring.' He saw her puzzled expression. 'Solicitors,' he said. 'I worked with petty crime, small claims and occasional family disputes.'

'And?' she said and shrugged. 'Would they tell me who the current owners are?'

'Yes, well, maybe for a small fee.' He sipped from his cup. 'I didn't do conveyance, that was Jeffrey's department.'

'I think my mother owns Russet House.'

'But she has been missing. How long did you say?'

'I didn't, but over fifteen years.'

'Complicated, dealing with the estate of a missing person.' He shook his head and said, 'There needs to be a death certificate and for a missing person a presumption they are dead. Do you know if she left a will?'

'I don't know. What about the solicitors will they know?'

'I'll ask Jeffrey to check their records.'

There was a thud behind a shelf as something landed on the floor.

Miss Ferguson came out from behind a storage aisle. 'Sorry. Sorry I didn't mean to disturb you,' she said.

'Oh, it's only you,' said George.

'I was just getting paper for the printer,' she said. 'Hello Laura.'

Laura responded with a smile and a half-hearted wave.

'I didn't hear you come in. You know if you had called, I would have brought you the pack up,' said George.

'Yes, I heard you talking and well sorry, I thought I'd . . . Okay, I better be off.' She turned, picked up the box, and rushed away past the shelves to exit the basement.

Laura finished drinking her coffee. 'I'll get started then.'

George nodded. 'I'll rinse these out.' He stood up and picked up the empty coffee cups. 'I've put the war records out on the table, you might find them useful.'

In the back room, her chart of the family tree lay next to the records from the Great War and World War II, listing the names of local men who had died.

She looked through the books and found the names of two brothers from Springfield Farm. Robert and Michael Dawson, her great uncles. They had been killed during the Normandy Landings. She sighed and searched through more pages, looking for Stewarts, but couldn't find any; perhaps she didn't have any great uncles on her mother's side of her family.

She copied the names she had found in the graveyard from her notebook onto the chart.

She thumbed through the parish records to an insert recording the marriage of William Charles Dawson to Claire Marie Wilcox, daughter of Mr and Mrs Matthew Wilcox of Oakwood Farm, on the 4th May 1918, at Kirkindale Parish Church.

Was Mrs Wilcox in the library a relative?

In the same year, she found the record of a marriage between Catherine Lynne Wollaston to Allan Brian Wilcox, son of Mr and Mrs Matthew Wilcox of Oakwood Farm.

On the old map, she found Oakwood Farm almost five miles south of Kirkindale, in the opposite direction from the Russet Barn.

She leafed through the second book with its meticulous handwritten entries, beautifully done by a skilled calligrapher. In 1952, she discovered the marriage of Allan Edward Wilcox, only son of Mr and Mrs A B Wilcox of Oakwood Farm to Margaret Claire Dawson, only daughter of Mr and Mrs W C Dawson of Springfield Farm.

Laura took a long deep breath as she studied her chart, Margaret Claire was her great-aunt and she had married a Wilcox. If she had children, they would be her first cousins once removed. Her father's cousins.

She was pleased with her chart. Now she had a history going back three generations of the Dawson and the Wilcox families. Her Great Grandparents William and Claire had four children: Margaret, Robert, Michael and Charlie. Charlie, her grandfather who lives on the family farm.

Next, she would search for details about her mother's family, the Stewarts. If she could trace her grandparents, would they know where her mother was?

She went back to the Gazettes and looked through the folders for the year, 1974.

In the wedding section, there were photographs of her mother and father. They had married in May. They looked so happy. Her mother's smile was warm and familiar. Had she seen this picture somewhere else? Perhaps there had been one in Russet House, but she couldn't remember seeing it. In the picture, her father looked so young, and like the handsome stranger she imagined from romance novels.

In the November issue she found a picture of Miss Diane Clarke married to Mr Edward David Wilcox, son of Allan and Margaret Wilcox of Oakwood Farm.

Diane wore a white wedding gown and Edward stood slightly apart in an awkward pose, his hands hidden in the sleeves of his suit. Looking closer, she saw a stern expression from the newly wedded Diane Wilcox. Perhaps she was cold as her dress looked ruffled in the wind.

She added the details to her family chart.

'Oh yes,' she said. 'Yes!' She punched the air. For years she had felt abandoned, an orphan, a forgotten child, and now from this family tree the past was coming to life. It was as if a curtain had lifted to signal the start of a play.

If Mrs Wilcox had children, what relation would they be? They would be second cousins. She would ask her later in the afternoon.

There was a knock at the door. She looked up and saw George standing in the doorway, and he waited for a moment before he came into the room.

'I heard you shouting,' he said. 'Is everything okay?'

'Sorry, it's like I've discovered the origins of a fresh world. One that was kept hidden for a long time.' She pointed at her partially completed chart.

'Exciting,' he said, 'can I look?' He picked the sheet up and examined her work. 'What about your mother's side?'

'I haven't done the Stewarts yet, that's next.'

'Another time then,' he said. 'It's lunchtime and I close up in the afternoons.'

She looked at her watch, then picked up her daypack. 'I'll have a sandwich by the river.'

'It's pouring with rain. Mrs Wilcox will be waiting for you in her office.'

Laura nodded, 'See you tomorrow then, bye.'

'Not tomorrow, Laura. I have presentations to deal with.'

'Okay, George, bye.'

§

Laura knocked on the open door and looked around the office, Mrs Wilcox was not in. She knocked louder, but no one appeared from the kitchenette. She went straight to the window where the albums lay on the occasional table. She turned over the pages to the colour photograph of the young Edward David Wilcox, (her father's cousin). He was the boy blacked out in the pictures she had found in the attic. She checked the names listed and matched Diane Clarke. It looks like she married her sweetheart from school, Laura smiled and chuckled. This was getting interesting as every piece provided an additional strand to her family background.

She opened her bag and took out her sandwiches.

'Oh, you're here,' said Mrs Wilcox. She strode across the office and took off her coat and shook off the raindrops. 'I bought us sandwiches and strawberry tarts.' She hung her coat on the corner stand and placed her wet umbrella to one side.

'Oh, I brought my lunch,' said Laura.

'I'll put the kettle on.' Mrs Wilcox put the food onto the table. 'You'll have a tart they are delicious and were Irene's favourites.' She rushed into the kitchenette and returned with a pot of tea, cups and milk.

Mrs Wilcox sat back in her chair. 'What did you want to ask?' she said and sipped her tea.

'Mrs Wilcox, it's about my mother's family.'

'Diane, please call me Diane.'

'Yes Diane. I mean my mother's parents, do you know them, are they still around?'

'They were lovely, but I think they retired abroad.'

'Abroad, but where?'

'They owned the Wheatsheaf Inn. Irene would have picnics in the garden.'

Mrs Wilcox nodded as Laura helped herself to a sandwich.

'Your mother would get us a bottle of cider and we would sit under the tree at the back of the garden. I say sit, we were hiding from her dad as he didn't know about the cider.'

'Where have they gone?'

'They sold the pub and I think they moved to France or was it the Canary Islands? I really don't know.'

'Why did they leave and did they know about me?'

'Laura, they retired before you were born. Oh, I think they knew about you all right, and Irene talked about going to visit them one day.'

'But she never did.'

'I wouldn't say that. Maybe she's with them now for all we know.' She added sugar and stirred her tea. The spoon rattled against the cup. 'She disappeared, remember. She left without saying goodbye.'

Laura swallowed, and the bread seemed to stick in her throat before it slid down her oesophagus. 'Who would know?' She stared at Mrs Wilcox who rattled her spoon, once more, against the cup.

Mrs Wilcox shrugged.

'I don't believe you, someone must know,' she said and then raised her voice. 'And if Mum is in Spain, the police would know.'

'Then ask them.'

'Maybe I will,' said Laura. 'Oh sorry, I didn't mean to be rude. Can I ask you about this photo?' She turned to the picture of the names carved into the tree bark.

'Oh my, yes.' Mrs Wilcox picked up the album. 'I forgot about this, we were just kids, a teenage crush. All the girls loved Billy.'

'I saw your wedding picture.'

'Where? I haven't brought them.'

'In the Gazette, married to Edward Wilcox, that makes Great Aunt Margaret your mother-in-law.'

'Yes, I expect it does.' She sipped her tea and watched Laura for a response. 'Yes, Edward took over the farm after his father died, Margaret moved to the farm cottage.'

'Great aunt.'

'Yes, Great Aunt Margaret. Would you like a strawberry tart? They are delicious.'

'Please. I would like to visit her.' Laura lifted the tart and placed it on a napkin. 'Can I have her telephone number?'

'Irene loved these tarts, she couldn't get enough.'

'It would be nice to meet Great Aunt Margaret.'

'Yes, I expect it would be nice. I'll take you, but not today.'

'Your children would be my second cousins.'

'Yes, I expect so. Sorry to disappoint you, but there are no second cousins. There are no children.'

'Oh! I'm sorry, that was rude of me.' Laura picked up the tart. 'It's just, I thought, the baby booties in the album.'

'No, you wouldn't have known.' She reached over and opened the album. 'Yes, those.' She turned over a few pages to a picture of a naked baby lying on a white rug.

'He's cute,' said Laura.

'She's cute. Yes, she is the baby I always dreamed of having.'

Laura watched the muscles relax on Mrs Wilcox's face and waited for a tear.

'So, what happened to the baby I mean.'

'The baby? It's in the past, I don't like to dwell on the past.'

'Sorry,' said Laura, 'I didn't mean to intrude, I understand.'

'No, it's okay. Where did you get that scar?'

'I fell onto a broken bottle when I was little.'

'You have a beautiful face, just as I imagined.' Mrs Wilcox stroked the picture of the baby.

'What was my mother like? Was she in trouble?'

'Certainly not! She was lovely, honestly. Now eat up.'

'If you were best friends, did she not confide in you?'

'All her secrets you mean?' Mrs Wilcox slammed the album shut.

'Yes, I expect so. Why is she missing?'

'Laura, I have something to show you, but only if you promise not to tell anyone.'

'What is it?'

'The police have never seen what I will give you, and you mustn't tell anyone for your mother's sake. Do you promise?'

'Why? You know where she is then, will you help me reach her?'

'Do you promise?' Mrs Wilcox stood up and looked down with a direct stare. 'Say it!'

'What?'

'For your mother's sake!' Wilcox took a step closer and glowered at Laura.

'Yes, I promise.' She blurted the words out impulsively and shuddered as a chill rippled down her spine.

'That's better.' Mrs Wilcox's expression lightened, and she smiled.

'What is it?'

'Some postcards.'

'From my mother?' Laura held her breath for a moment.

'Yes.' Wilcox walked to her desk and retrieved a white envelope from a bottom drawer. She gave it to Laura. 'Here, you can read them later. I believe your mother is alive and with a friend. Read them and see what you can learn.'

'You know where she is, don't you?'

'Oh Laura, no one knows, trust me, no one really knows.' She looked out of the window. 'It's stopped. The awful rain has stopped.'

'I don't understand, what is she hiding from?'

'Hiding? Yes, I suppose she must be hiding, but I've no idea.'

'What should I do? Where do I look?'

'Come and stay at Oakwood Farm. Once Irene knows her baby is with me, she might come home.'

Chapter Eleven

Back at Russet House, Laura spread the postcards across the dining room table and arranged them by date.

The earliest was dated the 5th October 1979, with a postmark from Folkestone. It showed a picture of a ship–The Horsa. A scrawled message on the back of the card reported how they were waiting for hours as the Sealink ferry was delayed because of the stormy weather. It was signed with a scribbled flourish.

Who were they?

The next was dated December 1979 and from Amsterdam. The message to Dear Diane was about ryebread and disgusting greasy sausages, but lovely soft cheese. They enjoyed their boat trip on the canal.

The May 1980 card was from Berlin. The weather was so hot they paddled all day in the Wannsee and watched a sounder of wild boar snorting and foraging in the Grunewald.

Laura wiped the cut on her arm with a piece of wet cotton wool and applied antiseptic cream to the wound.

She had left the library and took the Kirkindale to Marston bus; the driver dropped her at Springwater Lane. The early evening clouds had cleared, and the sunlight reflected off the wet tarmac along the lane.

She had stood on the grass verge as a tractor approached. Its yellow wheels took up the entire width of the narrow road, and she had taken a further step back. The vehicle swerved towards her. Had he not seen her? The glare from the tractor's windscreen had obscured her view of the driver's face. She slipped on the wet vegetation and had tumbled into the ditch where she cut her arm on a broken bottle. By the time she had crawled out of the ditch, the tractor had sped off down the major road. Was he the same man she had seen herding the cows? Was he Old Charlie?

From the table, she picked up the next card dated November 1980. They were at Lake Garda, in Italy, enjoying the refreshing Bardolino wine with soft bread, tortellini pasta and prosciutto hams. The picture showed a view of a hillside covered in vineyards and a background of mountains.

The last card was dated March 1985 and had a picture of a church named the Sagrada Familia. Dear Diane, the apples we bought today were delicious. We got lost in the fruit market. We are planning a visit to Milan for a few days. See you soon. The message ended with a scribbled flourish as on all the other cards.

Laura compared the cards, and they all ended with the usual; see you soon. This made little sense. Mrs Wilcox needed to explain what was going on. Why was it so important that she should tell no one about these cards? If they were from her mother who was she with?

She gathered the five cards and slipped them into their envelope. She went into the kitchen and placed the envelope on the sill by the sink. She filled the kettle.

The front door banged. Who had come into the house? She rushed to the hall. It was empty. She heard someone running on the gravel of the driveway. She dashed out of the front door. A brown and white collie trotted behind a man, who wore a Barbour jacket and flat cap. He sprinted around the bend towards the exit of the drive.

She went after them. 'Hoy! Hello,' she shouted as she ran to catch up with the intruder.

She looked up and down the lane, but the dog and its owner had found a gap in the hedge. She ran up the track and looked over a gate; they had sprinted across the field. She vaulted the steel frame; slipped in the mud and fell forward into a puddle. She got up and wiped her face with her hand. She saw that the man and his dog had reached the far end of the field. She stamped her foot and watched as the dog leapt a fence and the man hurdled over it. They both disappeared into the woods. A few moments later, she heard a vehicle engine start and a Toyota pickup drove out of the woods. It sped across the bottom of the field and through an open gate onto the road.

Back at the house, she locked the door and fastened the chain. She checked both the others, the kitchen patio doors, and the utility external door into the garden. She had locked them in the morning before she had left. Did the intruder have a key to the front door?

In her room, she discovered the bedding had been stripped from the bed and thrown across the floor. Someone had emptied her rucksack out and scattered the photograph albums over the mattress. She could not find her diary, birth certificate or passport. She had wrapped them in a T-shirt and pushed it to the bottom of her rucksack. She scrambled around searching among her clothes and found the T-shirt under the bed.

After this intrusion, she might consider accepting Mrs Wilcox's offer of a room at Oakwood Farm.

She stripped off her dirty clothes in the en-suite; washed and changed into her tracksuit.

She sat on the mattress as her legs were shaking. Someone was in the house when she had arrived back from Kirkindale. They would have heard her come in and listened as she made tea in the kitchen. He must have known she was in the dining-room. If the wind had not caught and slammed the front door as the person left, she may have blamed Scott for ransacking her belongings.

From under the bed, she dragged out the box containing the wedding dress and lifted out the silk material and shook it. Newspaper cuttings fluttered onto the bed and over the floor. The dress, although it had a few creases from the folds, appeared pristine and she held it against her body. It would fit, but she had no intention of trying it on. She draped it over the chair and picked up the front page of the 25th July 1979 Gazette. The headline read: "Kirkindale Reels from Shock". There was a photograph of Mrs Sophia Dawson and one of her daughters-in-law, Mrs Irene Dawson.

Laura stared at the headlines and slumped onto the bed. She read the columns. Tears trickled, then turned into a wash over her cheeks. She collected up the paper cuttings and sorted them in order and read over the various snippets.

An angler had found Sophia Dawson floating in the River Marrs, below the Mill Pool. Her head was brutally smashed. The angler had run all the way to the village to call the Emergency services.

The fisherman had reported seeing the family group earlier in the day, having a picnic by the pool, but said nothing more.

The investigation suggested the cause of death resulted from a sustained attack with multiple blows to the head. The police considered a bloodstained granite rock, lying nearby, was the likely weapon. When the police arrived, there were no signs of Mrs Irene Dawson.

When the police went to Russet House, they discovered Mary and Laura Dawson sat in the garden where they were eating ice cream with strawberries.

The group had been enjoying a family picnic at the popular site, the Mill Pool. Mary Dawson had taken her niece, Laura, back to the house to fetch some dry towels.

Laura wiped her face, although the tears continued. She took deep breaths. Why couldn't she remember the picnic? All she could picture was sitting on the swing being pushed.

> A later Gazette reported that the police had found no trace of the missing woman, and the local speculation concluded that she had either been abducted or ran away. The police were determined to trace Irene Dawson to explain the death of her mother-in-law and were concerned for the woman's own safety. The search of the surrounding area by hundreds of police and volunteers had found no trace of Mrs Irene Dawson. The investigation had confirmed that searches at the ports, both air and land, had not detected the woman leaving the country, but they couldn't rule out she may have escaped by clandestine means. Traveller groups and seasonal workers were being traced for information.

She looked through the rest of the cuttings, most of which were speculating about the death of Sophia Dawson. None reported any substantial advance in the investigation.

> In one article a journalist claimed, from inside sources in the investigation, how the police were convinced that Irene

> Dawson had murdered her mother-in-law. They were determined to trace her whereabouts and bring her to justice.

She turned over the newspaper pages, looking for an explanation. For what reason would her mother kill her grandmother? Had it been a terrible accident?

She lay back on the mattress and stared at the ceiling, forcing her mind to visualise the picnic. She saw herself splashing in the water, running around the large rock, sitting on a woollen rug, eating fairy cakes, and laughing. She could not have been alone, yet her mind refused to complete the scene. Was this suggestive speculation? Had she been at the picnic by the river, or had she been in the garden all the time?

She tidied up the room and made the bed.

She sat on the bed and spread the newspapers and cuttings out over the duvet. She read them over and over. Perhaps she had missed something important. There was the name of a policeman from Marston, Detective Sergeant Jackson, who was the investigating officer in the case. Would he still be around?

Mrs Wilcox had never mentioned the murder. Why not? She must know all about Sophia Dawson's murder. Perhaps she found the incident difficult to talk about and was waiting for an appropriate moment to say something.

Was her mum really a murderer? George must have known. Did he remove the newspapers in the archives to spare her the horror of finding out? She had to know the truth.

She heard a vehicle in the driveway coming towards the house.

Scott will expect a meal. She got up from the bed and went into the bathroom. In the mirror, she saw how red her eyelids appeared; she splashed water onto her face and dried herself with a towel. She dabbed face lotion onto her cheeks and rubbed it over her skin. Scott will notice she had been crying, but she'll explain that she suffers from hay fever.

The front doorbell chimed.

Chapter Twelve

Mary's eyes were closed, and her breathing was shallow.

'She wants to come and see you,' said Scott. He leaned forward in his chair by the hospital bed.

Mary lifted her arm and dropped it again. 'Laura was a lovely baby girl,' she said and turned her head to look at him.

'I'll bring her tomorrow if you feel up to it.'

'Yes please, but did you burn the box and newspapers?' she said. 'Tell me you did.'

The door to the ward clattered open.

'Dad!' said Mary. 'What is it?'

Scott stood up. 'Mr Dawson. I'll get another chair.'

'Aye well. Who is that you've got at the house?' Old Charlie pointed at Scott and then turned to Mary. 'How are you, lass?'

'It's Irene's Laura, Dad.' Mary said and attempted to sit up. 'She's come looking for her mother.'

Scott reached over and adjusted the pillows to help Mary get comfortable.

Mr Dawson sat by the bed and took off his hat. 'Aye, I was afraid of that,' he said and dusted his cap across his knees. 'She is a fine-looking woman, just like her mother. But it's trouble.'

'You've met her?' She reached for a drink. 'What is she like?'

Scott picked up a jug and poured water into a plastic cup and passed it to Mary. He said, 'She's searching the records in the library and listing her relatives.'

'How are you feeling?' Old Charlie reached out and touched Mary's elbow. 'I've been worried, and now this evil from the past.'

'Dad, what is it?' Mary waved her cup towards Scott. He poured her some more water.

'Tea, that's what you need,' Old Charlie said and tapped Mary's hand. He smiled.

'Scott, could you get us some tea?' she said and stared at him until he nodded. 'Please, from the café and not the machine. Please.'

Scott picked up his mobile telephone from the side table and left the ward.

Old Charlie followed Scott to the door and closed it. He checked if he could lock it, then he gave up trying. He came and sat by Mary's bed.

'Dad, I really don't care.' She lifted the cup and her arm shook.

He steadied the cup and held it to her lips. She took a mouthful and turned her face away. 'She wants to come and see me.'

'What for? We have nothing for her.' He put the cup down. 'Irene murdered Sophia. What will people think if we take this Laura in?'

'You don't know that! Dad, she is my niece, your grandchild, she's family.'

'She'll be a reminder to everyone, they'll point. No, no, she has to go for her own sake.'

'She was a lovely child, I want to see her.'

'Money, is that what she wants?'

'It was not her fault.'

'Aye, I want nothing to do with this Laura, tell her.'

'If you explain what happened and maybe, she'll understand. But I don't know what she'll do.'

'Exactly, I'll tell her what happened, that'll put an end to it.'

'No Dad, I'll tell her. You'll just lose your temper.'

'Well maybe. Aye, it would be better from you, just get her to go away.'

'We are her family, her home should have been with us,' said Mary.

'Aye, her mother's a murderer. You tell her that.'

'You don't know if that's true.'

'Don't I? Don't I know. This girl will stir everything up.' He slapped his cap across his knees.

'Oh Dad, it's not her fault, I'll tell her the truth and she'll understand.'

'You underestimate the truth. You tell her nothing of the sort.'

There was a knock at the door before it swung open and Scott carried in three polystyrene cups full of tea.

'Sugar and milk for all,' he said and placed them onto the side table.

Charlie Dawson stood up. 'Now you get better, lass. Remember what I said.' He waved away the offered cup of tea. 'Now, I must be off. Beasts to feed.' He walked out, leaving the door open.

'What was that about?' said Scott and offered the tea to Mary. She shook her head and leaned back. She closed her eyes.

'Well, just as I thought,' he said and sat down.

'Bring Laura tomorrow, please.' Mary coughed and cleared her throat. 'Before it's too late.'

'Too late! No, Mary, Dr Jamal says you're getting better.'

'Did you get rid of the newspapers from the attic?' She reached and grabbed his hand.

'Newspapers! From the attic. Yes.' He gently tapped her hand and she let go. 'Yes, I've burned everything, cleared the lot out.' He waited for some praise. 'I spoke to Anne, she mentioned that Laura has asked George to find out who owns our house.'

'I think Dad does. Yes, Dad owns the place. It was a wedding present for William and Irene.'

'So, you'll inherit the place.'

'Scott, I don't want to talk about this. Yes, you'll get the place when I die. Is that what you want me to say?'

'No Mary. Sorry, I'm just saying what Laura is up to.'

'I never thought I would see her again, and I never understood why they took her away.'

'Are you going to tell me what's going on?'

Mary closed her eyes. 'I'm tired, and I want to sleep.'

Scott studied her face. The strain of the illness had worn Mary out. He was certain, irrespective of Dr Jamal's optimism, that she was dying. Her pallor was ashen-grey like the colour of death, and her body was frail.

In the afternoons, he would stand by and watch as the physiotherapist and nurses helped her to exercise her limbs. They would lift her legs and move them back and forth to increase the blood flow through her muscles. Mary groaned and complained each time. She appeared to suffer more from the effort of moving rather than enjoy the treatment.

Mary gave a gentle sigh and appeared to relax into a deep sleep.

Scott walked to the window and looked out. There was a queue of vehicles towards the car park exit. Hospital visitors on their way to hot meals and comfortable beds at home.

Had Mary misled him about who owned the house, or had he over the years lived with a false assumption? There was no guarantee he would inherit the place now if Old Charlie owned Orchard View. The old man rarely spoke to him and even less after the incident with the bull calves. He rubbed at the scar on the back of his hand and although the wound had healed, on chilly days his thumb would feel numb.

He had warned Old Charlie about his lack of hygiene when ten of his calves went down with salmonellosis from contaminated milk powders. It was likely caused by the dirty buckets he used for the feeds. Perhaps he could have put it across to Old Charlie in a less forceful manner, as he had taken the accusations personally. In response, the old man had thrown a pitchfork at him. He had tried to deflect it but was too late and a spike cut and pierced the back of his hand.

With medication, treatment, and clean practices the animals recovered, but the relationship between him and the old farmer remained bitter and distant.

He went back to Mary's bed and picked up the patient's folder and flipped through the charts. There were no recorded changes to Mary's condition. Her breathing was shallow and regular, but her appearance was awful.

He couldn't help the disturbing thoughts which rattled around in his mind. He threw the folder across the room. Was he about to lose everything? Everything he dreamed about.

Chapter Thirteen

The doorbell chimed. Laura stood in the hallway and waited. Scott would have his house and car keys together on the same keyring. The bell chimed again.

In the dining room, she peered out of the window and through the overhang of ivy. A weathered, green Land Rover with a tattered canvas top was parked out front and a cocker spaniel sat by the rear wheel. The dog focused its attention on the person stood by the house door. Laura knocked on the window and waved to show she was coming.

She opened the door and the woman, who appeared to be in her sixties with a fresh healthy complexion, smiled. She rushed into the hallway with her arms wide, and the dog ran in behind her. She attempted to grasp and hug Laura, who stepped back and out of reach.

'So, it's true,' said the woman. 'Sorry, I'm Margaret.'

'Great Aunt Margaret?'

'Great Aunt, I expect I must be.' She laughed. 'Diane mentioned you'd arrived, and I wanted to meet you. So here I am.'

'Yes, please come through.'

It surprised and delighted Laura since, at last, a family relative had taken sufficient interest to visit her. The woman thrust her hand forward to introduce herself again, and the grip was firm.

She wore black stubby wellington boots, a floral dress, a short tweed jacket covered in dog hairs, and had a floppy bush hat pushed over her neatly tucked in hair. She slipped the boots off in the hallway. A toe stuck out through a hole in her left woollen sock.

'I was feeding the horses when Diane told me you'd arrived. Well, here I am.'

They sat at the kitchen table drinking tea with a plate of digestive biscuits between them. The spaniel, half asleep, rested its head on Margaret's lap.

'Diane told me about your project.'

'My family history. Yes, but I am also looking for Mum.'

'You look so like your grandfather,' said Margaret, 'and you have your mother's smile and such lovely hair.'

'A Dawson, but not like a Stewart?' said Laura. She felt a lump in her throat and got up from the table. At the sink, she filled a glass with water and took a few sips. She turned and stood to stare at the woman. It seems dear Great Aunt Margaret has come to gawp and satisfy her curiosity. Is she only interested in gathering tittle tattle for gossip?

'I was wondering, could tell me about my mother.'

'I've no idea where she is, if that is what you mean?' Margaret stroked the dog's head. 'Your mother was a wonderful girl, an exceptional artist. I have two of her oils at home.' She smiled and picked up a biscuit.

She dunked it in her tea before raising the cup to take a sip. 'I wouldn't be surprised if her landscapes were in the Marston gallery.' She placed the cup down, and it clattered on the table. The dog raised its head and looked at her.

'Sorry, clumsy me.' Her hand shook, and she laid it flat on her lap. 'The mention of your mother, poor soul. It gets to me.'

'Why did she run away?' Laura put her glass down and came to sit at the table.

'Oh Laura, something terrible happened, and she had to leave.' She picked up her teacup.

'You mean my grandmother's murder at the Mill Pool.'

Margaret dropped her cup, and it bounced off her lap onto the floor and smashed. 'You know!' She stared at Laura. 'Oh sorry, get me a cloth. I'll clean it up.'

'I've read the newspaper reports, but it doesn't say why.'

'They never do.' Margaret picked up the broken pieces of porcelain and placed them on the table. She wiped the floor with a tea towel. 'If you don't mind, I think it's best we don't talk about Sophia's death. It's not nice.' She took the wet cloth to the sink and washed it in running warm water. She had her back towards Laura, and she picked up the white envelope from the windowsill and slipped it under her cardigan.

'Why won't anyone talk about it. My mum is missing.'

'A murderer!'

'Missing, I mean she is missing.'

'Sorry Laura, I don't know. We have to let the past rest.' Margaret came across the kitchen and sat at the table. 'Please.'

'I will visit Mary tomorrow. I wonder if I'll recognise her.'

'Poor girl, she's been ill for a while now, ever since she fell off her horse, you know.'

'What can you tell me about my other grandparents and the Wheatsheaf?'

'The Wheatsheaf, yes, I remember Jean and Albert, they owned the place.'

'Do you know where they've gone?'

'They went bankrupted, and Charlie felt sorry for them, so he gave them money to start over in Spain.' Margaret shook her head. 'I heard they both passed away, but I can't be sure. Ask Diane she might know.'

'Aunt Margaret, why can't we talk about my grandmother Sophia's murder?'

'You already know, don't you?' Margaret scratched behind the dog's ears. 'I suspect Diane told you all about it.'

'I've only read the articles in the old copies of the Gazette. What really happened?'

'How much do you know? It's not nice.' Margaret pushed the dog off her lap. 'Blasted dribbler, that's the trouble with spaniels they dribble.'

The dog crawled under the table and laid by her feet.

'The news was on the radio that afternoon, what a shock. Poor Sophia.' She reached for another biscuit. 'They said Irene was missing. I phoned the house to speak with Mary, but it was the police who answered. They had arrested someone.'

'But they caught no one. Have they?'

'You must understand how everyone in the village was in shock. I went up to the farm. Diane and Ed were in the barn and what a state poor Diane was in.'

'I don't understand.' She poured the tea.

'No, I couldn't either. She was bleeding.'

'Diane was bleeding? What happened?'

'Ed said she had slipped in the byre and he took her into the house.' She shook her head. 'Drunk, she was drunk and gibbering about murder. I couldn't get any sense out of her.'

'What did she mean about murder?'

'Well, Ed had scratches on his face and a bruised eye. So what should I do? I left them to it.' She picked up another biscuit. 'It was the first time I had known them to fight.'

'I am not sure what this has got to do—'

'It was on the radio again next morning. All about the death at the pool,' said Margaret. 'I phoned Diane, and she was in hysterics. They had been the best of friends.'

'On the radio?'

'Yes, from the radio, where else?' Margaret dropped her biscuit. 'Sorry clumsy me. Look, let's talk about happier times. I'll help you with your family tree, how's that.'

'That would be nice.'

'You know, stay with me at the farm cottage.'

'Well, I could, maybe, but I am happy here.'

'Think about it. It will be pleasant company and imagine all the family gossip you could learn.'

An hour later Great Aunt Margaret left Russet House, and her Land Rover spewed a trail of black diesel fumes as she drove out of the drive.

Laura set about preparing dinner and she mulled over what her Great Aunt Margaret had told her.

Margaret had recently retired as a teacher from the Marston Grammar School and had known most of the children as they grew up in the village. She was knowledgeable, or was it gossip, about the affairs of many local families. Also, she knew the history of the Stewart side of Laura's family and gave her the names to add to her family tree. Unfortunately, they were dead or had moved away from Kirkindale.

She learned from Margaret that her grandfather, Albert Stewart, had a brother who lived alone somewhere up north, but she didn't know where. Also, she learned her grandmother, Jean Stewart, had a sister called Daphne who was living in Marston. Another great-aunt somebody or another was how Margaret described her. She didn't know if she was married, but her maiden name was Lister, just like her grandmother, Jean Lister.

Irene was an only child and, according to Margaret, one of the happiest pupils at the school. Diane, she said, was frequently bitter and carried grudges much longer than most children her age.

In the kitchen, the soup and the meatballs were in their pots, heated and ready. She intended to cook the spaghetti once Scott arrived back from the hospital. In the meantime, she took a mop and bucket and wiped the kitchen and hall floors where the spaniel had dribbled and left paw marks. She would love to have a dog one day, perhaps a Labrador, as they were soft and friendly.

She sat down and looked over the list of names from her mother's side of the family, a list she would add to her chart in the library.

Since George could not let her into the research department the next day, she planned a visit to Marston. First, she would visit Mary in the hospital with Scott and if she had time, she would visit the solicitors, the police station and perhaps search for her grandmother's sister.

She checked the time. Scott was later than expected. She was hungry. It would not be rude to eat on her own, and she could heat his meal for him later.

She heard the telephone ringing in the private area of the house. She ran and fetched the key from the utility room. She climbed through the hatch and rushed through the attic into the garage.

The glass door at the end of the corridor opened out into a hallway in the house. The door on the left was closed. Further on, a compact room doubled as an office and the telephone was on the desk. It had stopped ringing.

She had promised to call home but had not taken the opportunity so far. She picked up the handset and dialled.

'Jenny, it's me.' She smiled as the familiar voice replied with a gush of questions.

'Tell Mum everything is fine.' She always referred to Mrs McLean as Mum when speaking to Jenny, but she refused to call her mum to her face or for anyone else.

'No, I haven't found out yet, but I have a family history chart. Yes, it's almost complete,' she said. 'I should be home on Friday. Okay.'

The gravel crunched as a vehicle drove to the front of the house.

'Jenny, I'll call you later, bye.'

Back in the kitchen, she stood by the sink and Scott came in.

'Tea? I've just filled the kettle.' She was flushed from her exertion, dashing through the attic and down the stairs. In her hurry, had she replaced the hatch?

'How is Mary?' she said. She filled a pot with water to boil the spaghetti.

'The same and well, thanks.' He took his keys and unlocked the door into the private part of the house.

'Could I visit her tomorrow?'

'I'm not sure about tomorrow. Well, maybe in the afternoon. I'll speak with her and let you know.'

'Do you mind if I make a telephone call,' she said. 'I promised to call home and, well, I've forgotten so far.' She waited for a reply. 'I'll pay for the call.'

'Yea, I suppose so.' He pointed through the doorway. 'It's in the office. Five minutes long enough?'

When she returned, Scott was talking on his mobile telephone. He got up and locked the door into the private area.

'Look, I need to get back down to the hospital,' he said and finished his tea in one gulp. 'But let's eat first. It smells good.'

She twisted her spaghetti around her fork until it was too large for a mouthful; she watched him eat.

'Someone has been in the house,' she said. 'Whoever it was has stolen my passport.'

'What?' said Scott through a mouthful of food. 'What do you mean? Did they break in?'

'I think he had a key.'

'He, did you see him, who was it?'

'No, he ran off, but I saw his car, it was a pickup.'

'A pickup, lots of people have those around here.'

'Why did he have a key?'

'I think you should report your lost passport. Did they get any money?'

'No, but who would have a key?'

He picked up his mobile. 'I won't be back tonight,' he said. 'Sorry but I have to go. Make sure you lock all the doors, all the time.'

'I didn't leave them unlocked, if that is what you mean.'

'Be careful, Laura. I need to go.'

He put on his jacket and left the house.

Laura collected up the plates and cups from the table and took them to the sink. At least he had time to eat the spaghetti. It might be better if she took the bus into Marston and visited Mary. Why does she need his permission?

Chapter Fourteen

Laura sat on the bus as it wound its way along the narrow road to Marston. She admired the various views across the fields to the woodlands on the hillsides with their patchworks of spring-green shades. These scenic sights of natural beauty were the inspiration for her mother's landscape paintings, which showed her dedication and love for her art. She must have found this valley a wonderful place to live.

The letters from McCarthy and Sinclair were in her pocket, and these showed her mother was the legal owner of Russet House. She would ask the solicitors to confirm if this was true and ask if her mother had prepared a will. Last night, she read the letters over and over and she understood from them, her mother owned Russet House.

During the evening she scrutinised the newspaper articles, searching for some clarity about the murder of her grandmother. One snippet mentioned how an unnamed source had come forward, who claimed to have witnessed an argument between the Dawson women the previous day. The more she read, the more confused the story seemed. There was one article which suggested a sighting of Irene Dawson at a hostel in London. Another claimed that individuals from the traveller group were responsible for the murder of both women.

The shocking idea of her mother being a wanted person kept her mind racing all night and searching for explanations. It must have been a terrible accident, or as speculated, someone abducted her mother. These thoughts terrified her, but somehow softened her attitude towards an uncaring mother who had abandoned her only child. What! Was she an only child? She didn't remember there being other children at Russet House, and Great Aunt Margaret had not mentioned if there were. She should have asked her.

The acceleration of a car leaving the driveway had woken her in the early morning. She had leapt out of bed and crept down to the kitchen. The dirty plates from last night's leftovers were in the sink, and there were half eaten toast crusts in a cereal bowl. She shuddered.

Scott had come home late and eaten the remains of their evening meal. She had been in a deep sleep and had not heard him come home or make breakfast in the morning. Did he check to see if she was in the house?

What if the intruder was to return during the night? Before she got into bed, she had jammed the chair against her bedroom door but knew it would not survive a few sturdy kicks. The noise would wake her and give her time to get her knife.

Her meditation and the effect of the lavender fragrance on her pillows did not induce her usual relaxed sleep. Instead, her mind struggled to make sense of the newspaper reports and she tried to understand what might have occurred at the picnic. Images of people appeared as a jumble of blank faces; men in the orchards and women in the garden. She imagined her mother wandering in the woods. She wore a wedding dress and was calling for Laura. Eventually, exhaustion took over. Until the vehicle in the drive woke her.

The bus turned onto a side road and stopped by a thatched cottage where the driver sounded the horn a few times. The house door opened, and Anne Ferguson walked down the path and got into the bus. She saw Laura and came up the aisle and sat next to her.

'Hello,' said Anne, and she settled herself into the seat. 'It's a lovely day.'

'Day off?' said Laura and shifted her day sack by her feet.

'Dentist, just a check-up.' She opened her mouth wide to show her teeth. 'I had the braces taken out last month.'

'I had those when I was about fourteen.'

'So, did I,' said Anne, and she shuffled her bottom. 'The other bus has softer seats. Where are you off to?'

'I can't get in the research room since George is busy, so I thought a trip to Marston might be nice.' She gazed out of the window at the ewes and lambs in the field, oblivious of the passing vehicle. The bus drove over a narrow sandstone bridge and on the bank of the river, a man stood angling. He was swinging his line back and forth over the water; his hat obscured his face.

'I'll meet you after my appointment. Woolworths have a new range of clothes in this week.'

'I'm okay, I'm not after any.' Laura shook her head. 'Thanks, but I might not have time.'

'My cousin's getting married and I need a dress.'

'Do you know where Barrister Row is?' said Laura.

'No idea, but Brian will know. He knows everything.'

'Brian?'

'The driver, I'll ask him for you as we get off,' said Anne and laughed. 'He knows everyone in Marston. Do you know someone there?'

'I'm looking for the McCarthy solicitors.'

Laura saw the smug smile from Anne and realised she had done it again. She clenched her fist and slowly released it. She had let slip her reason for visiting Marston.

'People talk about you staying at the B and B, you know,' said Anne.

She had noticed the odd looks and stares she occasionally got, but decided the reactions were a natural curiosity whenever a stranger arrived in Kirkindale.

'I hope it's nice.'

'I mean my Uncle isn't like that, he's married and everything.'

'Yes, to my Aunt Mary.' She nodded. Scott would be her uncle.

'They say she left it too late for treatment. I saw her last week. She looked awful.'

'Do you know what ward she's in?'

'Ward, in the hospital, not sure. They keep moving her.' Anne fumbled in her handbag. 'Appointment card, it's here somewhere.'

The bus entered Marston and stopped in Market Square. Anne was first up and rushed forward to speak to the driver. Laura took her time and followed an elderly couple who were taking shuffling steps and holding onto the back of the seats as they moved towards the exit.

Anne was waiting on the pavement. 'Barrister Row is just around the corner from Fiddlers' Green,' she said and pointed towards a street off the far side of the square.

'Got to go or I'll be late.' She walked off, then stopped and turned. 'See you at Miller's café,' she called and pointed to the shopping centre.

Laura strode across the Square and walked on to Fiddlers' Green. Barrister Row was a single line of houses built with dark sandstone. On the opposite side of the road, a stone wall separated the pavement from the river.

There was a brass plate by a door engraved with black lettering; Number 8, McCarthy and Sinclair, Solicitors and Conveyance.

She went up the steps and through the open front door into the hallway. There was a sign which stated: 'Please Push for Attention.' She pressed the bell.

The three doors off the hallway were closed and opposite them, there was a stairway covered in a tattered and worn carpet.

She waited. A damp musty smell emanated from the faded floral wallpaper and its odour crept around her. She pressed the bell again.

A door opened and a tall woman with knobbly knees protruding beneath her mauve skirt looked at her. Laura returned the stare.

'Yes, dear!' The woman looked over the top of her glasses. 'Do you have an appointment? I'm not expecting anyone.'

'No, it's just a quick question.' Laura took out the letters from her pocket.

'No such thing, dear.' She tossed back the fringe that had slipped over her eyes. 'I can't see you just now. What's it about?'

'Russet House. George said, you might have the deeds.'

'Are you buying or selling, frankly you look like neither.' She removed her glasses. 'George! How is the old fart these days?'

A Persian cat appeared and rubbed itself against the woman's legs.

'He mentioned that Jeffrey would know.'

'Look, all right, dear. I'll give you five minutes, give me those.'

Laura held out the letters, and the woman snatched them from her.

'Come in dear, sit over there.' She pointed to a tartan covered sofa as she walked behind her desk and slouched into a white leather chair. She spread the letters over the polished surface next to two buff folders that were closed. A desk nameplate with gold letters on a wooden stand stated–Jeffrey Sinclair, LLB, Solicitor.

The office had a new beige carpet and at the far end, from the windows, was an unobstructed view out over the town's botanical gardens. The daylight through the windows filled the room with an airy atmosphere. Along one side of the room, someone had organised the filing cabinets with coloured alphabetical labels. A vase of fresh lavender stood on an occasional table beside an air freshener, which gave off an orange aroma.

'Where did you get these?'

'They were with my mother's things in the attic.'

'Your mother is Irene Dawson?'

'Yes, I was wondering if she still owned Russet House.'

'What is your name, dear? Do you have any proof of identification?'

'Laura, Laura Dawson. What kind of proof?'

'Mm, I remember these. What a bitter battle over the house, I must get Doreen to check our archives.'

'Would you know if my mother made a will?' Laura said and came towards the desk.

'Look dear, you can't just walk in here and—' She waved at Laura to sit back down. 'Sorry dear, let's make an appointment.' She took a diary from a desk drawer and flicked open the pages. 'One minute, where is your mother? What's happened?' She lifted her glasses and stared at Laura.

'She went missing in 1979 and I'm trying to find her.' Laura felt her eyes water, and she looked at her feet.

'Missing! Oh yes, now I remember. I'm sorry it was a terrible shock. A terrible murder,' she said, and flipped through her diary. 'I'll get Doreen to gather the files. How does Friday afternoon sound?' She looked up, expecting an answer. 'Oh dear, I don't mean to upset you.'

'Yes, Friday's fine.' She wiped her face with a tissue.

Jeffrey got up from behind the desk and gave Laura her letters, then waved towards the door.

'I'll see you on Friday, dear. Now bring proof of your identity, driving licence, passport, home address and anything about your mother.'

Jeffrey took hold of Laura's hand. 'Now don't worry dear, we'll sort this out.'

Laura nodded and froze as Jeffrey hugged her. She smelled the mixture of lemon oil and old spice.

'Now don't upset yourself, everything will turn out fine dear. It always does.' said Jeffrey and walked with Laura to the outside door. 'Bye dear.'

Laura crossed the road and looked over the wall into the water. A pair of mallard ducks swam across the river to a patch of weeds. She coughed to clear her throat and took deep breaths. She slapped the wall. She didn't mean to weep. Her thoughts about her mother as a wanted woman, and a murderer became overwhelming. What did Jeffrey think? She snorted and touched the side of her cheek where the silk material from Jeffrey's blouse had brushed against her face. Close-up she had seen a growth of stubble through the smear of concealer on the solicitor's face.

She walked along the pavement to a seating area overlooking the river bend. Where she unpacked her sandwiches and a small flask of tea.

Her next visit would be to the police station, where she would report the theft of her passport and stolen diary. She took out her notebook from her day sack and reminded herself of the name, Detective Sergeant Jackson.

Chapter Fifteen

The police station was in an ugly concrete building next to the ornate municipal town hall.

Laura entered through the main door into the reception area and walked up to the glass-covered counter. A middle-aged policewoman sat at a desk and when she saw Laura, she looked up from her reading and smiled. Her chair scraped on the floor as she stood, and then she came to the counter. She opened the glass hatch.

'Good afternoon, my dear,' said the policewoman. 'How can I help you?'

'Hello,' said Laura, 'I want to report a theft.'

'A theft, that's not nice, is it?' She reached down under the counter and brought up a pad of forms. 'Now, let's have the details.'

Laura gave her account of the intruder at Russet House, who had rummaged through her belongings and had taken her birth certificate, passport and diary.

'So, it was a burglary at Russet House,' she said. 'Now that name has stuck in my mind for a long time. I remember an incident there after I transferred from York.'

The policewoman searched among the forms under the counter. 'We don't seem to have any lost passport ones.' She shrugged and looked in a drawer. 'You must go to the post office. They'll have the forms you need to apply for a new passport.'

'Yes, I expect so.' said Laura.

'The registry office where your birth was recorded will provide you with a new certificate. You might need it for your passport application,' said the policewoman. She leaned on the counter and was holding her pen, ready to write. 'Now, what about money, or jewellery, was there anything else missing?'

'I think he had a key to the house.'

'Then my professional advice, Miss Dawson,' said the policewoman. She sighed. 'I am sorry to say you should change the locks on all the external doors. It may be expensive but for your peace of mind and security, you'll agree, it's worth the price.'

'Is it possible to speak to Detective Jackson?'

'Do you know him?'

'No, I'm following up on something I read in an old newspaper.'

'I see. Detective Sergeant Jackson has retired, and he won't help with your intruder. Don't worry, we'll place a patrol car in the area and if the burglar shows up again—'

'He was looking for my mother,' said Laura. She put her arms behind her back and formed fists, then she released them slowly.

'The intruder?'

'No, Detective Jackson. My mother is missing.'

'If you give me your mother's details, her name and when she went missing, I'll check our records.'

'Irene Dawson,1979.'

The policewoman dropped her pen. 'Irene Dawson! Yes, the name Dawson. Give me a minute,' she said and pointed to the seats in the reception area. 'I won't be long, take a pew while you wait.'

She closed the glass hatch and dashed through a doorway into a long corridor.

Twenty minutes later the policewoman returned and came out into the reception carrying a note. 'I spoke with my husband. That is Detective Jackson, well, Mr Jackson now that he is retired. He will meet you in Miller's café in about forty-five minutes,' she said. She passed a copy of the theft report to Laura. 'You'll need that, to show you've reported your stolen passport.'

She took the form, folded it, and put it in her bag.

'You won't remember me,' said the policewoman. She smiled and nodded.

'Should I?' said Laura

'Perhaps not. One of our detectives will be in contact in a few days. Someone will talk to you officially about your mother's case.'

'My mother's case?'

'Yes, she is a missing person, is she not?'

§

Laura approached Millers café and looked through the window to check if Anne had arrived. Why didn't she ask the policewoman to change the meeting place with the detective? She should have thought it through. She intended to avoid Anne, or at least make an excuse about her visiting a relative. If Jackson appeared first, she'll persuade him to go elsewhere. Pacing up and down on the pavement seemed ridiculous as anyone sitting in the café would notice, but then again would they care.

She pretended to read the menu in the window and saw Anne come through from the back of the café. She watched her wander around at first before she put her large Woolworth's bag down on the floor and sat at a table. A waitress approached and spoke with Anne.

There was an entrance into the café from the shopping alley she was not aware of. Would the retired policeman use it? She turned her back on the window and scanned up and down the street for Detective Jackson. He was going bald, has a light-fawn coat, and wears a woollen shirt. You'll know him when you see him; the policewoman had assured her. He was late.

Laura moved away from the café and crossed the street to a bookshop where she browsed the latest publications in the window. *The Rainmaker* by John Grisham, another, *The Horse Whisperer*. She couldn't make out the author. The book that caught her attention was *Anne Frank's Tales from the Secret Annex,* translated by Susan Massotty. She had read an earlier version at school and at the time had cried and lamented how horrendous life was.

She noticed a movement reflected in the glass and turned. Across the street, a man in a light-fawn coat entered the café. She dashed over the road and looked in through the window. The man was speaking with Anne, who shook her head and at that moment looked up and saw Laura at the window. Anne pointed and waved. The man turned and stared. Laura willed him to leave and come outside, instead she succumbed to the situation and entered the coffee shop. She smiled.

'Mr Jackson. Are you Mr Jackson?' Laura held out her hand.

'Yes, Miss Dawson, I believe.' He shook her hand.

'Her name's Laura,' said Anne. She moved her shopping bag to make room for them to join her at the table.

'Would you mind if we went for a walk?' said Laura. She let go of his hand and pointed to the exit.

Anne stood up and then immediately sat down when the waitress arrived with a tin of cola and a plate of chips.

'I'll see you later at the bus stop,' said Laura.

'Okay,' said Anne. 'On the bus.'

§

Laura led the way to the path by the river where she sat on a wooden bench. Mr Jackson hesitated before he sat on the seat. He stood and pulled up his coat's collar over his neck.

'I know where we should go, come on.' He set off along the pavement and waved back to her without looking. 'Come on, we'll go to my favourite pub.'

They walked back into the market square and down a side lane to the Farmers' Jug. They sat on the cushioned seats in a side booth. He took off his coat and folded it over a chair and called out to the barman. He asked for a Marston's Ale and a small orange juice for Laura.

'Christine told me who you were, and I had to drop everything,' he said.

'Christine?'

'The policewoman you met at the station.'

'I am pleased you came,' said Laura.

The barman brought over the drinks and placed them on the table.

'Thanks Frank,' said Mr Jackson, and he reached for his beer. He nodded towards Laura. 'This is better than sitting by the river. Besides, it looked like rain.'

'Yes, and it's warm.' she said and took off her jacket. Did the place need the open fire? 'And it's quiet.'

The threadbare high-backed chairs and stained tables in the lounge with its bare floorboards, dull wooded panels, faded woodland wallpaper and mirrors gave the impression of both décor neglect and antiquity. The glow from the burning coal added to the atmosphere of a lost Victorian period when, Laura imagined, there would be labourers at the bar who drank themselves into a rowdy stupor.

She had felt excited about her first visit to a pub with Jenny and her older friends. Unfortunately, it became an unpleasant experience when she had accidentally knocked over a drink. There was an outburst of profanities from a chubby-faced man before she could apologise and offer him a replacement drink.

'That's why I like it here, it's peaceful,' said Mr Jackson. 'Now you want to know about your mother, Irene Dawson.'

'There was a murder and—'

'First, tell me about yourself.' He sat back in his seat. 'You were the girl in the garden, the one Christine chased onto the swing.' He smiled. 'You won't remember.'

'I discovered your name in the Gazette. You were investigating the case.'

'We never found out what happened, or who killed Mrs Dawson.'

'My grandmother.'

'Yes. Have you come to tell me something? Has your mother been in contact?'

'Mr Jackson, I—'

'MJ, it's Malcolm but I go by MJ. I got called MJ during police training and it stuck.'

'I was wondering if you could tell me what happened.'

'What do you know? It's not nice.'

'I've read the newspaper reports. I don't need the detail, just what happened to my mum.'

'I spent thirty years in the police with lots of cases. This was the only one I never solved,' he said, and took a drink. He waited until it settled in his stomach. 'The investigation is still pending, regarded as an open case.' He coughed, then said, 'Pending fresh evidence. You know what that means?'

'They are still looking for—'

'Rubbish, it means it's filed and forgotten.'

'I was hoping you could help.'

'Don't you think I've tried, the hours, the days, months, and years.' He waved to the barman for another drink. 'Sleepless nights, wondering if I had missed something.'

He pointed at her orange juice and said, 'Do you want a top up?'

'No thanks.' She saw a sad look of defeat in his eyes. Or was it pity?

'Time goes on. Sometimes I think your mother magically disappeared. Well, that's understandable if she has something to hide.'

'Here MJ, take your time today.' The barman placed a fresh glass of beer on the table.

'Thanks, Frank, forever the hypocrite.' He looked up at the barman, and they both laughed.

'It must have been an accident,' said Laura. 'What has she got to hide?'

He stared at her and nodded. He picked up his pint and took a slow slurp.

'You know we never could decide on a motive, but it was not an accident.'

A man walked into the lounge and spoke with the barman. He then turned and saw MJ and Laura sitting in the corner. He came over.

'You're early MJ.' The man clapped him on the shoulder. 'I see you have some company eh, a pleasant change.' The man smiled at Laura.

She recognised his eye patch and corduroy trousers. He was the angler who had insisted she shared his catch of fish.

'Well hello, did you enjoy the trout?'

'Ah, yes it was lovely.' She looked away. It was lovely for the fox or the weasel that may have found it.

'You know Joe?' said MJ

'No, not really. We met by the river and he gave me a fish.'

'Joe, this is Irene Dawson's daughter, Laura.'

'Hell, what's happened? Have you found her?' Joe placed his hands on the table and leaned towards MJ. 'Well, did she do it, did she kill the old woman?'

'No Joe, nothing's changed,' said MJ. He raised his hands towards him. 'Get off Joe, you stink like an old badger.'

Joe took a step back. 'I've been digging for worms down the allotment.'

'Joe found your grandmother's body,' said MJ.

'Floating, and so peaceful like. Then I saw the blood leaking—'

'Okay, that's enough.' MJ interrupted him.

Joe stared at Laura for a moment. 'I'm sorry about your mother.' He tugged at his ear and then rubbed his one good eye. He turned back to the bar and collected a small box from the barman. 'Thanks Frank, I'll give these a try.' He went to the door and looked back. 'See you later MJ.' He exited, and the door clattered shut behind him.

'Joe posed us a dilemma during the investigation. We couldn't prove anything, but at one time we thought he did it.'

'Why?'

'He pulled the body out of the water and claimed he tried to revive your grandmother, her blood covered his clothes. So, we considered him a suspect.'

'Why would anyone kill my grandmother?'

'Now Laura, I'm not sure I can help you. Are you out to prove your mother's innocence?'

'Mr Jackson, I only want to find her.'

'Call me MJ, please. Let me tell you something that is not common knowledge.' He took a long drink from his glass. 'On second thoughts, maybe I shouldn't.'

'What is it?'

'Do you have any idea where your mother is? You see if you are in contact with her you should let us, I mean let the police know.'

'For fuck's sake! If I knew where she was—'

'No need to swear.' He stared at her. 'Sorry, it was a stupid question.'

'Someone took me away,' she shouted and then lowered her voice. 'I've no contact with my mum.' She gritted her teeth. 'My relatives abandoned me, and no one wants to explain why.'

'Joe found the body and heard people shouting at the Mill Pool, but he saw no one. At the time, we believed he had attempted to cover up what he had done. However, there was a lot of blood at the picnic site. The analysis showed traces of three people, but not one drop of Joe's blood, well he wasn't bleeding. No, Joe was innocent.'

'The articles in the Gazette did not mention the third person.'

'No, possibly not. The daughter said no one else was at the picnic, which contradicted the evidence.'

'What can we do to find out?'

'We? Unless there is fresh evidence, or your mother appears with the truth, there is nothing I can do. What do you expect?'

'I don't know. But I know that someone is not happy with me being here.'

MJ raised his glass at her remark and drank his beer. He turned and looked at the barman, who shook his head.

'Best have something to eat MJ first, I'll cook you a pie and some chips,' called the barman.

'Frank, you're an old woman sometimes.' He winked at Laura. 'People are not happy around here if you stick your nose into their business.'

'Someone ripped my tent, broke into the house, rummaged through my stuff and stole my passport,' she said. 'Explain that.'

'After all these years.' He grinned then moderated his expression. 'I wonder if your appearance has stirred the pot, so to speak.' He drummed his fingers up and down his empty beer glass.

'Then there are the postcards. They don't make—'

'Postcards!' He reached forward and touched her hand. 'Do you have them?'

'They are at the house.' She met his stare. 'They make no sense, and I am not sure what they mean.'

'I wonder if they are the same postcards I've already seen. They were a complete waste of time and money.' MJ looked towards the barman and shouted. 'Come on, Frank. Another won't do any harm.'

Chapter Sixteen

Scott's hands were shaking as he followed the nurse into the families' room. She took hold of his elbow and made him sit by the window.

'Now don't worry. Dr Jamal is on his way,' she said. 'I'll get you a hot drink.'

He accepted the coffee but spilt some over his knees, so he placed the polystyrene cup onto the floor next to the chair. He didn't want a coffee.

The nurse gave him a look of sadness. Or was it the professionally accepted expression towards people suspended in an emotional void? She left the room and closed the door.

Alone, he sensed peace in the stillness and then an overwhelming rush of despair. He kicked at the cup splattering its contents over the grey linoleum and then regretted his childish action. He fetched paper towels from the dispenser and wiped the floor to soak up the liquid in the absorbent material.

Dr Jamal came into the room, and Scott glanced at him but continued cleaning the floor. He ignored the doctor since at the moment he didn't want to hear the news.

'Mr Ferguson,' said Dr Jamal, 'please take a seat and I'll update you.'

Scott stood up and put the sodden paper into a bin. His hands had stopped shaking, and he dried them on a towel. He walked across the room and sat by the open window. He took a deep breath and felt ready to listen, even though he knew it would be dire news.

Dr Jamal slid a chair into a position opposite Scott and sat. He said, 'Mr Ferguson, your wife gave us all a scare through the night. Thankfully, there is nothing to worry about as we have settled her and made her comfortable.'

'How long?'

'We are moving Mary from the intensive care to a private room. She'll be more comfortable there.'

'Can I see her?' The words stuck in his throat; he gritted his teeth. He would not allow himself to cry in front of the doctor.

'Of course, you can. She is stable and awake,' said Dr Jamal. 'Come on. I'll take you through.' He pushed his chair back and stood up. 'We will move her later this afternoon.' He led Scott through to the ward. 'I'll leave you be,' he said and left.

'You look terrible,' said Mary as Scott came into her view. 'Is my husband here?'

He took her hand, and his smile shifted into a wide grin. 'Oh Mary, you know how much you mean to me.' He picked up a tissue and blew his nose. 'Sorry.'

'What's wrong?' she struggled to move up in the bed. 'You'd think I had run off with Dr Jamal. He is very nice you know.'

He adjusted the pillows and helped her sit back.

'Where would you run off to?' he said.

'New York or Paris. Shame, I'm still here.' She coughed, and spittle ran down her chin. 'You thought I had gone. Look, I'm getting better, see.'

He wiped her chin and mouth. 'You'll be home in no time.'

'Can't we live somewhere else, I'm so tired of the place.'

'What about the horses and the farm? The B and B.'

'Sell them. Sell the whole bloody lot.' She pointed to a nurse adjusting the air flow for a patient in the corner of the intensive care unit. 'Sister Death. Watch out for her.'

'They said they will move you to a private ward.'

'We can move to Iceland.'

'Iceland! It's cold there.' He patted her hand, 'Yes, we could watch the volcanoes and sit in the warm pools.'

'It was my fault.' She threw her head back and cried. 'If only we didn't need dry towels.'

'It's not your fault, now come on. Do you want a drink?' He poured water into a plastic beaker. 'People get ill and people get better. Just like horses.'

'No Scott, the picnic and Laura. She was a pretty girl.'

'It's over Mary, please—'

'Not yet! When I get out of here, I'll explain what happened.' She closed her hand around his wrist and gripped tightly as she tensed her entire body. 'You'll see.' She released her hold and relaxed back on the pillows with her eyes closed.

Mary's thoughts drifted to the time of the picnic. She was with Laura and they were sitting on the grass in the warm sunshine. They were making daisy chains and pretending to be little princesses, and their mothers wore daisy crowns. They were the queens of the valley.

They had thrown stones to skip them across the surface of the pool and Laura's stones went the furthest. Perhaps because she had picked small flat ones and was lower to the ground, or was it the flick of her wrist?

They had been laughing and giggling as they paddled through the water, splashing at each other. They had rolled around in the warm shallows. She left Laura behind at the water's edge and she swam across into the deep water. Laura screamed at her to come back. Her mother and Irene came over and put a towel over Laura's shoulders; it had slipped off into the water.

Scott leaned forward to brush the hair off Mary's forehead. She took a deep breath.

'Don't,' she said, keeping her eyes closed. 'I am so tired. You must tell her.'

She had swum behind the waterfall and climbed onto a ledge. Through the sheet of water from the waterfall, she saw the shape of someone standing by the river among the reeds. A woman was standing and staring at the group in the shallows.

'It was her.' Mary said. She opened her eyes and grabbed Scott's wrist. 'There was someone watching us.'

'It's okay,' Scott removed her hand that had gone limp. 'No one is here, the nurse has gone.'

'I know who it was, I'm sure. Scott, you must tell the police.' She moaned. 'Listen! Will you?'

There were four other beds in the care ward and their occupants had monitor wires and tubes attached connecting them to airlines, saline drips and heartbeat displays. Nurses moved between them checking and double checking and making occasional adjustments to the instruments.

'Don't mind me,' said a nurse as she smiled at Scott and pulled the screen curtains around Mary's bed. 'I'll be back in a minute.'

He leaned forward and gave Mary a kiss on her forehead; he felt her breath on his cheek and could smell its stale metallic odour from her dry mouth. He sat down and waited.

This was happening too fast. Mary had been in the hospital for the last six months and each day there was a possibility of her succumbing to cancer. This was happening too fast. He had not accepted the eventuality of sudden death. He shivered in a cold sweat. Was she on the point of no recovery? This was happening too fast.

A nurse pulled the curtains back and then she removed the monitor cables from Mary's chest.

She said, 'Okay, you can move her now.' She waved to the porters to come forward and take the bed.

The nurse patted Mary's arm, and she said, 'Mrs Ferguson, we are taking you for a ride. You'll like your new room, it is very nice.' She moved away as the porters manoeuvred the bed towards the open doors.

'You can come along,' she said to Scott, 'it's not too far and the other visitor can come in.'

'Who?'

'Oh, she's waiting in the family room. We couldn't let her in here since rules are rules.'

§

Aunt Margaret pushed open the door and strode into the side room. Scott stood up.

'Take this chair, I'll get another one,' he said. He tapped Mary on the elbow. 'Mary, look who has come to see you.'

'Oh Mary, how are you my sweet darling.' Margaret said and leaned forward to peck her on the cheek.

'Aunt Margaret, well, well I must be dying.'

'Don't say such silly things, dear.' She placed a newspaper and a small carton on the side table. 'Some fruit dear, red grapes, they'll do you the world of good.'

'Thank you, but there is no need. I can't eat them, anyway.'

'Just like your mother, bless her soul.' She reached into the bag. 'I love these, try them.' She slipped two grapes into her mouth.

Scott pulled up a chair and sat down. 'Dr Jamal is pleased with her progress.'

'Rubbish,' shouted Mary. 'He always says that I'm improving, but I feel worse.'

Margaret took hold of Mary's hand. 'Now stop it dear. We all wish you well.'

'Sorry, how are you?' said Mary, and she attempted to push herself into a sitting position. Scott adjusted the pillows and helped her up.

'Do you know Scott has a woman staying with him at Orchard View?' said Margaret.

'A guest for a few days,' he said. He reached for the water jug and half-filled a plastic beaker. He glanced at Margaret. 'You are a mischievous sort.'

'It's Laura Dawson,' said Mary as she reached for the offered beaker of water.

'I know dear,' she said and patted Mary's hand. 'I've met her, what a nice young lady. Isn't she Scott?'

'What is she like?' Mary took a long drink. 'Scott you promised, when will she come?'

'Well, she is tall like her mother and clever—' said Margaret.

'She was always a smart little child.' Mary interrupted. 'Irene adored her, yes we all did. Such a happy girl. Round and round the . . .'

'It is a shame she is looking for Irene,' said Margaret and she shook her head. 'She'll be disappointed.'

'How did you know she was staying at the B and B?' said Scott, and he reached for a grape.

'Really Scott, in Kirkindale. Diane told me, and I went straight round.'

'Scott, I want to see her,' said Mary, 'I never understood why they took her away.'

'Oh, that's obvious or have you forgotten. Charlie wanted rid of her.'

'Aunt Margaret! That's not true.'

'You didn't see him. Every time he looked at that child, you could see the loathing creep over his face. It was unnerving.' Margaret's hands shook. 'We thought he might do something.'

'Are you all right?' said Scott.

'Parkinson's.' She shook her head. 'Don't worry about me You should worry about Laura.'

'You mean Mary.'

'I know who I mean.'

'I saw someone in the reeds.' Mary wriggled around in the bed. 'The police didn't believe me, why? You must believe me, Margaret.' She pulled at a pillow.

Scott took her arm and helped her get comfortable.

'You were just a child,' said Margaret. 'Who did you think you saw? You weren't there. It was only the shock playing tricks with your mind, dear.'

'In the reeds, you know, I know you know. I must warn Laura.' She slid back down in the bed. 'I'm so tired I want to sleep.'

'Who did you see?' said Margaret. 'Warn Laura about who?' She patted Mary's hand. 'There dear, you have a nice rest.' She touched Scott's elbow and nodded towards the door. She stood, and the chair fell over. Scott placed it back onto its feet.

'Just a minute in private,' Margaret said and walked out of the room.

Scott followed her into the corridor. She closed the door.

'Listen, Scott, I don't think it would be the right thing.'

'The right thing, what do you mean?'

'To bring Laura here. It would upset both of them.'

'She wants to see her niece and after all these—'

'Scott! What will they talk about? Her murderous mother. No, Scott, I forbid it.'

'You forbid it!' Scott said and stared at her. 'You forbid it.'

'Yes, she is delirious, and you don't know what stories she'll tell.'

'But—'

'No buts, trust me, Scott.' She smiled. 'I must go. Tell Mary I'll see her tomorrow. The poor dear.' She turned her back on Scott and rushed off down the corridor.

Scott went back into the room and saw Mary was asleep. He picked up the newspaper and sat by her bed. Why should meeting Laura be so upsetting for Mary?

Chapter Seventeen

Laura requested the bus driver to stop at the junction to Springwater Lane.

'Thank you,' she said and got off.

He nodded a goodbye and closed the bus door before he drove on.

She was pleased to have made the return journey from Marston without having to endure the enthusiastic curiosity from Anne, who had not been waiting by the bus terminal as expected.

She hurried on along the lane. There was an electric chill in the evening atmosphere, as if a downpour was ready to burst from the ominous clouds. The birds were quiet. Perhaps they intuitively knew about the imminent storm and had taken shelter. The absence of their chirping and chatter along the hedgerows left an eerie silence. Should she run?

The day in Marston was productive, and she was pleased. The meetings with the solicitor and the retired policeman gave her a sense of progress towards finding out the truth about her mum. She did not want to believe that her mother was a suspected murderer on the run. Surely it can't be true.

She left the Farmers' Jug when Frank served MJ his meal of pie, chips, and peas. He had promised he would speak with the Chief at the police station and get permission to review the case files. It was the only one he had never solved, and as he spoke there was a sparkle in his eyes. He was smiling as Frank gave him an encouraging slap on his shoulder after he put the plate of food and cutlery onto the table.

A low rumble of thunder from further down the valley prompted her to pull up her jacket hood and increase her pace to a slow jog.

The Farmers' Jug had been peaceful and warm. She was usually nervous in pubs ever since her first evening out with Jenny and the incident of the spilt drink. Jenny and her friends had placated the man with a fresh pint of beer, but she felt uneasy among the loud crowd. The man had kept glancing at her with ugly glares and making lecherous gestures with his tongue. Although she had turned her back towards him, she still couldn't relax in the company of Jenny's friends. She had sensed she was being watched.

Later that evening, Jenny and her group went to the DJ Images nightclub, but she was underage and wouldn't get in. Besides, after the altercation with the man, it had spoiled the novelty of the evening. The boisterous crowd at the bar had become louder, and the atmosphere waned between good humour and menace. She had said goodbye and headed home.

The chubby man from the pub had stepped out from behind the church wall and he had grabbed her from behind. He had a tight grasp of her hair and forced marched her to a clearing behind the rhododendrons in the graveyard. He pressed a knife against her face, below her right eye.

'Scream and you'll be dead meat,' he had whispered. Stroking the knife against her face, he had said, 'Get them off.'

A dog had barked, and someone had shouted for Buster to come back. This distracted the man's attention. She had kneed him in the groin and stuck her thumbs into his eyes, then had felt the knife cut her cheek. He dropped to his knees, and she had kicked him in the face. He let go of the blade and rolled over onto his back. She picked up the knife.

A terrier came into the clearing and stood barking at them. A woman followed it and snapped a lead onto the dog's collar.

Laura turned back to the man squirming on the ground. She gritted her teeth and had raised the knife into the air. She stabbed down towards the body, but he had rolled to the side and she pegged his jacket to the ground.

The woman screamed for help while she had struggled to hold back the excited dog which was snapping and barking.

Laura had sprinted out of the churchyard and ran down the middle of the road, exhilarated and elated by her escape.

The effort of sprinting burned in her muscles until her legs lost their strength and shook. Gasping, she slowed to a walk. She still had the knife in her hand. Throw it, throw it away, but there was something empowering about holding it tight. She tucked the weapon under her waistband and jogged on until she reached home.

Back in her bedroom, she was both in tears and laughing hysterically. She should have killed him. She wanted to kill him, but could she have killed him? She wrapped the knife in a scarf and slipped it under her mattress.

The cut on her face was sore and bleeding. She had cleaned it in warm water and covered it with a large plaster. Later, she told Mr and Mrs McLean that she had tripped and cut her face on a piece of broken glass. They insisted on going to the doctors. A nurse in the treatment room had cleaned the wound with antiseptic, then applied butterfly stitches. She kept asking if she was sure it was a broken bottle that had caused the cut. There are people who can help if you don't want to go to the police. The nurse had been insistent.

She had no intention of going to the police. The woman in the churchyard had called her a murderer. Who would they believe? She was the one with the knife.

Her wound became swollen and infected and required continuous medical attention. It had left an ugly scar, and whenever she looked in the mirror she smiled. She knew she could fight back and win.

On the Wednesday after the attack, she had found it hilarious to read the article in the local Journal about an attempted mugging in the churchyard. The attacker had used a large Bowie knife and was described by the witness as a ferocious, fearsome thug. She compared the attacker to a Sioux Indian who was about to take a scalp. The police reminded the public that carrying knives was a serious offence.

Laura strode on down the lane towards Russet House. A momentary sheet of lightning made her jump and the perspective of the lane appeared to stretch away into the distance. It was not far now, and she should make it to the house before the clouds burst with the expected downpour.

She couldn't believe her mother was a murderer, although she understood how, in a certain situation, it was possible. The impulsive urge for self-preservation after feeling fear, helplessness and being humiliated was a reflexive retaliation towards revenge. She had felt that sudden surge of power over the man in the churchyard. Had she inherited a killer instinct from her mother? Although, she sometimes would wake at night feeling out of breath and terrified. In her dreams, the man had buried her inside a coffin while she was still alive.

It was only about a hundred yards from the house and the rain started with random drops. Over the top of the hedge, she saw the security light come on at the front of the house. She stopped and listened. She was expecting Scott to drive out from the access road. The light went out.

She found a gap in the hedge and crept through into the field where she followed the fence. She climbed over the wire into the garden and hid behind the chestnut trees. She lowered her jacket hood. There were no lights on in the house. She couldn't see if there was a car parked out front. She waited and looked around.

Lightning flashed, followed by a thunderous roar that shook the tree branches. A fox dashed across the garden lawn and scurried through the hedge by the entrance to the old path that led to the river.

She let out a sigh and pulled her hood back over her head. She looked down at her feet and saw the pile of cigarette butts. The rain became heavier. She ran, taking the keys from her pocket on the way. The security light came on as she sprinted across the gravel to the front door.

Inside the porch, she listened to the rain lashing against the door and its narrow window. She took off her jacket and gave it a shake, then picked up the letters lying on the mat. The outdoor security light went out. In the dark, she made her way to the hall and felt along the wall for the light switch. The outdoor security light came on again, with the noise of the rain she had not heard a car. She stood still and looked back towards the front door expecting Scott, but after a few minutes, the light extinguished.

In the dark, she made her way into the kitchen and stared out through the windows into the garden. Perhaps the fox had returned. The clouds had shifted towards the valley, taking the rainstorm away. She looked across the garden to where the hedges and bushes merged in the shadows; by the trees, she saw a faint glow from a cigarette.

There was a splash. She had let go of the letters, and they had fallen into the sink. She snatched to retrieve them before they became soaked among the unwashed dishes and threw them onto the table. She peered out the French windows towards the trees and watched for movement or another glow of light. Someone was watching the house. How long had they been out there, and why? Whoever it was must have seen her arrive. What did they want? How dare they!

Anger flushed through her; she dashed into the utility room and lifted the keys from the hook. She unlocked the door. She grasped the handle and stopped. She locked the door again. It would be mad to go out and confront the intruder, but she wanted to know who it was and what they wanted.

She ran upstairs to her bedroom, opened the window, and leaned out.

'Who are you?' she shouted. 'I can see you, what do you want?'

There was a glint of light from the shadow by the trees, and the cigarette end flashed as it dropped and tumbled to the ground.

The figure emerged and walked across the lawn towards the drive.

'I've called the police,' she called.

She leaned out of the window but couldn't distinguish the features of the person as a jacket hood concealed the face. The gravel crunched under the slow footsteps as the stranger headed out towards the lane.

She closed the window, switched on the light, and sat on her bed. What was it that prompted this vendetta if that is what it was? First, her tent was slashed then an intruder had stolen her diary and passport. Now someone was watching the house. Had this creep been waiting for her at the entrance to the driveway?

Downstairs, she checked to make sure that all the doors and windows were locked. She put the chain on the front door. The only way into the house would be through the garage and over the loft. Had she closed the door from the garage into the attic?

She rattled the locked door from the hall into the private rooms; the telephone was in the office. She fetched the keys and climbed into the attic. At the bottom of the stairway into the garage, the door was closed. She hesitated and decided against making a telephone call.

Back in the kitchen, she put the kettle on.

It was late, and Scott had not come home.

The letters on the table appeared to be official correspondence addressed to Scott, but among them was a manila envelope with her name neatly typed on a gummed label.

She switched on the radio and turned the volume low. She found the background music a comfortable distraction from thinking about the stalker in the garden.

The rain had eased to a drizzle, but there were occasional sudden squalls that rattled the roof slates and caused the tree branches to whip about in a frenzy. The noise made Laura jump and she would stare out expecting to see the unwelcomed figure smoking cigarettes by the chestnut tree.

She prepared sweet and sour chicken with plain rice, a dish that Mrs McLean would often make on Saturday evenings. With a fork, she picked at the food, eating small mouthfuls.

Had the stranger gone from the garden?

She served the remaining food onto a large plate and wrapped it in clingfilm. She would heat Scott's meal when he came home and warn him about the intruder lurking in the house grounds.

She went to her room, sat on her bed, and opened the manila envelope. Someone had returned her passport and birth certificate with a warning. "Finish your family research and leave. You are not wanted here".

Why?

She slept in her tracksuit and kept her trainers next to the door, ready to run. Every loud sound outside the house made her sit up. She lost count of the times she got up and looked out of the window. By now, whoever had been there would know that she had not called the police.

§

The chimes of the doorbell woke her. She sat up and rubbed at her eyes and then dropped back onto her pillows. The daylight shone through a gap in the curtains. She checked her watch; it was ten o'clock. The doorbell rang again. Scott!

She rushed down into the dining room and peeked out through the curtains. She saw a blue Mondeo parked in the drive, and a policewoman and a man in a tweed jacket were standing by the front door. She knocked on the window and they looked at her. She recognised the policewoman from Marston.

When she unlocked the front door, the man spoke before it was fully open.

'Detective Inspector Whitefield, Marston police.' He held up his warrant card and nodded towards the policewoman. 'Sergeant Christine Jackson, who I believe you've met.'

'Yes.'

'Nothing to worry about, Miss Lawson—'

'Dawson,' the policewoman corrected him. 'Sir, it's Miss Laura Dawson.'

'Sorry, slip of the tongue.' He straightened his tie and smiled. 'Miss Dawson. Yes. I would like to ask a few questions about your mother.' He looked up at the sky. 'Do you mind if we come in?'

In the kitchen, they sat around the table. Laura made them tea.

'I am aware you may have postcards from your mother,' said DI Whitefield. He added a spoonful of sugar to his tea, stirred it in, then added another spoonful.

'I'm not sure they are from my mother.'

'Let me be the judge of that.' He sipped his tea. 'My, you make a fine cup of tea.'

His cup clattered as he placed it on the table. 'Could I see them, if you don't mind.'

'Yes, they're here.' She stood up and went to fetch envelope she had left by the sink. 'Ah, I must have taken them upstairs.'

DI Whitefield nodded towards the policewoman. 'Sergeant Jackson, please go along with Miss Dawson.'

'I won't run away.' She looked at the policewoman and rolled her eyes.

In the bedroom, Laura searched for the white envelope while the policewoman watched.

'What's up?' she said. 'Come on Miss, we haven't got all day.' She walked to the side table and picked up the passport. 'Is this yours?'

'Yes, I—'

'So, it wasn't stolen, just mislaid, perhaps?'

'No, someone stole it. When I came home from Marston, it was on the doormat.'

'Home?'

'Back here I mean.' Laura threw her day sack across the bed. 'I can't find the postcards.'

'I see, were they also stolen?'

'Probably,' she said and saw the sneer on the policewoman's face. 'Well, they must have been.'

'Come on then, you can explain that to the Inspector,' she said and laughed. 'This will be fun, just like the last time.'

'The last time?'

'You don't remember, do you?' she said. 'I chased you around the garden, you were screaming for your teddy.'

'That was you?'

'Yes, I ripped my tights, bloody hell. You were small but fast. You ran off down the track, shouting for Numpty.'

'I had hidden it, I didn't think you could take me away without it.'

'Hidden, no you had lost it. We told everyone to search for it.'

'Did you find Numpty?'

'No.' She opened the bedroom door wide. 'Come on Miss, let's go.'

They returned downstairs and found DI Whitefield in the dining room reading the label on a bottle of wine.

'Ah good, right then, let's have a look at these cards.' He put the bottle back into the rack.

'Sir, she's lost them,' said the policewoman, and she walked over to the window and pulled the curtains further aside.

'Someone has stolen them,' said Laura.

'Stolen, eh? How inconvenient. Now listen, young lady, MJ reckoned these cards were new evidence, so don't be hiding them.'

'I'm not, someone stole them, like my diary and passport—'

'Your passport is upstairs,' said the policewoman.

'I know but—'

'Sergeant Jackson confiscate her passport. We'll check where she's been.'

'Been? Why would I come here if I knew where my mother was?' She saw the stern expression from the policeman and sat at the table. 'MJ said he had seen the postcards; don't you have copies in your records or something?'

'I'm sorry Miss Lawson—'

'Dawson,' said the policewoman.

'Sorry, Miss Dawson, but it is important to check.'

'I'll get my passport,' said Laura.

'I'll just take the details, Miss, no need to give it up, just yet.'

Chapter Eighteen

Later in the morning, she walked down the lane to catch the bus into Kirkindale.

She had considered visiting her grandfather at the farm, but would he speak to her? Mrs Wilcox gave the impression it was not advisable to stay at the B and B since Old Charlie hated her mother and because he was an unpleasant person. However, she was more concerned about the stranger in the garden than her grandfather's animosity. The visit can wait until another day.

It surprised her the police came so quickly since Sergeant Christine Jackson had suggested it would be a few days before a detective made contact. MJ must have stirred them into action.

She was embarrassed because her passport was not missing, and she could not find the envelope with the postcards. DI Whitefield had grumbled and mumbled about wasting police time and was sceptical about her motives. He suggested she was using the theft and postcards to provoke the police into action. He assured her he was fully committed to solving the murder.

When he had said that, she burst out laughing. She pointed out it has been almost fifteen years since the murder took place. DI Whitefield shook his head and stomped out of the house. He sat in the car for a moment before he shouted for Sergeant Jackson to hurry.

Sergeant Jackson was sympathetic and more concerned about Laura's safety than the missing postcards. She had suggested Laura find somewhere to stay in Kirkindale or in Marston. Better, though, she should go home and let the police deal with the investigation and the search for her mother.

At the lane junction to the road, there was a gate into a field. She sat on the gate and waited for the bus. There were half a dozen cigarette butts in a puddle, and she wondered if last night's prowler had also waited here and used the bus.

When the bus approached, she waved to the driver for him to stop. She paid her fare.

'Do you mind if I ask, did you pick up anyone from here last night?'

'Last night,' said the driver and put the bus into gear. 'I wasn't driving last night, sorry.' He checked his mirror and drove the bus on along the road.

'Who gets the bus from here?'

'Sorry Miss, you must sit down when the bus is moving,' he said and grimaced at her. 'Please sit down.'

At the stop in the village, she tried to speak to the driver again. He shook his head and pointed out the door. He was not interested.

She waited until the bus moved away before she crossed the street and went into the library. She rushed down the steps into the archives.

George was sitting at his desk with a pile of leather-bound books. He was recording details into a register.

'Good morning, George.'

'Ah, Laura.' He looked up from his work. 'Guess what, I found an old Parish Record book with the Stewarts listed.'

'Are these—'

'No, not these. It's on the table in the research room.'

'Thankyou.' She walked towards the back room.

'Wait just a minute!'

She turned and stared at him.

'I've made coffee.' He fetched the jug from the percolator and filled two cups.

'If you don't mind, I would like to get on and finish my research.'

'Milk? Yes, you take milk.' He smiled. 'Come on Miss Dawson, I've got something to tell you.'

'Laura,' she said, 'call me Laura.' She sat by the desk. 'What is it?'

'I called Jeffrey this morning.' He passed her a coffee. 'Be careful, that's hot. He tells me you came to see him.'

'Him?'

'Oh, don't be fooled. He's eccentric. Weird, I say.'

'Yes, I asked about Russet house.'

'We know, we know, but after you left, he had another visitor.' He took a sip from his cup. 'He told me his visitor was not pleased with you.'

'Who?'

'He wouldn't say. But the visitor suggested you leave Kirkindale for your own good.'

'Who was it? I could go to the police.'

'No, Jeffrey wouldn't say, client confidentiality and all that. I agree with you, but what could you tell the police?'

'I am not sure.' She noticed a sly shift in George's tone and a sullen look on his face. 'But if someone is making threats, I should know who.'

'Don't involve me, I'm just the messenger.'

'I see.'

'So, finish your family history research. The past won't change, so let it rest in peace, so to speak.'

'Yes, George,' she said and handed him her cup. She smiled and went into the back room.

The maps and records remained spread over the table as she had left them. The additional leather-bound book sat to one side. She opened it and searched through to find the details of the Stewarts dated March,1880. They owned the cotton mills in the village until the outbreak of WW1. Afterwards, there was a change of ownership and they renamed the mill as the Marston Union Textiles Co Ltd. She found this interesting but not useful in finding her mother's immediate relatives.

She wanted to find her Great Aunt Daphne Lister in Marston, but who would know her? There were lots of photographs back at Russet House, but none annotated with the names of the people shown. Would someone in Marston recognise her? Laura imagined herself in the Market Square asking strangers if anyone knew any of these women in the photographs, as if she had lost a cat. It was an excellent idea since her Great Aunt Daphne would visit the shops and use the banks or the post office. Surely, someone might recognise her.

There was a knock on the door and George walked in. 'Any use?' he said and pointed at the record book.

'Brilliant George, I think I'm finished here.' She rolled up her chart and slid an elastic band around it.

'Wait, I'll get you a tube for that,' said George. 'Don't worry about the maps and newspaper folders, I'll put them away.'

'No, I'll help.' She gathered her notebook and pens and pushed them into her day sack.

'Just leave the archives on the table. Let me get you a tube.' He turned and left.

She closed the newspaper folders and put one back on its shelf. George came into the room waving a cardboard tube like a sword, and he poked her shoulder.

'Leave them, I said!' He forced the tube into her hand. 'Sorry, here take this. I am precise on the order of the folders.' He smiled. 'I'm the one who has to find them again, and if they are not in the right place, it's frustrating.'

'George, you must have known about the murder of Sophia Dawson.'

He shook his head. 'Bitter times, Laura, it would be better if you left things alone.'

'Why, if it involves my mother, I have a right to know.'

'A right to know! Do you think people worry about the rights of murderers?'

'I don't believe my mother is a murderer.'

'Coffee is on, let's have an honest face-to-face chat.' He pointed towards the door.

§

Laura walked down the library steps onto the street. She hurried towards the river path. She wanted time to absorb what George had said about her mother. She sat on the wooden bench under the cherry trees and watched a swan swim upstream. Behind it, several cygnets struggled through the water, and the weeds trailing in the current.

The coffee tasted bitter, and she could not drink it as she had listened to George.

He had been the solicitor who had represented Joe Prince, the man who found Sophia Dawson floating in the river. For a while, the police were convinced he was responsible for the woman's murder. Later, the investigation proved he was innocent. However, he suggested information that pointed suspicion towards Charles Dawson as the culprit. Mr Prince had witnessed Irene Dawson and Charlie Dawson meeting by the Mill Pool and at the waterfalls frequently. Although it was many years before the murder, and Mr Prince couldn't say exactly when. He made a statement that the affair was consummated on many occasions.

George understood this to be a defensive move by Mr Joe Prince, and that he was deflecting the blame elsewhere.

The police investigation latched on to the motive as a crime of passion. It was suggested that Charles Dawson, when confronted about the affair by Sophia, murdered both his wife and his secret lover, Irene.

However, on the day of the murder, Mr Charles Dawson had been at an agriculture meeting for the judges of the Three Counties Show.

Another motive considered by the police was that an argument between the two women went too far. Since Mrs Irene Dawson was missing, she became a suspect.

Mr Charles Dawson denied the affair and took revenge on Joe. He beat Joe so severely that he spent a month in hospital and lost the sight from his left eye.

George had prepared the prosecution charges against Mr Charles Dawson, but the case never went to court. They arranged an out of court settlement where Joe Prince and his descendants received the fishing rights in perpetuity for the stretch of the River Marrs that passed through the Springfield Farm land. It was an affront to justice, George had said, that Mr Dawson, who had committed such a violent act of grievous bodily harm with intent, had convinced Joe to retract his complaint.

George had slammed his hand on the desk. He had shouted at her. They should not have allowed the out of court agreement. It was an injustice. He was adamant Mr Dawson deserved prison.

Laura brushed off the cherry blossom from her hair and lap. She pulled a tissue from her pocket and wiped the tears from her face and looked up; the swallows had arrived for the summer and were swooping above the trees, catching insects in flight.

She did not want to believe her mother was a murderer. What else was there to believe? George had apologised for getting angry, it wasn't with her and he moderated his tone. He had said sorry. Sorry for what?

Being angry or sorry that her mother was a killer on the run, and on the run for fifteen years?

'You be having a ciggy?'

She had not heard or seen the boy arrive. She leaned back on the bench and waved away his offered packet of Marlboro. She looked at his clean and highly polished shoes. He wore a fresh white shirt, a plain blue tie, and a light-coloured suit. It was a transformation from the scruffy clothes the same boy had worn the last time she saw him.

'You're looking very smart today. New clothes?'

'I know you be surprised.' He smiled. 'My sister's wedding, in the church, so boring and I needed a drag.'

'It's not nice.'

'I know it be boring.'

'I mean leaving the church for a cigarette.'

'I does what I want, it's none of anyone's business.' He lit up and took a long inhale.

'I can't stand the smoke, it's bad for you.'

'Bad,' he said, 'Yea, it be bad just like murder, it be bad.' He flicked ash onto the grass. 'Is it true your mum's a murderer?'

'Who said that?'

'Everyone knows, it be hush-hush. Anne says she's probably in jail.'

'Why in prison?' She stood up and faced him. 'If my mother was in prison, I would not be here.'

'Anne reckons once you be killing you can't stop.'

'I think you should go back to the church.'

'Na, they be ages.'

She picked up her day sack and walked away.

'Keep away from the Mill Pool, there be murderers there.' He shouted and laughed.

She put down her bag, strode back to the boy and balled her fists.

He backed away. 'Just be kidding.'

She punched him on the nose. He fell back onto the grass and grasped at his nose and glanced at her.

'I'm bleeding!' He scrambled to his feet and raised his fists.

'Yes, just try it,' she shouted, then lowered her voice. 'Remember, murder runs in the family.'

He cried. She took a fresh tissue from her pocket and gave it to him.

'Maybe you should improve your manners around strangers. Now off you go. Your sister's getting married.'

'Don't go to the witches pool it not be safe there.' He shouted over his shoulder as he ran off.

She felt disappointed with her reaction. She had lost her temper with a teenage boy, although he was taller than her. No doubt he'll go telling tales and people in the village will decide that the daughter is just like her mother. Perhaps it wasn't such a clever idea coming to Kirkindale. Jenny had said she should just forget the past and move on. How could she? Everyone has a right to a family and know who they are.

Mr and Mrs McLean were continually sorry and had forbidden her to ask them any more questions about her biological parents. The last time she had asked them about her actual mother, the discussion became heated and she had stomped off to her bedroom. She had hated them.

After the shale-gravel section, the path was muddy and slippery. She found a dry rock by the water's edge and sat down. It was peaceful. On the far side of the river, a waterhen swam oblivious to her presence, or perhaps it was used to the fishermen who dozed along the riverbank.

She had produced a chart with three generations of the Dawson family, but her mother's ancestry details were not completed on her diagram. Her grandmother's sister in Marston would know; if she could find her. Her maiden name was Daphne Lister, although she may have a married name. Would she have children? They would be her mother's cousins and she would like to meet them.

Regardless of Mrs Wilcox's advice to stay away from Old Charlie, she was determined to meet him and to learn what kind of man her father, William, had been.

Aunt Mary was ill, and she wasn't clear if she was the girl who once played with her at Russet House. She must be. How would she react?

Great Aunt Margaret was nice—

'Hello, it's you again. Do you want another fish?'

She turned and saw Joe holding up four brown trout dangling on a nylon rope.

'You made me jump.'

'I saw you with MJ, and he's all right for a bobby.'

'Yes, I expect so.'

'Sorry about your mother, she was a friendly woman.'

'How well did you know her?'

'Know her! Know her, not really.' He put his tackle bag and rods down by the edge of the path and then dangled the fish into the water. 'Got to keep them fresh, besides it keeps the flies off.'

'Nobody talks about my mother, except to say she's a murderer.'

'No, no, I expect they don't.' He leaned forward and tied the rope off on a turf of grass. 'She was lovely.'

'So, you knew her?'

'I wouldn't say know her. She would sit up at the Mill Pool arting.'

'Arting?'

'Painting or drawing or something. I'd ask what's it today. Just butterflies, or something like that, she'd say.'

'Can you tell me about the day you found my grandmother?'

'No. It was long ago. I told MJ everything so let it be.' He sat on the ground.

'I need to go,' she said. She stood up and picked up her day sack.

'Sit down and I'll tell you something.' He touched the side of his nose.

She sat and looked at him. Was this going to be a confession, or does he know the whereabouts of her mother?

'She'd come and sit by the pool and I'd share my tea, or I'd light a fire and brew up.' He fumbled in his pocket and brought out a half-smoked cigarette and lit it up. 'That day I was further down using a float, caught five but had to put two back.' He puffed on his stubby cigarette.

She stared at him. Was he only after some company or did he really have something to say? She wanted to hear anything about her mother. Something nice would be a bonus.

'I knew they were at the pool, I could hear them laughing and splashing and then it went all quiet.' He leaned back and closed his eye. 'I saw the blood first, and then she came floating. All still she was.' He sat back up and looked at her. 'You know I heard nothing except I saw someone across the other side running through the trees.'

'My mother?'

'That's what MJ kept saying. No, I didn't see them properly, I was pulling poor Mrs Dawson to the side.'

She felt a tear dribble down her cheek; so, it was true her mother was on the run, but where?

'Police said I did it.' He shook his head without looking at her. He pushed the remains of the cigarette stub into the ground with his thumb. 'I don't think your mother murdered anyone. She was a lovely, kind, and gentle woman. No, she wouldn't hurt anyone.'

'You are only saying—'

'What's your name?'

'Laura.'

'No Laura, I had a feeling creeping on me, there was someone else there. They killed the Dawson lady.'

'You think it was Mr Dawson? You told the police about an affair.' She took a tissue and wiped her face.

'They wanted to hang me. I said it to get them off my back.'

'So, it's not true.'

'Your mother was afraid.' He undid the front buttons of his waterproof jacket. 'It's getting hot. She had a secret and arting helped her relax. She told me the peace of the pool stopped her from having them nightmares.'

'Did she say what she was afraid of?'

'We don't tell secrets around here, no. We talked about the river, nature, and she knew about colours and that. She did my picture, still got it in the house.' He looked at his watch. 'Best be off, I've got the pigs to feed.'

He stood and retrieved his fish from the water; picked up his rod and tackle bag. 'Now you take care Laura. You've got your mother's face. It be a lovely smile.' He walked off towards the village and spoke without looking back. 'Bye now.'

Chapter Nineteen

Laura made her way along the paths winding through the gorse bushes and she followed the hawthorn hedge up the side of the field to Russet House. She crouched behind a hazel thicket and took her time scanning the area for any sulking intruders. She noticed the lawn was freshly cut with its edges neatly trimmed. The flower beds were dug over and new bedding plants were evenly planted in double rows.

She saw no one, so she climbed the fence into the garden and sneaked along the side of the path to the chestnut trees. Someone had cleared away the dried and loose foliage, including the cigarette butts that she had noticed the previous evening.

She crept through the rhododendron to have a look up and down the drive. She didn't see anyone hanging around, nor was Scott's car parked by the house.

She slipped the keys out from her pocket. She took a deep breath and then dashed across the lawn to the utility entrance at the back of the house. Once inside, she slammed the door shut and locked it. She ran through the hall to the front door. It was secure with its chain in place.

In the kitchen she filled the kettle, switched on the radio and turned the volume up. She went into the dining-room and stared out through the window. Her nerves ruffled the back of her neck. If someone was out there watching the house, they would now know she was home. What if he was already in the house?

She fetched a kitchen knife and stood at the bottom of the stairs.

'Hello, I know you are there!' Was she being ridiculous? She took one step at a time and once on the landing she looked up. The hatch to the attic was open.

She heard a vehicle crushing gravel as it approached down the drive.

Through the dining-room window, she watched a police Mondeo come to a stop by the front door. A policeman was in the driver's seat, and the passenger was Sergeant Christine Jackson.

They approached the front door and rang the bell; the chimes echoed through the house. Laura waited for a few moments in the hall by the stairs until they rang the bell again.

She opened the door and invited them into the kitchen. They remained standing on the granite flagstones by the front door, and the young policeman stared at her.

Sergeant Christine Jackson said, 'Miss Dawson, we have an allegation of assault. Did you attack a boy, Gavin Clarke, in the riverside park this afternoon?'

'Sorry, I didn't attack anyone.'

'Gavin Clarke claims you punched him for no reason. Now why would he say that?'

'Was that his name? No. Well yes, I punched him, but he deserved it.'

Jackson nodded towards the policeman who fumbled in his jacket pocket. He removed his notebook and flicked the pages open.

He said, 'Miss Dawson, it is a discretionary procedure under Home Office guidance that—'

'Dean get on with it,' Sergeant Christine Jackson interrupted. 'We don't need the rule book being thrown around.'

'Can I have your full name and date of birth?' He pointed his pencil at Laura and noted her reply. 'Oh, you are under eighteen years old.' He looked at Sergeant Jackson, who shook her head.

'Miss Dawson, I am surprised at you, but knowing young Gavin then again I could imagine someone might hit him,' said Sergeant Jackson. 'You've admitted the assault. However, if you apologise to his mother, then she might retract the complaint.'

'His mother! What if I don't?'

'Then Miss, I'll throw the rule book at you,' said Dean. 'You will receive a formal caution.' He grinned and nodded.

'I would advise you to apologise,' said Sergeant Jackson. 'Come with us and we can get this over with this evening.'

The policewoman pointed to the car as an invitation to Laura. 'Come on, let's go.'

§

Mrs Clarke had stood outside Hotel Marrs with her arms folded, a cigarette dangling from her mouth. She listened with a smirk as Laura apologised to Gavin and said she was sorry. Can they still be friends? Gavin stared at his feet and nodded. She didn't know why she said that, since she was not his friend.

His mother pointed out the bloodstains on Gavin's shirt and suggested Laura should pay for the dry cleaning. Before she could object, Mrs Clarke's husband came out of the hotel's front door. He demanded that the police leave them alone. He turned and belted Gavin behind his head and told him he wasn't to spoil his sister's wedding. Or he'll be for it.

A group of women were watching from a hotel window and chatting. It was obvious to Laura they were talking about her. As she got into the police car, she waved to them and saw Anne encouraging her group to wave back.

The police had taken her to apologise to Mrs Clarke, which she thought was an overreaction. How come the police acted immediately?

Afterwards, they returned her to Russet House. She watched from the doorstep as Dean drove the Mondeo up the drive. Its wheels spun in the gravel to find traction and then sped towards the lane.

She went into the house and heard voices. She stopped in the hall and listened. Who was in the house? Then she remembered she had left the radio switched on in the kitchen.

She made a coffee then fetched the boxes she had retrieved from the attic. She spread the photographs over the kitchen table and looked through them, searching for Daphne Lister. From her mother's wedding album, she removed group pictures of the bride, bridesmaids, and family members. Which of these people, if any could be Daphne?

She could only speculate that among the other women in the photographs one must be of her grandmother. Among the teenage girls in the pictures, surely one of them would be Mary Dawson.

She gathered her selection of pictures and placed them into her day sack, ready for the journey to Marston in the morning. If Great Aunt Lister was still living there, she would find her.

Chapter Twenty

Laura flagged the bus down at the end of Springwater Lane.

'A return to Marston?' the driver said. 'Did you find your young man?' He winked.

'Sorry, what do you mean?'

'Sam said you asked about someone from here the other night.'

'Oh, yes, a young man?' She placed the fare on his tray. 'Do you know him?'

'Stable lad from the farm, he goes to the Black Swan now and again.' He put the bus in gear and set off.

'I see,' she said and pulled by the momentum of the bus rushed to sit down.

From the stop in the Market Square, she crossed the road and went into the post office. She showed the staff the photographs of her mother's wedding and asked if they knew Daphne Lister.

'Couldn't say,' said one woman. 'Why don't you look her up in the phone book. You never know.' She pointed to the telephone box on the pavement outside the building.

Why didn't she think of that? Laura flicked through the pages of the telephone directory and found there were five Listers and one with the initial D. It could be Daphne. Perhaps she did not get married. She called the number and after ten rings she hung up. She copied the address into her notebook.

In the baker's shop, she showed the pictures to the women behind the counter, and they clustered together and looked at the wedding photographs. They chattered about the dated fashions of the clothes and hairstyles but recognised no one. She asked if they knew the way to the address she had found.

'Pass the Church and there be a lane along the side of the graveyard. Follow that until you reach the boat yard. Go left on the track, follow the river and it will bring you to Weir Cottage,' said the youngest woman.

An older woman said, 'Bit muddy that way, or you could follow the road—'

'No, Janice,' the younger woman interrupted. 'No, it would take ages. Go past the church, dear, it's the quickest.'

The track joined the road where Weir Cottage was the last house in the cul-de-sac. The grass on the front lawn was long and the flower beds beside the path were thick with marigold and geranium flowers. A scribbled note on the gate stated, 'wet paint'. She eased through the gap between the wooden gate and a fence post and walked up the path. Pots of wild garlic cluttered the archway leading to the front door. A 'wet paint' sign was stuck with Sellotape to a brass lion knocker, and the door was open.

'Hello, anyone at home?' she called. 'Hello, hello.'

'Here, over here dear,' shouted a woman kneeling by the fence.

Laura turned and looked across the garden. 'Oh hello,' she said.

'I didn't hear you open the gate.' The woman stood up and pointed her paint brush at the fence. 'Nearly finished.'

Laura walked across the grass to the woman. She appeared to be in her mid-sixties with a healthy tanned complexion and wore a dark headscarf holding back her hair. Green paint was splattered over her grey overalls.

'Hello, are you Daphne Lister?'

'I might be, but whatever you are selling I've already got it, thanks.'

'I'm not selling anything. My name's Laura and I want to ask you about my mother.'

'Your mother, oh dear, if you don't know your own mother, how should I?'

'My mother is Irene Dawson, I think you are my great aunt.'

'If it's money you want,' she said and dipped her brush into the paint pot. 'Well, I expect not. Look, let me finish this.' She turned her attention back to painting the fence and with her brush dabbed at a wooden post.

'I am Irene Dawson's daughter Laura.'

The woman stared at her. 'Yes, you said.'

'Excuse me, but are you Daphne Lister?'

'This is the last one. Now tell me, what do you want?' she said. 'Yes, I am Daphne Lister. Come on.' She picked up the paint pot and walked towards the back of the house.

Laura sat at the table on the patio and waited while Daphne had gone into the house.

She returned from the kitchen with a pot of tea and brought it out to the patio along with a plate of fruit scones spread with soft cheese. She had changed from her grey coveralls and was wearing trousers and a loose chequered shirt, which had colourful splodges of paint over the sleeves.

At the rear garden stood a large gypsy wagon. The cartwheels were painted a bright yellow and black. Ornate designs on the side panels were freshly coloured red and gold, and there were intricate wooden carvings along the frame edges.

'The caravan looks romantic, but is it practical?' said Laura.

'Practical, I grew up in that thing, it belonged to my father.'

'It looks new, do you still use it?'

'No, heavens no. I've renovated it for the Marston Museum. Someone spotted it and made an offer to buy it. Eh, I knew it was worth more.'

'Can I ask you about my mother and grandmother, what were they like?'

'The days we had on the road, me and Jean.' She lit a black cheroot and took a long drag. 'We never went to school, well not properly.'

'It must have been fun, travelling around.'

'I was cold and hungry.' She pointed towards the wagon with her cigar. 'I took six months to renovate it. What do you think?'

'It's pristine and looks colourful.'

'I remember Irene sitting there holding your hand. You didn't enjoy being up so high on the caravan.'

'My mother came here! I expect she did.'

'We would sit under that tree over there and eat apple crumble with cream,' she said. Her cigar had gone out, and she struck a match to relight it. 'You were only a baby, you won't remember.'

'I do, I sometimes see a horse and cart in my dreams.'

'Dreams. I have nightmares about that thing.'

'Is it not adventurous being a gypsy and living in a horse-drawn caravan?'

'Still, I'll be glad when it's gone.' She blew her nose on her sleeve. 'I feel sad though as I spent half my life in that bloody thing and it still haunts me.'

'Its history will be preserved now the museum owns it.'

'Oh, they don't own it. It's on loan. I'll get a monthly income. That way I'm still a gypsy,' she said and laughed. She then coughed and spat a mouthful of phlegm onto the grass. 'Your mother was Irene then?'

'She's missing, and I am trying to find out what—'

'Missing!' She turned her head and spat again onto the flagstones. 'Them Dawsons have done away with her. I don't like them, never have.'

'They say she is a murderer.'

'We heard what they said. Yea, everybody knows. No, I don't believe she would harm dear Sophia. She was a likeable woman.'

'But it was in the papers, my mum is a suspect.'

'I'd be off if I was you, or the Dawson lot will have you.'

'Why? I've done nothing wrong.'

'Irene used to come by here after school. We'd draw and paint. Good, she was.' She flicked her ash from the cheroot into her teacup. 'Murderer, perhaps she is. Irene, she was a wild one.'

'If you were gypsies and travellers, how did my grandmother end up owning the Wheatsheaf?'

'Albert owned the place. He was a lovely gentleman, enjoyed life he did. Jean, well, she played the violin and she could sing and flatter anyone with her voice.'

Daphne threw her tea onto the grass and refilled the cup from the teapot. She said, 'They met up at the harvests in the apple orchards.'

'I have pictures.' Laura took them from her day sack and spread them onto the table.

Daphne picked up each and her expression changed. She laughed and tears formed in her eyes. She wiped them away with her sleeve.

'We came every year for the apples. Albert, what a name. Well, he'd just be there every season with the other boys from the village and I think Jean fell for him.' She took a handkerchief from her pocket and wiped at her nose. 'Do you know what it's like to fall in love?'

Laura picked a photograph. 'Where was this taken, do you know?'

'Madness! You should never fall for it.' She took the picture from Laura's hand. 'Here in the garden, this was their house. A Stewart family wedding present.' She smiled. 'Imagine a rich Stewart marrying a poor gypsy girl. Jean did well.'

'I thought they owned the Wheatsheaf in Kirkindale.'

'Our folk disowned Jean at first, but life goes on. Jack, our pig of a father said, goodbye and good luck.'

'But you've settled here.'

'Albert worked in the boatyard for a while. When Irene was born, I stayed after the fruit harvest to help. It was hard work on the road trying to sell drawings and paintings. Hungry, I was so hungry.'

'Do you still paint?'

'That's what I do. You know, I earn more now than I did begging them around the doors. There is a little craft shop in Market Square that sells them for me. Some people call them masterpieces. Can you imagine?'

'Someone told me my grandparents went abroad, I mean Albert and Jean. Before I was born.'

'They loved their holidays, Spain, France, they even went to Greece.' She swilled the teapot around and stubbed her cheroot out on the plate next to a scone. 'More tea, I think. There was a road accident, so they told us, and we all went to the funeral in Valence. It was awful.'

Laura followed Daphne into the kitchen and ducked her head beneath the row of flowers hanging from a drying rack. There was a strong, sweet smell from the roses. On a table, fresh soap bars were lined up next to a pile of purple waxed paper with flora designs and small cardboard boxes.

Through a glass doorway, she could see an array of easels and a jumble of paint pots in the conservatory. There were artist's brushes and paint tubes cluttered on the tables.

§

Laura left Weir Cottage and dawdled along the river path towards the centre of Marston. On the way she reflected on her mother's family and on having part gypsy blood. Daphne had spoken about the closed family ties amongst the gypsy communities that ensured their autonomy and freedom to travel. Laura was convinced that her mother had somehow found refuge with the travellers. Perhaps she had changed her name and was living in fear of being caught and convicted of murder.

No, it couldn't have been a murder, it must have been an accident at the Mill Pool. What an odd feeling to think Mum was an outlaw. She enjoyed thinking of this version as it gave her a sense of euphoric happiness. She wanted to believe her mother was still alive. Where should she look?

Great Aunt Daphne had never married. According to her, the men from Marston were not interested in a rough gypsy woman. Or, she had laughed, they didn't like her goat meat. She used to breed Saanens for their milk and made cheese. Unfortunately, the animals often escaped from their enclosures and would terrorise the neighbours' gardens. She had to give them up for the sake of neighbourly sanity. Laura had smiled at her image of Daphne chasing goats out of people's gardens.

The younger relatives from her gypsy family occasionally visited and usually offered to work in her garden. She would overpay them for their slapdash efforts as she knew how difficult it was living on the road. She suspected it was their opportunity for a bath or a hot shower and a meal of roast chicken that encouraged their stopovers. However, Daphne had seen none of them for years, and honestly, she had said; she didn't care.

Laura followed the path past the boatyard and onto the bank of the river towards Barrister Row. She took her time, dawdling, letting the feelings of loneliness that had emerged in her thoughts to settle.

Her family, in Marston and Kirkindale, had continued their lives without a thought for her, she was snatched from her mother. Well, she was not snatched but was abandoned or at least forgotten. Certainly, she was not wanted by the Dawson family. She also noted how Daphne did not appear enthusiastic about her visit. She had remarked, “What do you want? Money?” This was Daphne’s immediate presumption. It was true, no one missed her or seemed to care.

Chapter Twenty-one

Mary was dozing, and her breathing was shallow. She felt a draught across her face and in her mind; it felt like the breeze that rustled through reeds by the Mill Pool. She imagined that she was there, sitting on the ledge behind the waterfall. She saw someone stood behind the long grasses watching her mother and Irene laughed as they splashed in the shallow water with Laura.

Lying on the hospital bed, Mary moaned as the dream became focused.

She dived out from under the waterfall and swam across the deep pool until she could stand in the shallows. She whispered to Irene that someone was watching them. Irene and Sophia looked across at the stretch of reeds on the opposite bank. They watched for any movement and said they couldn't see anyone.

Mary, it must be your imagination, Sophia had said and told her to play with Laura while she read her book.

Laura ran into the water, and Mary chased after her. They looked up and saw a woman stood among the reeds. Wisps of black hair and the swaying stalks of bull reeds obscured her face.

Mary gasped, she turned her head on her pillows, and her heartbeat increased.

In her dream she recognised who it was. She grabbed Laura's hand, and she squeezed it tighter and tighter, so tight that Laura screamed.

'Ouch!' said Diane, and she pulled her hand away. 'Are you awake?'

Mary opened her eyes. She felt drained and flushed. She saw Diane standing by her bed, looking down at her. Mary struggled around to sit up, and she groaned with the effort.

'Here let me help.' Diane lifted the pillows back and took Mary's elbow to ease her into a sitting position. 'I think you were having a nightmare. How are you feeling?'

'I'm feeling better. Where's Scott?'

'Scott has gone for coffee.'

'How long have you been here?' Mary said and leaned back against the pillows.

'Not long.' Diane lifted the plastic beaker from the side table. 'Would you like a drink? Scott said you might want water.'

'Yes, please.'

'Margaret suggested I should come and see what I can do.' She smiled. 'Get you anything like a book or some chocolate, I am sure Scott is doing the best he can despite—'

'Yes, he is. How's Edward?'

'He's busy as usual. He is getting the bullocks ready for next week's sale.'

'Have you seen Laura?'

'You know?'

'Have you seen her?'

'Laura, oh yes. She's lovely, and a smart girl.'

'Does she know?'

'She's in the library every day working on a genealogy project.'

'Laura is looking for her mother. Diane, you know that.'

'Yes well, she won't find her. She'll find her relatives and then leave.'

'Why leave?'

'Why should she remain here? Old Charlie won't let her stay.'

'That's not true—'

'Listen. It's important you get better. Let's not worry about the past.'

'The murder, you mean.'

'Can't you see what that girl has done? She is upsetting everyone. Please, Mary, let it go.'

'I can't, I saw someone in the reeds that day at the picnic, and I know who.'

'Don't upset yourself. You did everything you could. The police investigated and searched. It's over, let it—'

'I know Diane, I know.' Mary lifted her hand and pointed to the water beaker.

'What do you know? Please Mary, you must rest,' said Diane. 'Look, I've brought some grapes.' She took the packet from her coat pocket. 'Would you like one?' She pushed one into Mary's mouth, followed by a second and third.

'These are bitter and taste odd,' Mary said. She chewed them, and she turned her face away when Diane tried to push another into her mouth.

With a paper tissue, Diane picked up the rejected grape and placed it beside the others. 'I'll get rid of them if you don't like them.' She placed them into Scott's bag under the bed.

She grabbed Mary's arm just above the elbow. 'Who did you see? Come on, why do you think you know now?'

'Diane, you're hurting me.'

'Sorry,' she said and eased her grip. 'Are you going to tell the police?'

'Why were you watching us at the pool?' said Mary and she pulled her arm free. 'I know it was you. What did you do?'

Diane grabbed Mary's arm again. 'You've told them it was me. What do you mean me? Poor Mary, Margaret was right. You're delirious.'

'The police didn't believe me, but I know it was you.'

'Poor, poor Mary, you're not well. Your mind is—' She stopped talking when Scott came into the ward. He carried two paper cups with muffins balanced on the plastic lids.

'Here we are. Oh Mary, sorry I didn't bring you one. You can share mine.'

Diane waved away the offer of a cup.

'I need to be off, Scott,' she said and turned to Mary and took her hand. Mary pulled away. 'Take care, Mary. We want nothing to happen to you. Do we?' she said and walked to the door where she stood. 'Scott look after her, she's family and we all know how families should stick together.'

Diane looked back towards Mary. 'Get well soon. Remember, you're a Dawson,' she said and left the room.

'What was that about?'

'Nothing, it's just her way of being nice,' said Mary. 'I'll have the muffin. I'm starving.'

'No visitors for weeks and then they all come at once,' said Scott.

'When is Laura coming?'

'I'm not sure. Here, take the lemon one.'

Scott felt encouraged as he watched Mary eat the soft sponge. Her appetite had returned. He wasn't sure if this was the right time to talk about Orchard View. His check with the Land Registry showed Irene Dawson as the recorded owner. No one had made the application or followed the legal procedure of declaring Irene Dawson missing and presumed dead. How long does a person need to be missing before you believe they are dead? It was clear; he had no right of inheritance to Orchard View and if Irene had left a will then everything would go to Laura. Why couldn't Laura accept her orphan status and get on with her life, instead of coming to Kirkindale on the pretext of doing a family research project? Old Charlie was right, Laura must leave. Life was better when she didn't exist.

'That was lovely Scott,' said Mary, and she wiped her lips with the back of her hand. She took a mouthful of coffee. 'You know, I feel as if a world of guilt has washed away.' She smiled and cradled the paper cup in both hands under her chin.

'Mary, what do you mean by a world of guilt?' he said. He noticed the shift of her mood from the depressive demeanour earlier to an elated cheerfulness. Perhaps the visit by Diane has given her a new purpose with a positive outlook and distraction from the effects of cancer.

'It has been eating away in the back of my mind for years, and I've ignored it. They said I was only a child with a wild imagination. I believed I had seen a ghost.'

Scott smiled and nodded. She was rambling, but he liked her excited tone and expressiveness even though it made no sense to him. 'We all see ghosts in the darkest of times.'

'Don't make fun of me. Don't you see? Diane was at the Mill Pool when someone murdered my mother.'

'Then why didn't the police—'

'Oh Scott, they never believed me, and they never will.'

He shrugged. Aunt Margaret had warned him not to let Laura visit Mary, as they would only upset each other by talking about Sophia's murder. She was probably correct.

'There's a good programme about Shire horses on channel one tonight. Do you want to watch it?'

'It was Diane. I'm sure she was there.'

'I saw the trailer to the programme, and it looks interesting.'

'She must have been there. Oh Scott, Diane must know what happened.'

'How do you know this now?'

'I saw her in my dream, but it wasn't a dream. It was real, I saw her.'

'Oh Mary, a dream or a memory, I think you are upsetting yourself.'

'Don't Scott, please you must believe me.' She reached and grabbed his hand. She held tight. Tears formed in the corners of her eyes.

'I believe you. I do, Mary,' he said and patted the back of her hand. 'I need to go, I promised Michael I would attend an update at the vets.'

His availability for work was under scrutiny, and his partners wanted to recruit a replacement until Mary recovered.

Scott took the empty cups and put them in the bin by the sink. He headed to the door and said. 'I'm pleased you are feeling better, I'll be back later tonight.' He came to her, kissed her forehead, and said, 'Goodbye.'

Chapter Twenty-two

The brass plaque at No 8 Barrister Row gleamed from a recent polish. Laura climbed up the steps, two at a time, and walked into the hallway of McCarthy and Sinclair solicitors' office. There was a smell of fresh lemon mixed with the mustiness from the carpet and decrepit wallpaper. She pressed the bell and waited. She expected the door at the end of the hall to open and that Jeffrey would appear and usher her in. Instead, she heard footsteps striding across the floor above and a woman came halfway down the stairs. She stopped and looked over the bannister.

'Ah yes, you must be Miss Dawson. We are expecting you. Come on up.'

The stair carpet was worn, and the sacking frayed at the edges. Laura tripped at the last step onto the landing.

'Careful,' said the woman who stood by an open door. 'We are having new carpets fitted next week, and about time. I told Mr Jeffrey someone will trip and fall to their death and hopefully not me.' She pointed into the room. 'This way. Please take a seat.'

The room had a polished oak floor and rose floral curtains bordered the windows. Plant pots with geraniums sat around the hearth of the Victorian fireplace, and the stems showed a growth of buds with red petals peeking through.

Laura sat in front of the cluttered desk. The woman bundled the folders into her arms and carried the pile to a filing cabinet. She sorted the folders and slid them into various drawers.

An electric typewriter, and a telephone with a diary and notepad lay on a side table.

'I won't be a minute,' the woman said and picked up a collection of folders from the floor next to the window and cradled them into her arms. There were occasional squeaks from her plimsoles as she walked across the floor. She dropped the folders onto her desk and arranged them in tidy rows before she sat down into her mauve leather chair. She shuffled her bottom on the seat and pulled down on her blue flannel skirt and then pushed back the strands of hair that had dropped over her ears.

'Jeffrey asked me to answer all your questions,' she said and looked across at Laura. 'All your questions, he said. I'm sure.'

'It's about my mother and Russet House.' Laura did not know what to say but needed to say something. She wasn't sure if this woman knew of the situation.

'I know. Miss Dawson.' She pointed to the array of binders and files. 'I've brought out all the records if needed.' She spread out the folders and pushed them around like tarot cards, as if preparing to read Laura's future and fortune.

'Right, I've them all here,' she said.

'Is Mrs Sinclair—'

'Mr, it is Mr Sinclair, and no. I do all the work, he signs the letters, or if the occasion requires, he attends the courts.' She nodded and said, 'I get to go along on the difficult cases. It's all paperwork, I'm afraid.'

'Mr!'

'Sorry. Oh yes, he wears his costume sometimes. Jeffrey is a talented thespian with the Marston Drama Club. Honestly, I think he prefers women's clothes.'

Laura smiled and watched the woman as she opened a legal writing pad. She looked over forty years old and with threads of white in her auburn hair tied back in an untidy bun.

The woman saw Laura reading the engraved nameplate on the desk which stated–Miss D McCarthy ILSPA.

'My uncle is Ian McCarthy, the senior solicitor. Law runs in the family.' She tapped her pen on the notepad. 'Oh sorry, I'm Doreen, Doreen McCarthy, and I'll be dealing with your details. Now did you bring any form of ID?'

Laura passed over her birth certificate and passport.

'I will make a photocopy of these. I won't be a minute.' She picked up the documents and left the room.

Laura wandered over to the large paintings which hung on either side of the fireplace. She recognised the stretch of the River Marrs showing a family of swans in the water, and the painted detail of the feathers was intricate. There was no signature. The second painting was a landscape of the Kirkindale valley showing the orchards on the hillsides. The signature was, I Stewart.

'They are exquisite, aren't they?' said Doreen when she came back into the office. She went behind the desk and offered the documents back to Laura. 'I'll just file my copies.'

Laura accepted her passport and certificate and placed them into her bag. She sat in front of the desk.

'Did my mum have a will?'

'Oh yes.' Doreen opened a file and removed a sheet from a large envelop. 'It's just the standard format. What do you think of the paintings?'

'They're lovely,' said Laura. 'My mum painted the landscape.'

'She painted both of them. My uncle bought them at a school show. Yes, your mother was a very talented artist.'

'What do you know about the murder at the Mill Pool?'

'Yes, dreadful. What a shock, and unbelievable in Kirkindale.' She looked directly at Laura. 'I would never have expected your mother could do such a thing. She was so gentle at school.'

'You knew her?'

'Oh yes, we were in the netball team together. But we were not close friends. Unlike me, she was one of the clever ones. A teacher's pet, particularly in the art class.'

'What was she really like?'

'Lively, likable and even gregarious. She was normal, and I still find it hard to believe. We try not to talk about the murder of poor Mrs Dawson.'

'My grandmother.'

'Yes, I expect she was. Such a lovely woman.'

'I found these letters among her things,' said Laura, and she pulled them from her bag and out of their envelopes. She passed them across the desk.

Doreen looked at them and passed them back. 'No need, I have the original copies already filed.' She opened a buff folder. 'Yes, here they are. The dispute about the ownership of Russet House.' She flicked through the documents and then back to the last letter in the file. 'Yes, I remember this, quite a bad-tempered exchange. I'm afraid your grandfather wouldn't let go of the house after his son's death. Legally, from William Dawson's will, the house belongs to your mother, and she is the rightful owner.' She reached for another file. 'Here we are; she still is. I checked with the Land Registry, and our copy of the property deeds remain current. No change.'

'I want to know where my mum has gone.'

Doreen picked up a thick folder. 'I've compiled all the newspaper cuttings and the police reports. We had to after Mr Charles Dawson tried once again to get his hands on the house. We needed a death certificate.'

'I don't believe she is dead.'

'No, but she is missing and to activate a disposal on her estate and property rights we need the court to authorise a Presumption of Death Certificate.'

'I can't believe she is dead. I think she is with the gypsy community.'

'Mr Dawson couldn't get the situation resolved. His anger towards the police didn't help and eventually he gave up.'

'If Mum is dead, what happens to Russet House?'

'If there is a death certificate, then it is yours. Also, if I remember rightly.' She shuffled through the papers from the files. 'Here it is, we obtained Mr William Dawson's will during our investigations. According to our copy, it is likely you could also inherit partial ownership of Springfield Farm.'

'Really!' Laura shook her head. She couldn't grasp why the family sent her away and into care.

'The wording is ambiguous, but a legal argument could easily determine that William Dawson's share of the estate is passed onto you.'

'My father died in a farm accident.'

'According to the side notes by Jeffrey, it seems you may already have a claim on the farm. The documented deeds show shared ownership.'

'My grandfather may have changed his will.'

'Yes, but that only relates to his part of the farm, not William's or Mary's.'

'So, what do I do?'

'Find your mother.' Doreen stared at Laura. 'Sorry, that was insensitive.'

'I don't care about all this, I want to know what has happened to my mum, and where she is hiding.'

'I think everyone in both Marston and Kirkindale would like to know what happened.'

Laura's throat tightened. She swallowed and cleared her throat and said, 'Does everyone believe she killed my grandmother?'

'I'm sorry, Miss Dawson. I'm afraid so,' said Doreen. 'Let me see, from these notes; your mother owns Russet House and has a partial share of Springfield Farm.'

'So, I own—'

'You own nothing.' Doreen interrupted. 'Your mother is the legal owner.'

Laura rubbed her temples to ease her headache. She wasn't clear on the details, but it seemed as long as her mother remained missing the inheritance tilted in favour of Mary Dawson. Mary would have a claim on Springfield Farm and have control of Russet House. She didn't care, finding her mother was more important.

She felt a pang of loneliness, and a tear emerged to slip down her cheek. She looked away from the legal secretary.

'Laura, here.' Doreen stood up and passed her a tissue. 'I'm sorry these issues can become overwhelming.' She came out from behind her desk. 'Let me make you a tea or coffee.'

'Tea, please.'

'Tea and a scone. Then we'll discuss our next step.'

Chapter Twenty-three

Scott smiled at the nurse when she looked up from behind the ward desk.

'Hello Jean,' he said. 'How is she doing?' He knew the hospital staff in the cancer ward by name. Recently, a junior nurse had thought he was one of the hospital staff.

'Very peaceful,' said Jean. 'Mr Ferguson, the doctor was concerned about her cardiac readings, but it is nothing to worry about.'

He nodded and went into the private ward. Mary was asleep, and her breathing was soft and regular. He sat by her bed and opened the newspaper. Whatever was going on in the world was irrelevant to him. He turned to the crossword. Even the cryptic clues couldn't distract him from thinking about Laura and the murder at the Mill Pool.

Since Laura's arrival in the village, Mary has had some disturbing nightmares. In those dreams, she claims to have seen Diane hiding in the reeds and spying on the picnic group. Yet, her statement to the police was not specific about who she saw. Therefore, her account was dismissed as unreliable. So why would they believe her now? It made no sense to him. If Diane had been near the falls, would she not have told the police? He did not like upsetting Mary, but he would tell her that Laura could not visit just yet. Would Mary believe him?

He put down the newspaper and picked up the large envelope that Anne had given him. He slipped out the photocopies of the Gazette articles, which covered the details of the murder from fifteen years ago. He leafed through the reports.

They had a suspect, Joe Prince, and at first the police assumed he had killed both Sophia and Irene Dawson, but later he was proven to be innocent. Next, the hysteria of the media leapt on a family argument that resulted in an accident. In each case, there did not appear to be a motive. Both the women were inseparable and, as Mary had told him, they were the best of friends.

The newspaper articles did not mention Sophia Dawson's deep depression after the stillbirth of Robert. Mary had told him how the relationship between her parents had become increasingly difficult. Losing their baby was the catalyst for an unbearable bitterness between them, and this developed into a toxic atmosphere in the household.

When Irene announced she was pregnant, this news delighted Sophia and her mood had lifted. A grandchild was what she needed to regenerate her excitement and joy with life.

Old Charlie's bad temper got worse, and there were frequent arguments with William concerning the running of the farm. Whenever they started their heated debates, as they liked to call them, Mary would slip out of the kitchen and go to the stables and brush down the horses.

After William's accidental death, Mary went to live in Russet House. It had been Irene's idea as she wanted company and help to look after baby Laura. In all honesty, Mary had said, she was pleased to get away from the farm and the constant bickering between her parents.

Scott looked up as a nurse came into the room. She whispered, 'Hello, just checking.' She picked up the folder clipped to the foot of the bed and read the notes. She checked the drips and monitors and recorded details onto the loose pages.

'All's well,' she said and closed the door when she left.

Scott shuffled through the stories from the Gazette copies. There was a snippet with the story about a witness, but the police dismissed the statement as the fanciful imaginations of a hysterical Mary Dawson, aged 19 years. They concluded she had not been present at the location or witnessed the attack.

A police operation of collecting blood samples from all the local males did not discover the culprit. They decided that their investigations would concentrate on finding Irene Dawson, who they added was not a suspect.

A later article suggested that Irene had wanted to leave Kirkindale and join her gypsy relatives and the traveller community. Mrs Sophia Dawson had objected, citing her grandchild as the reason to stay. The newspaper article maintained how Irene's plan caused the argument which led to Sophia's death. Scott read this twice, and it seemed the reporter was writing on the information from unfounded rumours as the source for his speculation.

Scott stuffed the papers back into the envelope. The entire business would have laid dormant if Laura had not arrived in Kirkindale.

He reached out and held Mary's hand. She did not respond to his touch. Her face seemed paler than usual with a waxy appearance, and her skin felt cold.

He got up and went to the window. It was raining, and he was glad he didn't have to go out to a farm and treat sick animals in a muddy enclosure or in a dirty barn. His disruptive availability was not working for the veterinary practice, and Michael had suggested he formally gives up the post. This would allow them to recruit a temporary replacement until he could return full time. Effectively, he was out of work until either Mary got better and came home, or she died.

He was tired, and he yawned, a long yawn drawn out and exhaled from deep within his lungs. His fatigue was more the result of the mental strain and worry about Mary rather than his physical tiredness. Would she recover?

He heard her gurgle and went over to the bed, expecting her to be awake. He held and patted her hand. The alarms on the monitors burst into a series of intermittent high-pitched tones. He must have touched the sensors. The door swung open and two nurses rushed in, and they pushed him away from the bed.

'Could you please wait outside,' said Jean. She put her hand on his back and directed him out through the door. Dr Jamal came running along the corridor and pushed past him into the room. The door banged and closed behind him.

Scott felt a pang of fear shudder through his body, and he sat on the chair behind the ward desk. His legs were shaking. It'll be all right, he convinced himself; he had just accidently interrupted the monitor. Yes, that was the reason for the alarms. He knew it was serious when the nurses had reacted so quickly and had purposefully directed him out of the room. He placed his elbows on the desk and held his head. Tears of tiredness welled up as he sensed this was the end. At last this nightmare would be over. He shook his head, ashamed and feeling guilty for those thoughts. He wanted to get up and run back into the room to be with Mary. What were they doing? He closed his eyes and leaned back in the chair.

'Mr Ferguson, Scott.'

He looked up and saw Phyllis and Lynda. They were the MacMillan nurses he would occasionally chat to during the afternoons when Mary was asleep.

'Come into the families' room, Scott. We'll make a cup of tea,' said Phyllis.

Lynda came to him and took his arm. He shrugged her off.

'Sorry, I'm fine,' he said and followed Phyllis into the side room. He sat by the window. This is it, he thought, they will tell him something, something he already knew, something they would confirm. He waited, not really wanting to hear anything.

Lynda put the kettle on and arranged cups onto a tray.

'Now, we know Mary has had an adverse reaction,' said Phyllis, and she came and sat next to him. 'Jean called us and said Dr Jamal is working to settle her.'

This was the prelude, he thought, to lead him gently into the worst news, but they expected this. He felt a wash of tears stream down his face. Last week they had told him she was in recovery and there was a possibility of moving her to a convalescent ward. A place where she could build up her strength.

'Here you are, Mr Ferguson.' Lynda passed him a mug of tea. 'It's just as you like it, with two sugars and a drop of milk. Phyllis?'

'Coffee for me, please.'

The door opened, and Dr Jamal walked in. His eyes were watering, and he had a blank expression. He stared directly at Scott, who stood up. Phyllis took the mug off him.

'I'm sorry Mr Ferguson,' said Dr Jamal and shook his head. 'Your wife has had an unexpected relapse.'

'But yesterday you said she was much better.' Scott took a deep breath. 'Is she going to be okay?'

'Whatever caused the reaction has passed for the time being.' Dr Jamal nodded. 'I've induced a coma, and her pulse has settled.'

'Can I go through? I want to see her.'

Jean led the way. Scott went over to Mary and saw her face was a pale grey. He felt a wash of sadness creep over his head and drain down through his body. He leaned over her and kissed her cheek. He sat by the bed and sobbed. Was he feeling grief or was he relieved the pain would soon be over?

Jean put her hand on his shoulder for a moment and said, 'I'll leave you alone for now.' She patted him on his arm. 'She's peaceful, just asleep. I'll let you be.'

Dr Jamal was in the corridor looking in through the open door. 'Nurse,' he said to Jean, 'I need to go through all the notes. Mrs Ferguson should not have had that kind of reaction.'

Jean nodded. 'I'll bring them to your office in five minutes.'

'Bring all the medication records, please do. It is odd.' Dr Jamal stopped talking when he noticed Scott was listening and watching him. He ushered Jean out of the room and closed the door.

Chapter Twenty-four

The engine noise faded as the bus drove away towards Kirkindale, and Laura wandered up Springwater Lane. She enjoyed the warm evening breeze and the peace of the countryside. A skylark sang and she strained her eyes, searching the sky until she spotted the bird as a small hovering dot against the backdrop of the clouds.

She was delighted in finding Daphne Lister, but felt deflated to learn of her grandparents' deaths. She never met them, and they will remain a void in her life and an experience she has lost.

Daphne claimed the Dawsons were responsible for the murder at the Mill Pool, and they must have killed her mother. But there were flickers of humour in Daphne's eyes when she suggested Irene was living with the travellers in a caravan.

Where would she look for the gypsy community? If she found them, would they help to find her mother or else be uncooperative and fearful of the consequences? She imagined a moment of overwhelming joy when she found her mother alive and living in a horse-drawn caravan. But would her own mother trust her?

She watched a man come down the lane; he wore a flat cap, a black Donkey jacket open at the front and moleskin trousers. He appeared to be in his early twenties with an old-fashioned dress sense, or else it was the preferred country style for many people in Kirkindale.

'Hello, you must be Laura,' he said and approached her.

She could smell the tang of his aftershave. He had neatly knotted his woollen tie at the collar of his chequered shirt.

'Yes,' she said and took a step to one side. 'You've missed the bus.'

'Doesn't matter, I'll walk. I always get a lift.'

'Bye then.' She walked on. She did not hear him move and sensed he was watching her. She resisted her temptation to run or turn around and see what he was doing.

'I heard in the Swan you're looking for your mother.'

She wheeled round to face him. 'My mum, yes she's missing.'

'I know, well I wasn't here then, but Anne told me all about the murder.'

'Okay, well, enjoy your walk. I need to get going.'

'Just to warn you. Stay away from the farm.'

'Stay away! What—'

'Mr Dawson doesn't like visitors, he's a lunatic if you ask me.' He took off his hat and smoothed the Brylcreem on his hair. 'I work the stables and horses and do a bit of gardening.' He kicked at a stone on the road. 'I cut the grass around Mr Ferguson's place yesterday.'

'Were you behind the trees?' She stared at him.

'I didn't know he had a visitor, sorry if I scared you.' He laughed. 'I thought you were a burglar.'

So, he knew all about her and she was the subject of gossip around the bar in the village.

'Have you worked here long?'

'About five years or thereabouts,' he said, twisting his cap in his hands. 'Why don't you come down to the Swan, I mean would you like to come? Anne will be there and, well, it's up to you.' He put his cap back on and shrugged. 'If you like.'

'The bus has gone and I'm tired.' She smiled and shook her head. 'I don't fancy walking.'

'I always get a lift on the road,' he said, 'and the last bus back.' He straightened his cap and pulled his jacket closed. 'It must be lonely in the house. Come on.'

'I'm exhausted, maybe another time.'

'That's what they say, bad blood breeds ignorance.' He walked closer towards her and spoke through his teeth. 'They say your mother was a witch.'

She took two steps away from him and slipped her hand into her pocket to find the house keys. She took them out and clenched them in her fist.

'A witch. Is that what they think?'

He grinned. 'Come and tell them it's not true.' He looked at the keys in her hand and stepped back. 'Well, if you're tired, maybe another time then.'

'Yes. maybe.'

He strode off down the lane towards the road and glanced over his shoulder. 'I'll be seeing you, bye.' He shouted. 'Name's Tommy if anyone should ask.'

She watched him for a moment until she was certain he would not turn back, then she jogged along the lane. At the entrance to the driveway, she stopped and checked that Tommy was still walking away. She dashed down the middle of the drive and ran across the garden to the rear door and entered the utility room. She slammed and locked the door.

There was a chill in the kitchen, and she touched the radiator; it was cold. The outdoors felt warmer than the interior of the house. The thermostat in the dining room was turned off, so she turned up the setting. Next, she checked the front door was locked. In the hallway she listened for any movement of someone in the house, but all she heard was the water gurgling as it was pumped around the pipes. This reminded her of the day when her foster father became frustrated as he tried to bleed the radiators. Then he realised he was doing it in the wrong order.

She made a hot chocolate drink and sat at the kitchen table with her new hardback notebook, a replacement for her stolen diary.

She had made notes on Daphne's recollection of her time with her mother, and she noted the names of her relatives among the gypsies. The travellers could be anywhere at this time of the year, suggested Daphne. They might be picking fruit in Kent or Scotland. They move around to where they can find work, and they could be in Ireland. The men were a versatile group of tradesmen without qualifications. Daphne had said that they were not interested in schools and didn't like to settle with folk.

Was her mother dead and done away with as Daphne said? She took a long hard breath and felt a surge of despair and her eyes welled. She sniffed and wiped her face with the dishcloth.

Scott was not home but would expect a meal to be ready. She made a fresh vegetable soup, following Mrs McLean's recipe of chopped fried bacon, lentils, onion and enough carrots and potatoes for everyone.

After her meal, she took a cup of warm chocolate up to her room and sat looking out the window. The fields along the valley, carved out by the River Marrs, and the wooded hillside in the distance provided a wide vista unlike the rows of brick houses surrounding her foster home. What would her life have been like had she grown up here? Tonight, for instance, would she be in the Swan enjoying the company of friends and discussing their lives? She might enjoy the gossip about who was dating who or planning to escape to the city or taking an adventurous trip around the world on a gap year. Did people from Kirkindale go to university or else just live their lives farming and riding horses? This was an unfamiliar world from her restricted town existence.

She was on a gap year and taking this opportunity to visit the place where she was born, to find her mother, and meet her relatives. She had told Mr and Mrs McLean she was backpacking around Europe with friends, otherwise they might have stopped her from visiting Kirkindale. Perhaps they knew about the murder and were trying to shield her from the horror. Why couldn't they have explained and told her the truth?

She was unwanted and forgotten by the Dawson family because of the Mill Pool murder, but she was just a child. Why was she being punished?

A tear dropped into her hot chocolate, and she laughed for a moment.

She had confided in Jenny about her plans and trusted her not to tell Mrs McLean. She was a wonderful woman and a kind foster mother, but discouraged Laura from searching for her biological parents. Mrs McLean told her to wait until she was older and wiser and then she would understand. Understand what? What she meant was to wait until Laura was mature enough to deal with the emotional upheaval, suggesting she would be a shuddering emotional wreck on meeting her mother. Who cares? She had to find her mother. This obsession upset Mrs McLean and she would often sit with Laura and persuade her to concentrate on her schoolwork, think about university and a career and then perhaps a nice professional man. The latter would break the tension and make them laugh.

She had a deferred place at Manchester University and was determined to use some of her gap year to discover her identity.

She saw a man and his collie dog walk across the field; he swung his stick in time with his step as if on a military parade ground. She leaned forward and touched the glass and watched. The dog trotted by his side with its ears pointed towards the sheep which were grazing at the bottom of the hill. The man turned his head and glanced towards the house. Laura pulled back from the window. Did he think he was being watched and did he see her? The man was her grandfather who, according to Tommy, was a lunatic. Tomorrow she would go up to the farm and visit him, and if he doesn't want to talk, she will refuse to leave until he does. She wanted to meet him and ask why she was sent away.

She was his son's daughter and his grandchild, and she would face up to him and ask why he disowned her.

She took a box from under the bed and searched through the pictures, separating them into various groups of events. Yes, she had a family, and these pictures were proof that they existed. They abandoned her and she needed to find an explanation. Why does a mother's crime get passed onto their children?

If her grandfather refused to see her tomorrow, she could go to the hospital and visit her Aunt Mary, who may explain the reasons they placed her into foster care.

She packed the photographs back into the box, putting her father's picture in last. The evening was getting dark, but before she switched on the room light, she went to the window to close the curtains. Outside in the garden a fox sat looking up at the house. She watched it for a moment and then realised from its reaction to her appearance at the window it knew she was there. The fox kept its stare on her. She felt a tingle creep over her skin. Her breathing was short and erratic as the fox strolled towards the utility entrance. She knew she had closed it. Could a fox open a locked door?

She closed the curtains with two quick pulls and rushed down the stairs into the kitchen.

The fox sat on the patio, looking in through the French windows. She slapped the glass door in front of the fox. It yawned and laid down, all the while watching her, and it stared at her with its head resting on its front paws.

Laura fetched a class of water and dragged a chair over to the window. The fox stood and trotted off down the garden to the hedge by the old track. It sat facing the house. After what seemed like minutes, the fox slipped through the hedge and out of her sight.

Chapter Twenty-five

Scott did not return home last night, so rather than go to the hospital and see Aunt Mary, Laura decided on a visit to Springfield Farm. She knew her grandfather was hurting about the murder at the Mill Pool. Perhaps she could get him to talk and get him to discuss the past. A past she desperately wanted to understand. Why was her grandmother murdered? Why does anyone murder? Yes, in the moment of desperation she might have killed that idiot in the graveyard, but that was more about survival and panic. Is that what happened, did someone panic at the Mill Pool?

The track to the farm was a mixture of broken tarmac and compacted gravel with water-filled potholes. There were sections where tractor tyres had carved deep ruts into the grass verges.

She walked alongside a field where five black horses were grazing. They raised their heads and looked towards her and they trotted over to the fence where they jostled each other for Laura's attention. There was a pleasant smell of their musky animal sweat as they snorted and nudged to get in close. Their ears twitched back and forth, and they shook their heads to deter the flies from landing around their eyes. She reached up and stroked the nose of the nearest horse, which neighed in protest and nodded, releasing a cloud of dust from an untidy mane. Its salvia dribbled over her hand and splattered onto her face. The animal stamped its hooves into the ground, and it reared and gave a long neigh before it ran off into the middle of the field. The other horses whined and walked away. Had they mistaken her for someone else?

She expected a dog to meet her, or at least bark when she walked into the farmyard. She knocked on the house door and waited; there was no response, so she knocked again and much louder. She rapped on a window and looked through into the kitchen. The room appeared clean and organised; there was a folded newspaper on the table.

She glanced around the yard and saw a tractor with large yellow wheels parked by the stables; she walked across to the building. Inside, horse stalls lined both sides. There were reins and saddles draped over the pen doors. Someone had recently washed the floor and there was a smell of soap.

'Hello,' she shouted and waited. She heard animals moving about in the shed beyond the stables and went to have a look.

Old Charlie and Tommy were forking silage into feeder troughs and the bullocks had their heads through the rails and they grabbed mouthfuls of the preserved grass. She watched the men continue their work. Since neither of them had noticed her, she waited until they reached the far end of the shed and had cleared all the silage from the central aisle.

'Hello,' she called, 'I . . .' She didn't know what to say as the men were startled. They glared at her and she waved. 'Hi, I thought I would come and say hello. I'm Laura and—'

'I know who you are,' shouted Old Charlie. 'There's nothing for you here, so bugger off.'

Tommy pulled his cap down over his eyes. He swapped his pitchfork for a wide brush and swept the remains of the silage across the floor.

She walked towards the men and stopped within arm's distance from Old Charlie.

'You're my grandfather, why don't you—'

'Just like your mother.' He interrupted. 'Don't listen to nobody. Now bugger off.'

She picked up the pitchfork that stood against the pen railings.

The bullocks were snorting and scuffling as they chewed at the feeding.

Tommy stopped sweeping. 'I'll take that,' he said, and stepped forward to reach for the fork in Laura's hands. She pulled back and raised the prongs towards the men.

'Did you kill my mother?' she shouted. 'Well!'

'I've been expecting you,' said Charlie. He grabbed the pitchfork and pulled it free from her. 'Now, we don't want trouble.' He passed it to Tommy.

She took two steps back. 'I want to know what happened to my mother.'

'I know,' said Charlie. 'Tommy, when you're done here, check the sheep. You!' He pointed at her. 'You better come with me.'

She strode with him across the farmyard and a collie dog appeared and followed them into the kitchen. She sat at the kitchen table as instructed. The dog slumped onto a tattered blanket in the corner.

Charlie filled the kettle. He stood by the sink and stared at her while the water boiled. He masked the tea in a Picquot pot.

'You've grown into a pretty, young lady,' he said and passed her a mug of tea. 'Help yourself to milk and sugar.' He pulled a chair out from the table and sat.

'I—'

'Do you take milk?' He interrupted her and passed the milk bottle. 'Now just listen.'

She poured a dash of milk into her mug and looked up at the old man. He appeared to have softened his expression and showed a smidgeon of a smile.

'No one expected to see you again,' he said. 'People would hate you for what your mother did.'

'Hate a child?'

'For your own sake I sent you away. People don't forgive around here.'

'But . . .' she felt the word choke in her throat. 'Did I not belong here?'

'Being a farmer, you learn the strength of cruelty.'

'What was my mother like?' She stared directly at him to read his reaction.

He tapped the table with his fingers. He took a handkerchief from his pocket and wiped at his eyes, then blew his nose. He composed himself and said, 'There is nothing for you here, go back home.'

'I have. I've come home.'

'Has anyone told you about—'

'Grandmother's murder at the Mill Pool.'

'You know! I don't believe Irene killed my Sophia.'

'I am so pleased you said that. Everyone else thinks she did.'

'Everyone. No, Irene would not kill. She was gentle like a lamb.'

'So why did she run away?'

'Irene bothered no one,' he said. 'There were people jealous of her artistic talents and this got worse after she married William.' He got up from the table. 'Here, just wait a minute.' He left the room, and the dog followed him out. He returned with a large photograph album and he opened it on the table.

'It was the gypsy blood people objected to.' He shook his head. 'I was against Will marrying her, but somehow she was just . . .' He clasped and wrung his hands. 'Charming and strong minded.'

Laura sipped her tea. He was talking, and she did not want to interrupt him.

'You wanted to know about our family.' He pointed to the first set of pictures. 'That's our wedding, look how young Sophia is, and the carriage. My own Friesians, magnificent horses. Mary manages the herd and gets a good price for every animal she sells.'

Laura listened, and her thoughts whirled as Old Charlie described the background to each of the photographs. She was the baby on his lap who reached up and pulled at his cheeks. It was her birthday cake with one candle. She was the girl on a tricycle being pushed around the farmyard. There was a picture of a black horse with a child on the saddle. Her grandfather held the reins. Snippets of memory were returning of her time on the farm, and this album triggered the return of her childhood memories. She lifted the mug of tea to her chin to conceal the tremble of her lips.

The telephone in the hall rang. Old Charlie shook his head and said, 'It can wait.'

She understood how this gentle man was a bitter, lonely farmer. His only son was killed in an accident with a bull and his wife murdered and left in the river. The warnings to stay away from him were based on pity and because of his angry attitude.

He turned through the pictures, telling her of where and when. She listened and concentrated on the sound of his rasping voice. A dam burst as the origins of her life flowed through her body in emotional waves that erupted in tiny sobs. The sight of the tears on the old man's face made her cry in overwhelming happiness. She had found her family. When there were no more photographs, but only newspaper cuttings, he closed the album.

He came around the table and pulled her up off the chair towards him. He hugged her and although the moment only lasted a second; it seemed as if it contained eighteen years of missing love and warmth.

The telephone in the hall rang persistently. 'Damn phone, it can wait,' he said.

'I'm so sorry Laura, so sorry.' He wiped his eyes with a kitchen paper napkin and took hold of her hand. He smiled and said, 'Come, let's talk to Sophia.'

They went through to the living room, and he pointed to a portrait of her grandmother above the fireplace.

'Sophia, look who has come to see us.' He reached up and touched the painting.

She recognised the gypsy caravan in the background, and she stepped forward to read the artist's signature.

'I know,' he said, 'I wanted to burn it, but she is so beautiful.' He turned to her. 'I've placed a memorial block at the waterfalls above the pool. I should show you. Sophia adored the place. She spent a lot of time there with Irene, painting or reading.'

The telephone rang.

'Please, take the album. Do you want it?' He waited for a reply.

Laura shook her head. 'Don't you want to keep it?'

'I think you should take it. Is it not what you came for?'

'What about my mum?'

'There are drawings in here. I want you to take them, please.' He opened a drawer and took out a large envelope. 'It would be best if you left Kirkindale, since there is nothing but bitterness here.'

The dog barked and dashed to the door. They heard a vehicle draw into the yard, and Old Charlie went into the kitchen and peered through the window.

'Ah! What the hell does he want.' He put on his jacket. 'I expect he is checking up on my bull calves, he never gives up.'

She followed him out and saw Scott get out of his car and come towards the door.

'You said next month.' Old Charlie walked towards the byre. 'But seeing you're here, come on this way.'

Laura stood in the doorway and watched Scott; he was pale and clasping his hands and then rubbing at his face.

'I've not come about the calves,' he shouted and rested on the bonnet of the car. He folded his arms.

'No. That's a surprise. I've nothing else for you to be sticking your nose into.'

'Can we please go inside, I've something to say.'

'I've nothing to say to you,' said Old Charlie. 'Whatever it is just say it and be off with you.'

'Your cankerous old bastard,' Scott screamed, and punched the bonnet of his car.

Startled pigeons took off from the coop behind the byre.

'Don't shout at me!' said Old Charlie, and he pointed at Scott. 'What do you want?' He turned towards the stables. 'I've got work to be getting on with.'

'Mary's dead.'

'What?' Old Charlie came back towards Scott.

A Land Rover raced into the yard and skidded to a stop. Great Aunt Margaret got out and dashed across to them. 'You know then, I called twice and . . .'

Charlie threw his hands up and turned away from everyone. He strode into the house.

'Tea, that's what we need,' said Margaret. 'Come Laura, kitchen.' She looked at Scott and went to him. 'I'm so sorry,' she said and hugged him.

He accepted her hug for a moment and then pushed her off. 'Yes tea, the answer to everything.' He got into his car and turned it around in the yard.

'Scott, come back,' shouted Margaret. 'Wait!' She slapped at the side of his vehicle.

The car sped off down the farm track, skidding sideways in places before it reached the tarmac lane where it then accelerated towards the main road.

Chapter Twenty-six

Great Aunt Margaret made tea in the kitchen and tried to placate Old Charlie. He was raging and reminiscent of his hellish bad luck. After he had recovered from his manic outburst of grief, he composed himself and talked about the funeral. He spoke of a horse-drawn carriage to carry the coffin to the church and on to the graveyard. The wake must be in the stables, and he was insistent.

'Whatever you like,' Margaret said. 'Mary would like that.'

'Take the bloody album. I never want to see you again,' he shouted at Laura.

They left him in the living room, sat by an unlit fire with a second full glass of brandy in his hand.

Margaret persistently insisted that Laura must come home with her and stay at the Oakwood Farm cottage. She declined the offer and asked Margaret to stop by the driveway to Russet House.

Margaret called out of the Land Rover window, 'Laura, you must come and see me tomorrow afternoon. No buts.'

Only after she agreed to a visit, and she promised, did Great Aunt Margaret wave goodbye. There was a sound of crunching gears from the Land Rover as it sped off down the lane, trailing bursts of exhaust fumes.

Laura walked down the gravel drive. Scott's car was not at the house as she expected. Where was he?

Inside, Russet House was pleasantly warm as the afternoon sun had heated the kitchen through the windows. She sat at the table and spread out her collection of photographs and ordered them into family groups and compared them to those in Old Charlie's album. To see her mother and grandmother side by side in the many photographs contradicted the ideas of animosity as reported in the various newspaper articles. The why and who?

For what seemed like a sudden shock, she burst out crying and grabbed a paper towel to wipe her face. Mary; she had missed the chance to visit her in hospital and now her poor aunt was dead. Her grandmothers were dead, and her father was dead. Her mother was an assumed killer and missing.

At midnight, she packed the album and photographs back into their boxes and slipped them under her bed.

She had waited up for Scott, but by now it was clear he was not coming home. Where was he and was it any of her business?

§

Next morning, Laura strolled through the field towards the river and watched the fog slide down the valley. As the day warmed, the haze rose above the wooded hillsides and eventually cleared. By the time she reached the bottom fence of the field, the remaining pockets of mist had evaporated, leaving a clear view across the dale.

She followed the stone wall upriver away from the Mill Pool and pushed through a wooden kissing gate onto a pathway; it led to the top of the gorge. From a viewpoint, she watched the water flow around boulders and stream over the edge of the fall. Further up and to one side of the path there was a polished granite memorial on top of a hillock. A fresh display of flowers lay at its base. She read the words aloud.

In
Loving Memory of
Sophia Anne Dawson
25th July 1979
A loving wife and friend to all
Never Selfish, always kind
These are the memories
She left behind.

Someone had trimmed the grass on the hillock and rose plants grew in the surrounding flower beds. This was a beautiful place. She stroked the granite stone. The murmur of the water over the falls added a musical tone to the atmosphere of tranquillity. Her memories flooded through her thoughts.

Her grandmother pushed her on the swing in the garden. They had sat together on a woollen rug on the lawn eating ice cream and strawberries. Her mouth watered as she remembered the taste of apple crumble and the smooth custard her grandmother once served in the farm kitchen. They had been throwing snowballs at each other in the yard and needed to warm themselves up.

Her eyes welled, and she wiped her nose. The emergence of memories of her grandmother unlocked her forgotten time as a child. She had images of the hens, which seemed like large frightening creatures, as she followed her grandmother to collect eggs. In the old barn, they counted the chickens together, more than once before they agreed on ten. Why had she forgotten those times? She blew her nose as a euphoria of sad happiness engulfed her.

There was a cough, and someone stumbled further up the track. Whoever it was, would disturb her privacy of memories that touching the granite memorial had released. She wanted to be alone. She sneaked behind the mound and lay down among the dried pine needles beneath a group of fir trees. She waited.

There was heavy breathing from someone on the hillock and the occasional clicking of a camera.

She had thought about asking Jenny to borrow her Compact 35mm, but forgot in her rush to catch the train.

The person left the hillock and walked away. Laura crawled out from under the trees and followed the stranger down the path towards the Mill Pool. She caught up with him at the stile over the dyke and saw who it was.

'Hello, Detective Jackson,' she called.

He looked up and saw a grin on her face. He smiled and shook his head.

'I'm getting too old for this,' he said and struggled to swing his leg over the barrier of the stile. He caught his foot on the step and tripped; he lost his balance and fell into a gorse bush.

'Careful!' said Laura, and she suppressed a laugh.

He pulled himself free from the gorse and took a handkerchief from his pocket. He wiped his brow.

'Hello Laura, it's a nice day for a walk,' he said and picked up a tattered leather briefcase. He opened it and took out a manila envelope. 'It's Mr Jackson, although I like the sound of Detective.' He pulled out a folded map. 'Please call me MJ.'

Laura leapt over the stile and jumped down next to him. 'What's that?'

'The scene of the crime,' he said, 'have a look.' He placed the map down on his briefcase and knelt beside it. 'I want to go through all these points, just to compare the location with the documented detail.'

'Thank you, MJ,' she said and knelt to have a closer look.

'For what?'

'Opening the investigation.'

'Oh, it has never been closed, just filed under unsolved.' He coughed. 'I convinced the boss to let me have another go. Do you know what he said?'

She looked at him and waited for the answer.

'Under supervision MJ. Imagine, bloody cheek of the man.' He burst into a fit of coughing. When he recovered, he said, 'No budget, no expenses and a progress report every two days.'

'If it helps to find my mother, then I appreciate your help.'

'There are two places I want to look. Miss Mary Dawson claims to have seen someone. The investigation had dismissed her statement as a conjecture.'

'Why, if she saw someone then why don't you believe her? Who did she see?'

'I believed her, but she was muddled. She said she was in the middle of the waterfall. Look here.' He pointed to the diagrams drawn on the map section. He shook his head. 'To see the person here.' He pointed to a red circle on the diagram. 'She would need to be standing half-way up the waterfall.' He looked at her. 'What do you think?'

She thought nothing and waited for him to elaborate.

'Miss Dawson said she was swimming. Do you think anyone could swim up this falling water?' He shrugged. He pointed to a cross on the diagram. 'Here is where she saw someone. Let's have a look.' He picked up the map and his briefcase.

By the pool, he pointed to the area of bull reeds and the central position of the waterfall, which were marked on his diagram. They walked by the edge of the pool and past the large boulder in the clearing.

The tongue twister, *Round and round the rugged rock the ragged rascal ran*, flashed in her memory. Hide and seek. Where would they hide? She walked around the large stone a few times; it seemed smaller. She was sure it was once enormous. She placed her hands on its rough surface.

MJ watched her for a moment and then carried on comparing his diagram with the layout of the site. He pointed with his arm to the different positions and walked around, turning the diagram to align with the bull reeds.

'It's no use. I can't see how Miss Dawson saw what she saw,' he said and looked across at Laura. She was hugging the rock with her eyes closed. 'When you're finished kissing the witches' stone you—'

'Hide and seek,' she shouted, 'we would hide somewhere.' She walked around the boulder twice, then ran to the base of the falls. 'In here, I'm sure.' She climbed up the side of the cliff face, then screamed. She called, 'Yes, yes in here.' She squeezed her body through a gap between the rocks.

'Laura, Laura.' MJ walked up to the waterfall. 'Come out, Laura. Laura!' He climbed up a few feet and slipped on the wet surface and tumbled back down onto the grass. He shouted again, 'Laura!'

It was ten minutes before Laura pushed out from between the rocks. A green slime covered her hair and the bottom of her trousers were wet.

'There is a ledge,' she said. 'Behind the water there is a ledge. We used to hide there, I know, I know. Mary took me in there once. We were hiding.' She wiped the gunge from her hair.

'What the bloody hell were you doing?' he shouted.

'A ledge, I have found—'

'Another two minutes and I would have gone for a rescue party,' he said.

'That is where Mary was when she saw someone.'

'Don't do that again. You scared the hell out of me.' He sat down on the grass and pulled a thermos flask from his briefcase.

'I remember the hide and seek we played, no one ever found us.'

'I thought you had slipped, and the water dragged you under into the pool.' He took a sip of coffee. 'Do you want some?' He offered the cup to her and reached into his bag for a paper wrapper with sandwiches.

'Good,' he said, 'she must have been telling the truth.' He passed her a sandwich. 'It's potted salmon, nothing but the best.'

She took a large mouthful of coffee and gave him the cup back.

He flicked through his notes. 'There were fingerprints found among the bloodstains on a rock. Unidentified prints from an unknown suspect.'

'So, Mary was telling the truth.'

'It took years to collect samples and chasing the travellers was the worst.' He refilled the coffee cup, and said, 'We never matched those prints.'

'What, you believe my mother was involved with someone else. Why?'

'Why? We never decided on a motive.'

'My mother didn't do this.' She stared at him as he finished his coffee.

He nodded. 'Now the other place I want to search is the sluice from the old mill.' He pointed to his diagram and said, 'It is here. Above the falls.'

'Why! Did Mary mention that as well?'

'No,' he said and rummaged through his notes.

'Ah, here. Scout had gone berserk. Well, I am not sure berserk is the right word, but that's what the handler has noted.'

'Scout?'

'The dog,' he said and flicked over the page. 'A German Shepherd, there is even a photograph with the PC. Here look.'

'Ah, that's nice,' she said. 'What did they find?'

'A fox's den. I wished the dog could have talked.' He turned over his notes. 'They put the incident down to Scout's excitement around the animal scent.'

‘Oh. You think they missed something.’

‘Well, the handler insisted the dog had found something.’ He flicked over the notes. ‘Looks like no further action was taken.’

‘Probably a waste of police time.’

‘You sound like my old boss.’ He stared at her for a moment. ‘No, you wouldn’t understand. They train the dogs to find bodies. Dead or alive.’ He turned the diagram around and pointed in the path's direction. ‘Come on, let’s have a nose.’

The area of the old mill was undefined on the ground. But the police diagram showed a channel from the river towards the waterfall which on the ground looked like a shallow ditch. The area was overgrown with brambles and nettles, nevertheless, MJ matched the rows of the depressions to the line sketched on the drawing.

‘I expect photographs were too much to ask for,’ he said, turning the fold of the paper over. ‘I think the fox’s den is further down towards the river.’ He scrambled over the rubble piled in places along the remains of the sluice.

Laura carried his briefcase and followed him over the rough ground. She was elated with the retired detective’s enthusiasm, or maybe it was the buzz she felt from the coffee. She was sure there was a drop of alcohol in the drink, an Irish coffee without the cream.

The valley looked picturesque from where she stood, a place from where her mother may have painted her landscapes. She sat on a large stone to admire the view.

MJ stumbled about and swore when he tripped into some brambles.

A peregrine falcon swooped across the sky and hovered above the gorge. Laura watched as it circled, and she listened to its calls. The bird moved upriver and its regular high-pitched note faded. There was a gentle murmur from the river. She picked up the briefcase and scrambled off the rocks towards the bramble patch.

'MJ,' she called, 'where are you?' She stepped to the side of the thicket into a bog and saw MJ's footprints sunk into the black mire. There was a wide groove gouged through the mud into a hole among the nettles.

She looked around and shouted, 'MJ!'

She moved forward, taking her time as each step squelched in and out of the soft ground. At the edge of the opening she called, 'Mr Jackson. Are you all right?' She put down the briefcase and knelt on it and leaned forward. 'MJ can you hear me.'

There was a groan. 'Hell, bloody hell,' he shouted. 'I'm okay, nothing broken.'

Laura ducked back to avoid an object thrown out from the hole. MJ's hands appeared and reached up, clawing for a grip in the soft mud, then his head and shoulders followed on. He pulled himself out of the hole. Laura leaned forward and grabbed his arm. She helped him across the bog.

'Did you get it?' he said and crawled past her onto the stones and stood up. His hair, face and clothes were coated with grey and black patches of dirt and slime. He rubbed the dirt from his face. 'Well, did you catch it?'

'Let me help,' she said and took his hand to lead him over the stones onto the grass by the wall. She took a napkin from the briefcase and wiped at his face. He snatched it from her.

'Go, get the bone,' he said. 'What a mess.' He opened his briefcase and took out the coffee flask.

Chapter Twenty-seven

Next day, Laura sat in the garden at Russet House. She saw the vehicles drive through the field and she ran to the fence for a better look. There was a large police van followed by a Land Rover towing a trailer with a digger. She wanted to watch the excavation of the sluice and to see the bones as they were pulled from the earth. MJ had warned her to stay away.

She had called him late last night, desperate to know what was happening. He confirmed the bone was a femur from a human left leg. He had said; the Chief had tasked a mobile incident unit to coordinate the work at the ruins. The forensic anthropologists were on the way, and someone had informed the local amateur archaeologist group who wanted to be involved. Opportunists, MJ had said. Unfortunately, the Chief had assigned him to sifting through the statements in the case files and had ordered him to conduct a review of every aspect of the original investigation. He was to determine what pieces of evidence they may have missed fifteen years ago, and the job would keep him busy for a few days.

He advised her to stay away from the dig site since the press had been informed and the reporters will turn up. If they knew who she was, they would pounce on her with a barrage of questions. They are relentless. MJ advised her to keep away from them as the experience would not be pleasant. She should stay at home and be patient.

Yesterday at the Mill Pool waterfall, she sat with MJ with their backs against the wall drinking coffee. MJ smelled of peaty earth. When he had been walking along the old sluice channel he had slipped in the mud and fell through the soft ground. He had scrabbled for support and the first solid thing he grabbed was the bone.

They had stared at the bone. It lay on the grass in front of them, and neither of them was sure what to say. The appearance of the mud-coated object with a ball joint and knuckled ends was recognisable as a bone and from its size, a human bone.

'No,' he had said, 'It does not mean what you think, might not be your mother, could be anyone, maybe from an ancient burial, maybe the owner of the mill way back from centuries ago.'

'No, it's not my mum.' she had said. Why didn't he stop talking? She wanted to tell him to shut up. Her mother was a fugitive on the run, go Mum run, keep running. But the find might explain why her mother was missing; could it be possible that her body had been rotting in the mud near the waterfall for the last fifteen years? Let it not be true.

She paced around the garden. The telephone rang inside the house, and she ran across the lawn and over the patio into the kitchen. Since Scott had not come home, she had left the door into the private section of the house open. She was too slow and missed the call.

She rushed back into the garden and watched more police vehicles drive down through the field towards the river. What would her grandfather think? She assumed the police had his permission before they drove across his land.

She walked up and down beside the garden fence and felt the knot in her stomach tighten. She found the entrance to the old path where she smelled an ammoniacal decay and covered her nose with her hand. She pushed through the unkempt privet to the weather worn wooden gate cloaked with moss and ivy. An animal track tunnelled through the undergrowth of brambles. She knelt and peered into the space under the mass of the thorny thicket to where she saw a fox.

Roused by her presence, it got up and yawned and stretched its body. It turned and ambled through the mesh of stems from the wild rose, brambles, and hawthorn. The overgrown hedgerows gave the animal a perfect cover to travel unseen from the house to the river, but the lingering odour of damp musk betrayed its presence.

She used the gate for support and stood up. As a child she had wandered between these hedges when the footpath was clear of nettles and the vegetation cut back. On the day of the picnic, Aunt Mary had pulled her along as she protested. They were returning from the Mill Pool to fetch dry towels, and she had struggled to free her hand from Mary's grip. She had left Numpty behind, and she had wanted to go back for her teddy bear.

The memory flashed across her mind; she had hidden Numpty at the picnic.

Mary had promised they would have ice-cream if they ran. They raced, and she had been first through the gate which she banged shut to stop Mary from catching her.

The only flavour left in the freezer was raspberry, and together they had sat on the grass in the garden while they ate. Afterwards, Mary had pushed her on the swing with the sun on her face while she sang. What was she singing?

An image came to her, the police had arrived, and someone was to take her away. She didn't want to go without Numpty, and she had run down the path towards the river. She had been screaming as the woman came chasing after her. Where had she left her teddy? A policewoman sprinted over and caught her. Later, they took her away from Russet House.

By the dilapidated gate, she eased the foliage aside and pushed through the hedge into the garden. She saw him and stood still; had he telephoned earlier?

Scott was sitting on the patio steps drinking from a large glass. He gave a lack lustre wave with a bottle. It seemed like a gesture of dismissal rather than a sign of acknowledgment.

She crossed the lawn and sat next to him.

'Did you find any?' he said.

'Find what?'

'More bones buried at the bottom of the garden.'

'You've heard.'

'You can't see police vehicles around Kirkindale and not wonder what is going on.' He took a drink of whisky and refilled the glass.

'It might be an old burial site from the mill,' she said. 'It could be.'

He got up. 'Are you hungry?' he said and went into the kitchen and shouted. 'I've brought some eggs and bacon.' He drank the contents of his glass.

She followed into the house. 'I'm so sorry about Aunt Mary, I wished—'

'You wished you saw her.' He nodded at her. 'Well, you didn't!'

'Sorry.'

'There is to be a post-mortem.' He found a frying pan and placed it on the cooker. 'Dr Jamal has asked for one. Covering his back, I expect.' He refilled his glass.

'Sorry.'

'She really liked your mother. Did you know?'

'Well, I expect so.'

'No doubt you'll be happy once they dig your mother out.'

Laura sat down at the kitchen table. Why did he say dig her out? She watched him crack two eggs into a bowl and mix them.

'Omelette?' He waited a moment for her reply. 'Omelette it is then.' He layered bacon onto a plate and put it into the microwave. 'There's bread on the table, put some in the toaster. Please.'

She turned her back to him. Her lips trembled. Why did he say that? She dropped four slices of bread into the toaster and then filled the kettle. Why did he say that? She saw the kitchen knife in the sink, and she picked it up. She wiped it on a tea towel and then slipped it under her sleeve.

'After we eat, I would like you to leave.' He shook his head. 'It's just that I would rather be on my own for the time being.'

'I am not leaving.'

'Good luck with that.' He poured some egg mixture into the pan. 'You might be better off down at the Black Swan.'

'I'll leave after Aunt Mary's funeral.' She rubbed at the knife handle.

'I want you to leave. Today!'

'Why did you say it was my mother?'

'Oh, come on.' He tipped an omelette onto a plate. 'Here you have the first one.' He cracked another three eggs into the bowl.

Laura buttered the toast. 'My mother is alive.'

'So, where is she?'

'I am sorry about Aunt Mary. I wanted to see her, I wished.'

He stirred the pan. He had his back to her. 'You wished. We wished you had never existed.'

'Meaning?' She dropped her fork on the table and stood up.

'Nothing.' He stirred the mixture in the pan. 'Mary had something important to say, but you missed your chance.'

'About my mother?' She sat down and took a bite of toast.

'No. About your grandmother's murder.' He tipped the omelette onto a plate. 'Mary was convinced she saw Diane.'

'Mrs Wilcox?' She waited for an answer and watched Scott eat his meal.

'If you pack all your mother's stuff, I'll arrange the removals.'

'There was a witness statement, but the police didn't believe her.'

'Who told you that? She saw someone, and she told me it was Diane.'

'You must tell the police.'

'Must! I don't think so.' He took another mouthful of whisky. 'You need to leave.'

'I am not leaving, this is Mum's house.'

'I know, I checked with Jeffrey Sinclair. Yes, you're a sly one.'

'If anyone should leave, it should be you. This is my mother's house.'

'Your mother's house. Well, she'll have to evict me. No, you should go.'

'I'll go once the investigation is over.'

'You should leave Kirkindale. Think about all the trouble you've caused.'

'I caused! Good grief. Ever since I can remember, I wanted to find my mum.'

'She is not here, so go look somewhere else.'

'When I find her.' She stood. 'She will claim this house.'

'And if she shows her face here, she will end up in prison.' He threw the empty whisky bottle towards the sink, and it smashed on the floor. 'Enough,' he shouted and leapt up causing his chair to fall over backwards. He swept the plates and cutlery off the table.

They stared at each other.

'Sorry,' he said and picked up the chair. 'Just go, I need to be alone.'

She collected up the broken crockery pieces and placed them in the bin.

'I'll leave tomorrow.'

He stood up, walked around the table kicking the chairs aside and left the kitchen.

She dropped the knife into the sink.

She heard him in the dining room shouting incoherently and thumping the furniture. She rushed through to the hall and up the stairs to her room. There was no point in barricading the door because it would trap her in the bedroom. She grabbed at her possessions and stuffed them into her rucksack. Her tent was in the utility room and there was no time to fetch it.

She returned to the hallway and heard Scott in the dining room, sobbing. Should she speak to him and offer some comfort? He gave a loud agonising scream and began ripping at something.

She ran out through the front door and past his car and then on up the drive towards the lane. She jogged along the lane to the road and waited for the bus.

Scott had said; "We wished you had never existed". She could only believe he said those words to hurt her, to create a sense of guilt and illogically pass the blame for Mary's death onto her. When she had wanted to visit the hospital, he had suggested Mary was too ill for visitors and it would be upsetting. If anything, it would have been a surprise for Aunt Mary, and for them both. Why did she listen to him? She should have gone to the hospital and visited Mary. It was too late now.

There it was again; a memory of eating ice cream in the garden and being pushed on the swing by Mary. What was the song?

The bus stopped, and she lifted her rucksack in through the door, and the driver smiled as he took her fare to Marston. She looked past him and saw a green Land Rover turn down the lane towards Russet House.

Chapter Twenty-eight

Laura walked up the steps into the library and met Anne coming down the stairs.

'Mrs Wilcox won't be in today,' said Anne. 'She's upset about Mary.'

'I never went to the hospital,' said Laura. 'I feel terrible.' She followed Anne to the reception counter.

'Yes, I know,' said Anne. 'Poor Aunt Mary, she was so young.'

'Hello Laura,' interrupted George. 'I've just made a pot of coffee in my den.' He handed Anne a pack of printer paper. 'I expect you waste most.' He turned to Laura, 'Come and have a coffee? I've found more archives about the parish, and there's an excellent section about fruit pickers and farm workers, very interesting.'

'She's looking for Mrs Wilcox,' said Anne. She tore open the packet of printer paper. 'She's got the flu.'

'The flu. A sniffle more like,' said George, he turned to Laura. 'I'm afraid she's a bit of a hypochondriac, the slightest of excuses and she stays at home.'

'I hear they've found your mother,' said Anne as she loaded paper into a printer tray. 'Is it true, you found the bones?'

'What!' Laura glared at her. 'No, it's not my mum, probably just some old bones.'

'I expect it is an ancient burial they've found,' said George. 'Now don't worry Laura. Many places had family graves at one time.'

'Don't you think it strange,' said Anne, 'finding them now after all these years.'

'Ignore her. Let's have a coffee and afterwards see what you can find in the records.'

'Would you mind George?' said Laura. 'I promised to visit Great Aunt Margaret.' She wanted to leave the library and run away. 'Tomorrow, I'll read them tomorrow.'

'Yes, tomorrow.' He smiled. 'Coffee tomorrow then.'

§

The cocker spaniel leapt towards Laura. It jumped up and down with its tail wagging furiously. She held out her arms to deter the dog from licking her face as its hind legs scrambled and skidded for traction in the loose gravel of the driveway.

'Laura,' called Margaret, standing at the doorway. 'Come in. Don't mind Jasper, he can be boisterous. Come in.'

Bunches of lavender and herbs hung from a ceiling pulley, and Laura ducked under the flowers and the damp tea towels to reach the kitchen table.

Margaret grabbed the kettle and spoke as she filled it. 'Poor Mary. How are you taking it?'

'I'm not sure.' She fiddled with a piece of string on the table. 'Do we know when the funeral will be?'

'I'm glad you came.' said Margaret. 'I wasn't sure you would.' She patted the dog's head. 'Rarely do we get visitors at our cottage.' She ruffled the dog's ears. 'Do we, Jasper?'

'I was wondering if you heard—'

'Just a minute, dear.' Margaret reached for some cups from the dresser and placed them on the table. 'Biscuits?' She rummaged in a cupboard and brought out a large tin of cream and chocolate assortments, and she squinted to read the label.

'They're still in date.' She opened the lid. 'Help yourself,' she said and pulled a chair out and sat at the table. 'Lovely to see you again.'

Laura took a biscuit. 'Yes, thank you.' They only saw each other two days ago at Springfield Farm. 'I expect you've heard.'

'Heard?' Margaret poured tea into the cups. 'Not yet dear, Scott doesn't think they'll allow it soon. It depends on the result of the post-mortem. I expect.'

'I'm sorry, I thought Mary had terminal cancer.'

'I know dear.' She leaned forward and touched Laura's hand. 'Why don't you come and stay here until afterwards? We'd love your company. Wouldn't we, Jasper?'

'It's okay,' she said. 'I was wondering if you knew—'

'You shouldn't stay on your own, not up at Russet House.' Margaret interrupted. 'You should meet Edward, you haven't met him yet.'

'My cousin?'

'No, your father's cousin. Diane's husband.'

'That would be nice, but I was wondering if you had heard that Mary saw Mrs Wilcox at the pool.'

'Diane.'

'Yes. Did Diane see anyone at the Mill Pool?' Laura twisted the string around her fingers. 'When my grandmother was murdered.'

'You should ask Diane, not me dear.' She picked out a cream biscuit and fed it to Jasper. 'He doesn't get the chocolate ones, mind.'

'I expect the police will want to interview her.'

'What has brought all this on? Now Laura, the past is the past, we can't change what is not our fault.'

'But what if someone murdered my mother?'

'Your mother murdered, I don't think so. What have people been telling you?' She selected a wafer biscuit and took a bite. 'She's on the run because, well, who knows.' She lifted the teapot. 'More tea?'

'No, thank you.'

'Now, no more talk about murders and cancer.' She pushed the biscuit tin towards Laura.

The telephone rang in the hallway.

'I won't be a moment,' said Margaret, 'help yourself to more tea.' She mumbled through a mouthful of biscuit as she left the kitchen. She closed the door.

Laura sipped her tea. It was strong with a bitter taste like an unripe olive and made her mouth feel dry. It was awful. She took her cup and tipped its contents into the sink. She wondered if Margaret had added herbs to the tea mixture, and she lifted the teapot lid and saw the flat leaves of what looked like nettles. There was also an aroma of lavender. She wrinkled her nose and replaced the lid. Margaret had not touched her tea, and it was getting cold.

The door opened, and Margaret returned to the table. She took the teapot and her cup and put them into the sink. She turned to face Laura and folded her arms across her chest.

'That was Diane calling from the farm. The police have interviewed her.'

'Yes. The police have been digging around the ruined mill.'

'What? What has that got to do with Diane or Mary?'

'With Mary? She saw Diane at the Mill Pool and the police have found some bones.'

'So, when were you going to tell me?'

'About the discover at the waterfall?' said Laura.

'Your Aunt Mary is lying in the morgue!' Margaret pointed at her, 'And all you care about is your selfish mother.'

'I'm sorry.' Laura stood up. 'I think I should go.' She walked towards the door and Jasper followed on behind.

'Sit!' Margaret ordered the dog. 'I am disappointed in you, Laura. Don't you realise what you've done?'

'What have I done?'

'Just get out! For your own safety, go back to where you came from.'

Away from the house and on the farm track, she ran. Tears trickled down her face. It wasn't her fault. Even Great Aunt Margaret had said they should forget about the past. She slowed to a fast walk towards the village. She would take the bus to Marston and find Detective Jackson.

Chapter Twenty-nine

Laura sat in the Farmers' Jug with a glass of ginger beer gripped in her hands. MJ kept talking, but she had stopped listening. Her mother was alive. He was wrong, he must be wrong.

The excavation at the mill site above the waterfall had uncovered a short tunnel under the rock to a cavity beneath the cliff. The forensic team found the remains of human bones scattered over the dirt floor of the cave.

'Laura, we need a DNA sample from you,' said MJ. 'This afternoon.'

There were three skeletons found; a woman and a male child who died over two hundred years ago and a second female skeleton who possibly died within the last ten to twenty years.

'Also, there is something we would like you to look at,' he said. 'Laura, are you listening?'

The examination of the skeletal remains showed no signs of traumatic injuries on the child; however, some vertebrae of the older female were contained in a deteriorated strap. It was proposed the cause of her death was by strangulation.

A gold ring was discovered on a phalange of the more recent female, and the likely cause of her death was sustained blows to the skull.

'It's not my mother.' Laura wiped her face with a napkin.

'Let's not speculate.' MJ took a large slurp of his beer. 'A DNA test will confirm it is not your mother.' He put down his glass. 'I'm sorry, but one way or the other we need to eliminate that possibility.'

'The ring,' she said. 'What about the ring?'

'The police are working on that.' He finished off his beer. 'Come on, let's go, there is something you need to see.'

§

At the police station in the interview room, there were items in polythene bags tagged with the details of their discovery. Each label had a crime scene evidence number.

'Do you recognise this?' MJ picked up a package and held it out to Laura. 'This was found wrapped in material. Possibly a towel.'

'What is it?' Laura turned the bag over a few times, trying to make out the detail of a ragged leather purse. It was dirty, and the edges were chewed in places.

'Does it look familiar?'

She stared at him. 'Why, should I know?'

He pushed another polythene wrapped item towards her. This one had a faded photograph. The picture was indistinct but appeared to be a girl sitting on a gypsy wagon holding a teddy bear. 'This was in the purse, and I'm surprised it survived. Have you seen it before?'

She shook her head, then squinted to make out the form of the toy. With both hands, she grasped and held it tight to her chest. She welled up and tears formed. Where had she hidden Numpty?

She had searched everywhere in her foster home for her teddy bear until Mrs McLean bought her a new one. The replacement sat on a chair in the corner of the bedroom untouched. A reminder of her loss. There was only one Numpty.

'Hang on,' said MJ. He left the room and returned with a box of tissues. 'Well Laura, what is it?'

She took a tissue, blew her nose, and nodded. 'I am the girl in the photograph.'

'It was found in the purse or pouch thing, possibly it is your mother's.'

The door opened and a woman carrying a small metallic suitcase came and put it on the desk.

'I'm Sandra,' she said and smiled. 'I am here to take a saliva sample from you, Miss Dawson.' She opened the case and took out a pad of consent forms. 'First, you have a choice, you may decline as the purpose is to determine the identity of an unknown person. I understand you believe the deceased maybe your mother.'

'No, it is not my mother. She is alive.'

'Laura, please. This will determine definitively,' said MJ. 'We can then continue the search.'

'How can you prove this skeleton is my mother?'

'Great question. There are many detailed examinations and checks,' said Sandra.

'Just trust the experts Laura,' said MJ. 'We don't need the details.'

'The lab will do its best,' said Sandra. 'Although the results are not yet one hundred percent as there is still a lot of experimentation on the extraction of DNA from old bones, but teeth prove a useful source.'

Laura blew her nose with a tissue and allowed the forensic technician to take swabs from the inside of her cheeks.

'It's stuffy in here,' said MJ. 'Come on, let's go. We need some fresh air.' He took the bag from her and placed it on the table. 'We'll leave this here for now, okay.'

'So, please tell me, how will you know?' Laura pulled another tissue from the box.

Sandra glanced at MJ, who nodded.

'Briefly.' She packed the saliva containers into her case. 'We can compare medical records of missing persons and compare healed injuries, if any. The ante-mortem is where someone has had a broken bone during their life.' She closed her case and sat on the edge of the table. 'The forensic anthropologist is working on the details, but it is difficult to determine post-mortem damage to the bones because of scavenging animals.'

'How did the person die?'

'Trauma at the time of death, peri-mortem injuries which may have contributed to the death of the person. Sorry, it requires a fuller analysis before we are certain of the true nature of the injuries.'

'When will you know?'

'There are some teeth recovered and we are waiting for the forensic odontologist to complete his report.' She fiddled with the catch on her case. 'It takes a lot of effort to bring together all the medical and dental records.'

She waited until Laura blew her nose. 'You understand your mother is a person of interest.' She nodded towards MJ. 'The police investigation determines how quickly we work; we collect as much evidence as possible including family DNA samples for comparison.'

'Okay Sandra, I think Laura has got the message,' said MJ. He pointed towards the door.

'Laura, we are doing all we can. We will also analyse all the historical evidence collected from the scene as DNA profiling has advanced since the time of the original investigation,' said Sandra. 'We will do our best for you.'

'I am sure my mother is alive,' Laura said and followed MJ's direction towards the door.

Sandra picked up her case and followed them out of the room.

§

A low grey cloud shrouded the sky and drops of rain splattered onto the pavement. Laura shivered and walked away from the police station.

'If we hurry, we'll get there before the downpour.' MJ turned up his coat collar and quickened his pace towards the Farmers' Jug. 'I hope Frank's got some logs on the fire.'

MJ collected a pint of Marston's beer and a glass of tonic water from the bar. He carried them to a corner table where Laura sat.

'What did Mrs Wilcox say?' Laura accepted the tonic water and placed the glass on the table. 'She was interviewed, wasn't she?'

'Who?' he said, 'Nothing to do with this case.'

'But Scott told me it was Diane Wilcox who Aunt Mary saw on the day of the murder.'

'The witness statement doesn't record who she saw.'

'But you can find out. Speak to Scott and Mrs Wilcox.'

'Now Laura, I am not the investigating officer,' he said and took a large mouthful and swallowed. 'Besides, she was being interviewed about something else and not this case. Anyhow, I wouldn't tell you even if I knew.'

'What else? I might ask her myself.'

'No! You won't and don't meddle.' He took a sip of beer, then coughed. 'That went down the wrong way.' He placed his glass on the table. 'Leave it be, Laura, once the DNA results are complete, we'll know.' He shook his head. 'This was the only case I never solved in twenty-nine years.' He sat back in his seat when the barman arrived carrying a tray with two plates of fish and chips with garden peas.

'Ah, Frank, you're a star.'

'It is not my mother. I just know it,' said Laura, and she unwrapped her knife and fork from the napkin.

'There is a third blood sample that was never identified. They also found hair caught up in the skeleton's ring.' He added salt to his chips.

'Hair, what hair?' She put her cutlery down with a clatter. 'Do you mean it's Mrs Wilcox's?'

'No, I did not say that.' He pointed with his fork at her meal. 'Come on, eat up.'

'Please, can you tell me?'

'I know nothing, remember, I'm retired.'

'You found the bones.'

'We found the bones. Okay, I'll see what I can find out. That's enough for now.' He picked up his knife and fork. 'This is the best fish in Marston, so eat up.'

Her food stuck in her throat. She believed her mum must be alive somewhere and living with the traveller community. What if she is wrong?

If MJ will not reveal what Diane Wilcox said in the police interview; then she will ask Diane herself.

Laura watched MJ as he ate. She pushed the peas around on her plate.

'I'll give you a lift to Springwater Lane after—'

'Mr Ferguson wanted me to leave,' she interrupted. 'I'm staying in Marston.'

'Where?'

'With my great aunt.' She sipped at her tonic water. 'Great Aunt Daphne at Weir Cottage,' she said.

Chapter Thirty

Laura stood in the hallway of Weir Cottage. She heard Daphne talking in the kitchen and a second voice replied. She waited by the door and strained to hear the full conversation.

'You need the Coroner's certificate of Evidence of Death. Yes, it may take a few weeks for approval. The liaison officer will be in touch, Mrs Lister.'

'It's Miss,' said Daphne. 'Damned if I'll ever need a man around the place, they are a useless lot.'

'Don't take my word for it though, Miss Lister, it's not my responsibility.'

'Well, goodbye and thanks for your help.'

Daphne came into the hallway. 'Ah Laura, this lot are just leaving. Put the kettle on, dear. I won't be a minute.'

Laura recognised Sandra, the forensic technician, but not the policewoman. She smiled and watched them leave through the front door.

'Bye, mind how you go,' Daphne called to them as they walked away.

She returned to the kitchen and sat at the table. She took a drink of her herb infusion.

'It looks like you found poor Irene's bones,' she said.

'No, it's not my mother.' Laura poured the boiling water into a teapot. 'Let it not be her.'

'Coming here sticking their prods in my mouth. I told them it was the Dawsons that killed her or them Wilcoxes or that fisherman. He hid her under the waterfall.'

Laura slammed her hand on the table. 'Did the police say who it was?' She sat down and helped herself to a cup of tea.

'Where's mine?'

'Sorry, I thought you were drinking herbs.' Laura poured tea into a mug and passed it with the milk jug to Daphne.

'They don't know who it is,' said Daphne. 'I mean it's just bones.'

'What was that about a death certificate?'

'I'm not sure.' She reached over and touched Laura's arm. 'I've lived here for so long and since Jean died. Well, I'm settled and well, I'm not sure what will happen.'

'What are you talking about?'

'This was Jean's. I mean your grandmother's house. I'm sure you didn't know. Them Dawsons will chuck me out.'

'Hell! How many more places? Does my mother own this place?'

'Not sure, but I expect she does.'

Laura got up and walked out into the garden carrying her tea. The caravan had gone, leaving indentations in the ground where it stood for years. The vacated area was untidy and needed attention; the ruts required to be filled, overgrown grass and nettles to be cut back or roots dug up, and all the neglected detritus from beneath the body of the wagon required clearing away. There was a rusted tin full of worn paint brushes with their bristles hardened together. There were empty paint pots and used sandpaper stuffed in bags and the material rubbish remains from the work done on the restoration of the caravan's wooden panels.

'The museum boys came this morning,' said Daphne. She sat by the table on the patio. She opened a box of chocolate biscuits. 'Come and sit with me. There is something you need to know.'

Laura emptied the contents of her cup onto a flower bed and walked across the grass to the patio. She sat down with a thump and almost tipped the chair over.

'Careful,' said Daphne. 'Irene let me live here rent free. She was kind. But once the Dawsons divide up the estate, I'll be out. I expect Old Charlie and Mary will share the spoils.'

'Daphne, I'm not interested. Besides, Aunt Mary has died.'

'The cancer finally got her. Poor girl.'

'She didn't care about me so why should I bother.'

'You hard-nosed little brat.'

'My mother is alive and so what has changed?'

'What if it is Irene bones at the waterfall?'

'I know, they found a purse with a photograph of me and my Numpty.'

'Your teddy,' she said. 'Wait there.' She went into the house.

She returned with an album and opened it out on the table.

'Ah, it is here, I thought so,' said Daphne. She turned the album towards Laura. 'Look there you are.'

The picture showed a small girl sat on the driver's seat of the gypsy caravan holding a teddy bear.

'I gave you that, it was on your second birthday.'

'Numpty,' said Laura. 'The picture means nothing. I still believe my mother is alive.'

'Believe what you like. If you have any sense, you'll find out if your mother had a will.'

'Is this what I need to know?' She turned over the leaves of the album.

'Yes, and no. Your mother had enemies, lots of them.'

'I don't believe you. Why?'

'Enemies, maybe that's strong. People who didn't like her, maybe.'

'You haven't listened to anything I said.' She placed her cup on the table. 'Aunt Mary has died.'

'Poor girl.' She selected a chocolate digestive covered with coconut flakes. 'Do you have a boyfriend or maybe a special man?'

Laura touched the scar on her face and shook her head. She turned over to the next picture It showed a naked baby lying on a white rug. 'Whose baby is this?'

Daphne leaned over and smiled. 'Don't you recognise her? Of course, not. It's you, my dear. Your mother's sweet baby, Laura.'

'Me!' She turned over the page. The next photograph showed her mother sat on the wagon cradling the baby.

'Men, I don't blame you, they are a useless lot.' She held her hand over her mouth to catch the crumbs from her biscuit. 'While we were painting, your mother would tell me all about her troubles.'

'Don't blame me?' Laura turned the pages back to the baby lying on the rug. 'Where was this taken?'

'Let me have a proper look.' Daphne grabbed the album. 'You were a lovely baby. That was here in the garden. See, there's a wheel from the wagon.'

'But Diane Wilcox has the same picture.'

'Really! Wilcox. She was never friendly. Why would Irene give her a copy?'

Daphne spoke for about thirty minutes about how Irene had endured abuse and childish hatred from Diane Wilcox.

According to Irene, the village teenagers often met at the Mill Pool. Once Diane told a captive audience about her sexual adventures in the woods. All the girls listened and were jealous when they discovered who she was with. Diane relished their attention and told them the details about her lover and what they did. Then, rumour and gossip in Kirkindale spread among the girls about Diane's pregnancy, and Diane blamed Irene for betraying her confidentiality.

After months the bitterness intensified, and they had fought after school at the Mill Pool. Diane came off the worst. Later in the evening, the ambulance rushed her to the hospital with heavy bleeding, and she lost a child. There was a hysterical search through the village to discover the man responsible, but Diane would not cooperate. Her parents suspected William Dawson, but he confessed to kissing Diane and nothing more.

When Irene married William, if you believed the gossip, it was to spite Diane.

'Rumours, bloody rumours.' Daphne said, and she poured her tea out over the grass.

Laura continued to turn over the pages of the album. She stopped listening to Daphne.

'It was not true. Irene and William were in love.' Daphne laughed. 'Is that what they call it?' She picked up the cups and walked across the patio to the kitchen door. 'Come on, Laura, let's get dinner on. I'm famished.'

A van stopped on the road and backed into the garden. It parked in the space left by the gypsy wagon. The driver got out and waved to Daphne.

'Where's it gone?' the man shouted. He strode across the lawn. 'Daphne, who's taken my pride and joy?'

'You what?' She took a step back to avoid him, but he grabbed her in a tight bear hug, and she dropped the cups.

'Mark, get off! Will you get off? You pig.'

'You know you love me.' He released her and turned towards Laura. She stood, and her chair fell backwards.

'She's Irene's girl, Laura,' said Daphne. 'Now you behave, or I'll clatter you.'

Mark sat down and put his feet up on the table. 'Irene's baby, I've heard about you.' He searched the pockets of his Donkey jacket and found a small pipe and a tobacco pouch.

'Do you know my mother?' Laura said and righted her chair.

'None of your pot smoking here, Mark, I'm telling you,' said Daphne. 'Put it away and get your feet off the table.'

'Well, get the kettle on,' he said and winked at Laura. 'Proper tea, none of your stinking weeds.' He swung his legs to one side and sat forward. He offered a hand towards Laura. 'Nice to meet you.' She ignored his gesture. He put his pipe back into his pocket. 'I never met your mother.'

'You must have a nose like a vulture,' said Daphne. 'Come for a meal, have you?'

'Ah, Daphne, the thought of your chicken pies makes me want to give up the adventures of roaming the world.' He took off his Wigens cap and brushed back the thin hair wisps over his balding head.

'Your mother was an artist,' he said and winked at Laura. 'She painted as if it were magic. If you saw people in her pictures, they came alive.'

'You never met, you said. Where is she?'

Mark looked at Daphne and then turned to Laura. 'I'm sorry, I've no idea.' He slapped the table. 'Now come on then where's this dinner you promised.'

'Parasite,' said Daphne, and went into the house.

'I heard they found human bones, down at the river,' he said to Laura. 'We all remember, you know.'

She stared at him for a moment. This man knows the truth; he must, why is he here?

'Can you tell me about my mum? What do you remember?'

'The police hounded us all the way to Kent, they said we were hiding something, first they said we murdered old Mrs Dawson.' He took a packet of cheroots from his jacket, and he offered one to Laura. She shook her head. 'Then they said we kidnapped somebody, and they had blood traces.' He took a flick-knife from his pocket and trimmed the end of a cheroot. 'They get damp and don't light proper.' He struck a match and lit his cigarillo.

'Whose blood? Did they trace my mother to your caravans?'

'No! No, they took lots of samples, and just from the men,' he said. 'I thought maybe women don't bleed or something.' He blew a long line of smoke into the air. 'Oh, we were all murdering suspects all right.'

Laura moved her chair and sat upwind to avoid the drifting swirls of murky smoke.

'We did nothing, and they blamed us. Worse, we were no longer welcome in Marston or Kirkindale. Old Dawson dug out his orchards and there was no work left.'

'But you knew my mother,' she said. 'What do you remember about her?'

'Nothing really, I knew Jean before she settled and rarely saw the baby Irene or Daphne much after that.'

'Which group is my mother with?'

'Oh, you never give up, do you,' he said and sucked on the remains of his cheroot. 'I know they think she killed the old woman. Now, that is hard to believe.' He stubbed the cigar out on the table.

'If she is on the run, then good luck to her. If she came to us, yes, I would hide her.'

Laura got up and walked towards the house, and halfway across the patio she turned and looked at him. 'Thank you, Mark,' she said and went into the kitchen.

Chapter Thirty-one

MJ stood at the front door of Orchard View and for the third time rung the bell. It was frustrating listening to the musical chimes echo through the hallway; he was sure he had heard the tune somewhere before. There was no answer. He stepped across to the window and pulled aside the ivy leaves and peered into the house. A picture frame lay in splinters and pieces of a torn painting canvas were scattered over the dining room table.

He strolled along the side of the house into the rear garden and onto the patio. He tried to open the French doors leading into the kitchen, but they were locked.

He should have telephoned and made an appointment. He shrugged, it was just as well he had asked Frank to keep a steak pie for him. It was one of the popular lunchtime dishes in the Farmers' Jug.

He cupped his hands against the glass door and looked into the kitchen. The chairs lay on the floor, broken plates and cutlery littered the table and the fridge was on its side; its contents had spilled out, and egg yolks floated in a pool of milk.

He had come to interview, that was too formal, he had come to speak with Mr Scott Ferguson. He wanted to discuss what Mary remembered about a woman she saw in the reeds. Unfortunately, she had passed away so any opinion from Mr Ferguson would be considered hearsay, but he would let the criminal justice system deal with what is permissible evidence. All he needed from Mr Ferguson was pointers to help him find whoever had been hiding in the reeds. Something he should have done fifteen years ago, if only he had followed up on Miss Dawson's statement. Why didn't he? It was a reminder of his inaptitude at the time. He clenched his teeth. He had missed an opportunity in tracing a witness to the murder of Sophia Dawson. He regretted his mistake.

He returned to his Corsa at the front of the house and saw a police patrol car come down the driveway. It skidded sideways and blocked the exit. Two policemen and a man in a suit got out. MJ didn't recognise them. They put on their hats as they came towards him.

'Good morning, sir. Are you Mr Scott Ferguson?' said the police Sergeant.

'No, I—'

'Is Mr Ferguson at home?'

'I've rung the bell a few times,' said MJ, and he shook his head. 'There was no answer.'

The policemen went to the front door and pressed the bell. They heard the chimes playing inside the house.

The man in the suit leaned against the car and lit a cigarette. He stared at MJ and then said, 'I've seen you before.'

MJ walked over to him. 'Would you mind?' He pointed at the cigarette. 'I've given them up. A quick drag wouldn't do any harm.'

'Now I remember. You are Detective Sergeant Jackson.' He passed him the cigarette and retrieved another from his packet. 'I was at your retirement bash.' He grabbed MJ's hand and shook it. 'I was in uniform then, John Davis. Detective Constable these days.'

'We'll look around the back,' shouted the police Sergeant. Davis waved an acknowledgement and watched the uniformed men walk across the gravel towards the garden.

'Yes, retired.' said MJ, 'What do you want with Mr Ferguson.'

'Not really your concern, sir,' said Davis. 'Would you mind telling why . . .' He turned and looked at the garage. 'Can you hear that?' He rushed over the yard and tried to open the garage door.

'Over here,' Davis shouted. 'Hoy! You two.' He waved to the policemen. 'Over here, one of you go around the back and get in through a window or somehow.'

Smoke crept out from the gaps above the door. DC Davis hammered with his fists on the steel door. He shouted, 'Is there anyone there?'

MJ ran to his car and fetched a wheel brace. He levered it on the garage door handle and after two quick jerks he broke the lock. He pushed the door up on its rollers and a thick cloud of exhaust fumes billowed out. He coughed and stepped back.

The police Sergeant covered his nose and pushed both MJ and Davis aside. He dashed into the garage, then rushed back out.

'There's someone in the car,' he said, and took a few lengthy breaths.

Davis looked at MJ and grabbed the wheel brace from him, the police Sergeant grabbed it from Davis.

He shouted, 'Sir, I'll do it. You call for an ambulance.'

Davis ran to the patrol car as the second policeman came from behind the building.

'Sanderson come here,' said the Sergeant, and he returned into the garage. He smashed the driver's window and yanked the car open. He reached in and turned the engine off.

Sanderson pushed the Sergeant aside and leaned into the car. 'Hell, what a stink, he's been sick.' He recoiled at first, then returned to check the body for a pulse on the neck and wrist.

MJ took a few steps into the garage, Davis placed his hand out. 'Best stay back, Mr Jackson, sir. Let the uniforms handle it.'

§

They left the body in the car until the medical examiner and forensic team had completed their examination. The ambulance crew then loaded the cadaver into their vehicle and drove off.

The police Sergeant discovered the entry into the house through the garage and kicked the door open. He entered the premise to conduct a preliminary search of the building, and then he declared it vacant and safe for the forensic team.

'What did you want him for?' said MJ as he signed his statement; an explanation of why he was at the house.

'Who?' said Davis.

'Scott Ferguson.'

'Do you know the man?'

'No, I've never met him.'

'So, until we identify the body, formally that is, I don't know this man either.'

'Don't be offhanded with me, Davis.'

'Sorry sir, yes. Just a few questions about his wife. The pathologist report states she was poisoned.'

'He poisoned his own wife!'

'I never said that,' Davis lit up and blew smoke rings. 'There were suspicious items from the hospital. Not your concern.' He read through MJ's statement. 'Ah, the murder at the falls, I heard from Marston, they've finally decided on a motive.'

MJ followed Davis through the house and walked into the kitchen.

'Looks like someone has had a fit of temper,' said Davis.

'A motive. Did you say?'

'A case of a lover's tiff. The dead woman's husband.'

'Mr Charlie Dawson, hell! So Joe Prince was right,' said MJ. 'No! He had an alibi. Old Charlie was at an agricultural show that day.'

'Sorry sir, maybe you got it wrong,' said Davis. 'Mr Jackson, you're retired. You should go home.'

'Don't patronise me.' MJ turned his back on Davis and headed to his Corsa. 'I didn't get it wrong.' He mumbled and opened the car door.

Chapter Thirty-two

Laura ambled along the road towards Oakwood Farm. The warm spring air and the smell of the scent of the wild rose from the hedge row soothed her thoughts. She would ask Mrs Diane Wilcox, what happened at the Mill Pool and if she saw who had killed her grandmother? How would she phrase the question, and how would she know if the answer was the truth?

Perhaps Mary was wrong, perhaps Scott had misunderstood what she had told him. Perhaps it wasn't Diane in the reeds by the pool, but someone else.

She stopped and leaned on a fence post. In the field, Ayrshire cows looked up from their grazing and sauntered across to her.

It was a hundred yards more to the house and to a possible confrontation with Mrs Wilcox.

A cow leaned forward and tried to lick her hands and face, and she turned away. She strode on towards the farm.

In the courtyard she expected a dog to bark or at least meet her; didn't everyone have a dog in the countryside? By the front door of the house, she took two deep breaths before she rang the bell. There was no answer, so she pressed the button again. No response.

She crossed the yard and made her way between the house and the byre. A yellow and green coloured John Deere tractor stood next to an empty hay shed. She looked beyond the buildings to the woods where on the hillside she saw a stationary Pickup. Nearby, a man and his dog were herding sheep.

Behind the house was a walled garden. She scanned over the cast iron gate at the recently mowed lawn and the surrounding flowerbeds with fresh bedding plants. Further back there were rows of raspberry canes tied to wires, and alongside raised drills of earth lined a vegetable patch. On the sandstone patio by the house was a picnic table, where someone had set out cutlery and a teacup. There was toast in a rack.

Mrs Wilcox came out of the house and looked across the lawn. She waved and walked over to the gate. 'Oh Laura, I am glad you've come.' She undid the bolt and let Laura into the garden.

'I hope you don't mind,' said Laura.

'No, I don't mind. Please come in. I'm just having breakfast, or brunch if you like.'

They walked to the patio, and Laura sat on the wooden bench by the table.

'Would you like a tea?' said Mrs Wilcox. 'I better get another cup.' She went into the house and returned with a bottle of vodka and two glasses.

'No thanks, not for me,' said Laura. She sipped her tea and watched as Mrs Wilcox poured half a glass of vodka and added some orange juice. She stirred the drink with her index finger.

'I've not been sleeping well,' she said. She swallowed a large mouthful. 'Ah, that's better.'

'I want to ask you something.'

'You sound like the police.' She drank another mouthful of vodka. 'I am pleased you've come. Edward can collect your things later. Here, have a piece of toast.'

'Collect my things?' said Laura. 'No, no, I'm not coming to stay.' She put down her cup.

'You must. Where else can you stay after what has happened?'

'Poor Aunt Mary, I never got to meet her.'

'Come and stay with me. Russet House is a bitter place, and I can't imagine Scott is in any mood for company.'

'I'm staying in Marston.'

'In Marston, why there? Not with the gypsy lady. I hope not. No, you must come home here.'

'You know Daphne then?'

'She was your mother's art teacher or guardian. Here, do have the toast.' She passed the butter and marmalade to Laura.

'Can you tell me about my grandmother's murder?'

'Poor Mrs Dawson. How terrible for you.'

'They have caught no one.'

'It was awful. Everyone was shocked.' She drank her vodka mix. 'I'm sorry about your mother. You realise she is a suspect.'

'I don't believe my mum killed anyone.'

'You don't know. I offered to take care of you, but Old Charlie refused and he sent you away.'

'Mary told Scott she saw you among the reeds.'

'Saw me! Mary, poor Mary,' said Mrs Wilcox. 'We should not speak about her, not after what Scott did.' She poured another glass of vodka.

'What Scott did? I don't understand.'

'He poisoned Mary. Imagine! She was already dying and Scott, well, what else.'

Laura shook her head when offered vodka. She refilled her cup with tea and picked up a piece of toast. Was it true that Scott had poisoned Mary?

'Perhaps it was the chemotherapy and her body just couldn't cope,' said Laura.

'No, they found evidence of toxins.' Mrs Wilcox nodded. 'It's hard to believe. The police asked me so many questions. Oh, God.'

'I can't imagine anyone so cruel.'

'Yes, that's it. He put her out of her misery.'

'What!' Laura dropped her toast onto the table. 'I never went to see her.' Her hands shook. She could not believe what Mrs Wilcox had said. She didn't believe Scott would poison Mary. 'What did the police want with you?'

'They questioned all the relatives and everyone who visited her. Just routine, they said.' She refilled her glass without the additional orange juice. She sipped her drink. 'Besides, you never knew Mary.'

'I remember she pushed me on the swing.' She tried to grasp her memories but could not form a clear image of anyone's face. They remained as shadows, no matter how hard she tried to picture them.

'I'm sorry.' Mrs Wilcox finished her drink of vodka, refilled the glass, and added a splash of orange juice.

'Mary saw you at the pool when—'

'Oh please, enough.' Mrs Wilcox got up and sipped from her glass. 'Come, let me show you.' She carried her glass and bottle into the house. 'I've kept your room ready. You'll love it, trust me.' She put the bottle down on the kitchen table.

'Thank you, and that is kind,' said Laura, 'but I am not coming to stay here.' She followed Mrs Wilcox through the kitchen and up the stairs.

'Here, I've kept everything the same.' She opened the door into a nursery. 'Edward wouldn't allow me to adopt. A little girl was all I wanted.'

The faded curtains on the bay windows showed scenes from the jungle book and matched the pattern of the bedspread. A wooden rocking horse with a leather saddle stood to one side of the room, and an array of dolls lined the shelves on a bookcase.

'I don't remember this as my room?'

'Now you are older, we can change the décor to your liking.'

'I'm sorry, but when I find my mother, I have no intention of staying in Kirkindale.'

'I decorated this room for you. You should have been my baby.'

'Sorry!' Laura looked around at the toys. 'I'm sorry, I think we should go back downstairs.'

Mrs Wilcox blocked the doorway and pushed Laura back towards the window.

'You don't understand.'

'No, I don't.'

'I lost my baby boy. He ignored me. No one listened.' She prodded at Laura's forehead with her finger. 'When I married Edward, we almost had a baby, Lilly. That was her name, Lilly. Imagine my joy, a baby girl and then . . . it was so unfair.'

'Diane, I am sorry, really I am.' She walked across the room and saw an old teddy bear. She picked it up. There were dark stains along its back, and its ears were torn and ragged. 'I am not a child, I am not your child.' She watched Mrs Wilcox finish her drink and placed the glass onto the bookcase.

'Not just one, but every bloody time. One miscarriage after another.' Diane knocked the glass off the bookcase. 'Your bloody mother did this to me.'

'I'm sorry Diane, I am sure—'

'Sure! What do you know?'

Laura turned the toy over and read the embroidery on the label; *this belongs to Laura Dawson.* She sat down on the bed.

'See, you remember. I gave you that teddy on your first birthday.' Mrs Wilcox smiled. 'See, they should have let you stay.'

Laura pushed the toy to one side. She remembered; they were playing hide and seek.

Round and round the ragged rock.
The ragged rascal ran.

They were playing hide and seek, and Numpty was hiding behind the rock at the pool. That was where she had hidden Numpty. She picked up the teddy. Yes it was, it was Numpty.

'Where did you get this?' Laura stood and pointed at Mrs Wilcox. 'Tell me, where did you get this?'

'It's just a toy.'

'No, it is not just a toy. It's mine, and you took it from the Mill Pool.' Laura tightened her jaw and ground her teeth. 'You were there. Mary was right.'

She recognised the diary on the side table; she picked it up. 'This is mine.' She shouted. 'You stole my diary!'

'Accusations, dear.' Mrs Wilcox laughed. 'You have your diary, so no one has stolen it. It was here in your room.' She picked up and fidgeted with the empty glass.

'Why do you keep saying that? This is not my room.' Laura picked up the teddy and backed towards the bay window.

'Don't you care after all I've done,' said Mrs Wilcox, and she grinned. 'Just like your mother and that fool William.'

'My father.'

'Oh dear, he wouldn't listen, I tried to tell him but then Duke butted him.' She went to the wardrobe and opened the door. 'I tried to help. I did, they know I did. Something jammed the gate, I told them the bull—'

'You were there!'

'He wouldn't listen, I tried to tell him the truth about you. Lies, he screamed at me.' She took a long wedding dress from the wardrobe. 'He should have married me. We were in love.'

'You watched the bull kill my father.'

'I saw him. Yes, and I hated him because he wouldn't listen.' She held the dress against her body. 'I loved him, he promised. He wouldn't listen.'

'You could have saved him.'

'Our baby, Ryan, was his, but he lied.' She replaced the dress into the wardrobe and closed the door. She turned and shouted at Laura. 'He promised.'

'What truth about me?'

A vehicle drove into the farmyard. Laura looked out of the window. The Toyota Pickup stopped by the house. A brown collie sat with its head out of the passenger door window, its tongue hanging loose. A man wearing a flat cap got out of the vehicle and he carried a split shotgun over his arm. He walked towards the house and gave a short whistle. The dog leapt out of the vehicle and followed him.

'That'll be Edward,' said Mrs Wilcox. 'Why don't we go downstairs. He wants to meet you.'

Laura picked up the teddy and diary, and she followed Mrs Wilcox down to the kitchen. She had Numpty in her hand. Run, she should run and find MJ.

Edward stood in his woollen socks by the sink, his wellington boots were by the door and the dog laid on a rug in the corner. It sat up panting and watched them as they came through. Edward turned from washing his hands and stared.

'Edward, this is Laura.' Mrs Wilcox went to the table and picked up the vodka bottle. 'Isn't she pretty?'

'That's enough, Diane.' He grabbed the bottle from her and poured the liquid into the sink. 'You really need to get a grip.' He threw the empty bottle into the bin. 'Now, Laura, it would be better if you left.'

'She knows!' Mrs Wilcox laughed. 'Look, she has her teddy. Remember, I told—'

'Diane, shut up.' He turned to Laura. 'This is your fault. Give me that.'

'No. This is mine, and it is proof.'

'It is the proof of nothing.' He locked the outside door. 'Keep it.'

'I need a drink.' Mrs Wilcox said and left the kitchen.

'I already found your stash of bottles, there are none left.' Edward shouted to her and looked at Laura. 'She is not well. Why are you here?'

'Aunt Mary saw Diane at the pool. She might have witnessed my grandmother's murder.'

'Can't you let it rest.' he said and sat at the table. 'We live with this horror and have gone over it a hundred times. Really, I am sorry about your grandmother.'

'I need to know the truth.'

'The truth,' shouted Mrs Wilcox as she returned into the kitchen with another bottle of vodka. 'I hated your mother. She was a vile, selfish bitch.'

'Diane!' Edward went to her. 'Stop it, you need to sleep.' He took hold of her wrist and tried to wrestle the bottle from her. 'Take your pills. You need to rest.'

'Get off me.' She pushed him away. 'Tell her. She wants the truth, tell her.'

'What is she saying?'

'Nothing Laura, she is very upset. Mary's death was a shock.'

'She knows Edward. Mary saw me. Edward, she knows.' She sat at the table sobbing.

He turned towards Laura and shook his head. 'She is not well and is confused.' He looked at his wife. 'She has not been well, you understand Laura. She is not well.'

'Bloody hell, it was an accident,' shouted Mrs Wilcox. 'Just tell her what you did with that bitch.'

'Diane, enough,' screamed Edward.

'What do you mean an accident? Please tell me?' said Laura.

'You need to leave. I warned you not to come to Kirkindale,' said Edward.

The dog sat up and stared at the door. They heard a vehicle drive into the farmyard.

'What was the accident?'

'Nothing. Don't listen to Diane. Mary's death has traumatised her,' said Edward. 'You need to go.'

'Who cares about Mary, what about me? What about my babies?' Diane grabbed at the vodka bottle.

Through the kitchen window, Laura saw Great Aunt Margaret get out of her Land Rover.

Chapter Thirty-three

MJ sat at the back of the police briefing room. The Chief ordered him not to get involved, and he was there only to listen. Just one word, the boss had said, and you are out.

DC Davis presented a progress and update on his investigation into the murder of Mary Ferguson, (nee Dawson), at the hospital.

"The suspected motive of an early inheritance for the husband, Scott Ferguson, was now invalid after the discovery of his body in the garage at Orchard View.

At first, they considered this as a case of a rather sad, and unfortunate, murder-suicide. However, the initial toxicity results show traces of the piperidine alkaloid, coniine, and a high level of alcohol in the dead man's blood and organs. This alkaloid was identical to a toxin listed on the Mary Ferguson post mortem report. The Scott Ferguson PM report has recorded there were no trace of monoxide poisoning as expected. He was already dead before someone started the vehicle engine.

Someone had locked the internal door to the garage from the inside of the house."

MJ fumbled with his briefcase and it dropped to the floor. Everyone in the room turned and watched him.

'Do you mind,' DC Davis called. 'What's the matter?'

'Sorry, just looking for a pen.' MJ smiled.

Davis shuffled through his briefing notes and turned over a flip board sheet to show a list of tasks and questions. He continued with his presentation.

"The grapes found in a bag at the house contained a high quantity of the same poison. I want to know; who bought the grapes? Where did the poison come from, and how did it get into the grapes?

There was a woman, Miss Laura Dawson, who had been staying at the B and B. She apparently left the place prior to the body being discovered. We need a statement from her."

MJ raised his hand. DC Davis looked at him and stopped talking.

'If I could offer—'

'No. No interruptions.' DC Davis shook his head. 'I'll take questions when I am finished.' He continued with his briefing.

"According to Mary's aunt, Mrs Margaret Wilcox, Miss Laura Dawson visited the Kirkindale library to trace her family history and had also visited solicitors McCarthy and Sinclair in Marston. Where, we understand, she made enquiries about her mother's will and ownership of Orchard View.

So far, we have no evidence to link her to the deaths, but she remains a suspect until we eliminate her involvement." He folded up his notes.

'As you are all aware a Detective Chief Inspector will arrive to head our investigation.' Davis grabbed at his millboard. 'Until he arrives, let's see what we can find out.'

DC Davis read out a series of tasks and nominated them to individuals in his team. He looked across the room at MJ and shook his head. 'We can speak later, there is no time.' He left the room and took his flip board with him. His team followed on behind.

The next briefing was by Detective Sergeant Fiona Mycroft, regarding the murder of Sophia Dawson.

She started by thanking Detective Sergeant Michael Jackson, retired, for his persistence in following up on the historical case and his discovery of the skeletons.

MJ stood up. The officers seated in the room ignored him.

DS Mycroft elaborated on the progress of the case.

"One of the skeletons found in the cave above the waterfall on the River Marrs has been identified as the remains of Mrs Irene Dawson, nee Stewart. The DNA comparisons with samples from her family members and examination of her dental record prove this is the case.

The DNA profiles showed with certainty that Laura Dawson is the daughter of Mrs Irene Dawson - deceased.

During the original investigation we compiled a large DNA database from samples from all the local males, and some men of the traveller community. Much of this information has been destroyed, except those samples recorded in relation to criminal convictions for other offences.

An important match of DNA evidence supports a hypothesis that the elder Mrs Dawson may have discovered an affair between her husband and her daughter-in-law. There is the speculation of a confrontation between the women at the pool. It is factual that Mrs Sophia Dawson was severely injured and drowned and, not subject to fact, Mrs Irene Dawson may have been seriously wounded and possibly hid in the cave and died from her injuries."

'There was a witness statement,' interrupted MJ.

'Please sir, I am not taking questions,' said DS Mycroft, and she returned to her brief.

"From the case records, a witness statement mentions a person, as yet unknown, was seen among the reeds. The original investigation could not identify this individual at the time because the witness statement was not consistent. Unfortunately, the witness was Mary Dawson, who has now passed away."

'I think I can help there,' MJ called out.

'Please, no interruptions.' DS Mycroft wagged her finger towards him. She carried on.

"The DNA from other blood samples collected at the scene, by the pool, have not been attributed to any individual. However, this confirms the presence of someone whose involvement may or may not be of significance.

A forensic archaeologist team has confirmed the other skeletons are from an earlier period and are not considered being connected to the Irene Dawson case. The Marston Archaeology Society have generated a project to study the archived records from the seventeen-century and are considering a preliminary archaeological dig on the site above the waterfall."

Once again, she thanked MJ for his involvement.

'Can I have a quick word?' MJ stood up.

'Not now, perhaps later,' said DS Mycroft. 'Please leave. I need to allocate tasks.' She looked at him and when he didn't move, she pointed towards the door. He picked up his briefcase and left.

§

At the station, The Chief formally thanked MJ for his efforts and informed him that his involvement in the Sophia Dawson murder case was no longer required.

A dismissal, disguised as a warm handshake, was all the thanks he got. When he walked down the steps, the door to the police station slammed behind him. Was it the wind? He marched off down the street towards the pub.

'He had not solved the case. It was his case and he would to see it through. Sod the Chief,' he spoke as he walked.

He was certain it was a vicious murder, and the hypothesis of a fight between the women was ridiculous. He saw the body of Mrs Sophia Dawson in the morgue, and only a few hours after they had pulled her from the river. Her injuries were severe and not what he would consider as minor bruising as the result of a fight between two women. They had been good friends. What was the fresh DNA evidence that proved an affair?

MJ pushed the door open into the Farmers' Jug. He waved to Frank behind the bar and received a nodded acknowledgement in return. He took off his jacket, hung it over a chair next to his usual seat in the corner, and placed his briefcase under the table. Frank brought him a Marston's beer and a plate with fish and chips.

'Thanks, Frank,' he said.

'We've all heard. Sad news about the Fergusons.' He slapped a tea towel over his shoulder. 'A nice couple, I liked them,' he said and returned to the bar.

Breadcrumbs coated the fried fish, and the chips were piping hot. MJ buttered a slice of white bread and poured brown sauce over the chips.

When he'd finished eating, he pulled a file from his briefcase and leafed through the pages. The possibility of an affair between Old Charlie and Irene Dawson had been recorded on Joe Prince's statement, but this was dismissed as Joe later indicated he was mistaken. Old Charlie had denied any such thing.

He read through the record of Joe Prince's witness statement; it seemed a bit jumbled since the focus was on the premise that he was a suspect.

MJ folded the document open at the section he was looking for.

Joe had been fishing near the pool and had seen Mrs Irene Dawson painting just above the falls. Old Charlie had arrived and spoke with her, they were laughing; he didn't hear what was being said. It sounded like giggling at first, then some angry screaming. He didn't see where they were but thought they had gone under the fir trees. After a while Mrs Irene Dawson had appeared, she was crying, and she was rearranging and pulling her clothes back on. She sat by her easel for a while, not painting, just staring and sobbing. He didn't see her leave as he fell asleep by the reeds. He caught no fish that day.

MJ replaced the file into his briefcase. He would need to clarify with DS Fiona Mycroft what the important DNA evidence was that supported her suspicion of an affair. It didn't seem clear to him.

The incident, as Joe remembered, took place in 1975, a few years before the murder of Mrs Sophia Dawson. For that reason, the original investigation assessment dismissed this section of Joe Prince's statement. It was not accepted as being relevant.

Chapter Thirty-four

Margaret tried the kitchen door and then hammered on it with her fists. She glanced through the kitchen window and knocked on the glass. She turned and rushed towards the front door. From within the hallway she shouted, 'Edward! Diane! They've found Irene.'

'Did you hear me?' She stood at the hallway door into the kitchen.

The dog ran to her and reached up with its front paws. Margaret grabbed them, dropped them, and patted the dog's head. It yelped and with its tail tucked between its legs; it scuttled to its rug in the corner.

Margaret looked at Diane sat at the table with her head in her hands, then she noticed Laura.

'Edward, what's going on here?' said Margaret. She went to Diane and held her shoulders. 'It's all right, dear. Have you been drinking again?' She stared at Edward. 'I told you, don't you listen.'

'She knows,' shouted Diane, and she pointed towards Laura.

'Hell!' Margaret turned and glared at Laura. 'What's happening, Edward?'

'Diane knows who murdered my grandmother,' said Laura and took a step back towards the exit into the hallway.

'Murdered. Yes, your mother is the murderer.' She put her arms around Diane. 'Edward will take you upstairs, you need to sleep.' She glanced at the shotgun by the door.

'I heard on the radio,' said Margaret, 'that they've found a skeleton.'

'It was an accident, she told Laura it was an accident,' said Edward, and he took Diane's arm and then recoiled as she struck out at him. 'Stop it. Come on, you need your pills.'

Margaret picked up the shotgun.

Edward stepped forward and stood between Margaret and Laura. 'Laura, you best get out of here. Mum, it's not loaded.'

'Get me some cartridges.'

'No, Mum.'

'That pesky fox has been at my chickens again, I want to borrow it.' She placed the gun onto the table. 'What the hell did you think I would do.' She laughed and looked towards Diane. 'Edward, please take her upstairs. Now Laura, come and sit here. We need to chat.'

'A chat? What happened at the pool, what did Diane see?'

Edward led Diane out of the kitchen.

'She is not well, she imagines things, things that upset her.'

'I believe you.'

'There now, see, I knew you would understand.'

'No, I believe she is not well. Also, I believe she saw what happened.'

'She saw nothing. Well, the police have a skeleton, the rumour is, it is your mother,' said Margaret, and she sat at the table. 'Happy now?'

'I've proof Diane was there.' Laura held up the teddy bear. 'She took this from the Mill Pool. How do you explain that?'

'Oh please. Everyone and the police know your mother murdered dear Sophia. Stop your nonsense.'

'I want Diane to tell the police what she knows.'

'Oh Laura, I know it is hard to accept, but the only people who know what happened are dead. The police are not interested.'

'I am taking this teddy to the police, and we'll see what they say.'

'My advice dear, just burn it. Don't you realise what will happen?'

'The truth, I will learn the truth.'

'Trust me, it is better to accept a lie than invent the truth.'

'My mother as a murderer. That is the lie.'

'You shouldn't have come. See the pain you have caused poor Diane.' She pointed to a chair by the table. 'Come and sit . . . you need to know.'

'What?' Laura pulled a chair away from the table and sat.

'Sophia was the most forgiving person I have ever known.' She stroked the shotgun barrel. 'Your mother told her what Charlie had done. She forgave him, but he denied everything.' She picked up the gun and split it. 'Sophia had lost baby Robert and when you were born, she treated you as her own. She moved into Russet House to be with Irene and Mary.'

'What had he done?'

'It was a tough time for everyone.'

'A bull had killed my father. I expect my mum was distraught.'

'William, yes he didn't know,' said Margaret, and she stared at Laura. 'We all knew except William, and I wondered for how long.'

'What are you talking about?'

'William lied about getting Diane pregnant, we all know. She was only a child.'

'What's that got to do –'

'It was my fault and Diane wouldn't let it rest.'

'Your fault?' Laura sat down. 'Are you saying you killed Sophia?'

'Oh, don't be ridiculous. No, I let slip what Sophia said about Charlie.'

'What! What about Charlie?'

'Diane thought it was her chance with William and make him leave your mother.'

'If it was an accident, you need to tell the police.'

'Oh, Laura, you are young. Don't spoil your life.'

'I need to know. What happened to my family?'

'Family! That's just it, Laura, you mustn't destroy the family. We must forgive and forget many things in our lives.'

'I want to hear what Diane knows?'

'Oh, Laura, she is not well, you can't believe what she says.'

'I don't care, I am going to the police.'

'There's no need. We will let Diane rest, and tomorrow she can explain everything.'

'If you know, can't you—'

'You need to hear it from Diane.' She reached to touch Laura's hand. 'It's not what you think.' With her other hand, she pulled the shotgun onto her lap.

'Do you know?'

'Ah Laura, why don't you stay tonight and tomorrow we can explain.'

'Stay tonight! No.'

'We kept a room for you, we have been waiting . . .'

Laura rushed into the hallway and out through the front door.

She heard Margaret shouting from the kitchen. 'Edward! We have to stop her. Edward!'

Laura sprinted down the farm track towards the road. In one hand she had Numpty and in the other her diary. She heard shouting from the farmyard and a vehicle engine start.

Chapter Thirty-five

MJ knocked on the door and since there was no response, he walked into the incident room.

DS Fiona Mycroft was sitting on the edge of her desk and staring at a mesh of diagrams on an array of white boards. She looked round when she heard MJ bump against a chair.

'Ah, MJ. What do you want?' She pointed at the boards. 'I'm busy.'

'Looks like a spider's web, does it make any sense?'

'I can't get the motive to fit. How do two women who have lived together for years turn on each other? Why?'

MJ looked at the scribbled diagrams. The word money caught his attention. Lines spiralled out to a chain of tasks: the will got from solicitors, coincidence (no such thing), Laura Dawson–background checks to follow.

'Miss Dawson's reason for coming to Kirkindale,' said MJ, 'was to discover the whereabout of her mother and relatives.'

'Yes, then she found out about her inheritance.'

'What? So, her plan was to kill off her relatives and claim the house and farm.' MJ put his briefcase on the table and took out a folder. 'A master stroke of revenge from a callous, scheming psychopath. Is that it?'

'You're one to talk. What motive did you originally have for Sophia Dawson's murder? None!'

'Maybe not, but it wasn't an inheritance scam.'

'Opportunity and motive. Mr and Mrs Ferguson were in somebody's way.'

'Irrelevant to the Dawson murders.'

'Most people take a lifetime to accumulate half of that.' DS Mycroft drew a question mark beside the word inheritance. 'We are still waiting for a copy of Irene Dawson's will.' She watched MJ open a file on the desk.

'Here read this.' He pointed to the statement from Joe Prince.

She picked up the folder and read the paragraph; she nodded. 'Yes, this corroborates the affair and the DNA results.'

'Are you going to let me in on the secret?'

She ignored him.

MJ looked over the board listing the detailed background of the Dawsons. He pointed at the notes: the farm accident of Mr William Dawson, killed by a bull. Witness–Diane Wilcox.

'Not much luck in this family. I remember this. It was a terrible time for them.'

'You know MJ. It's odd, why go into a bullpen and lock the gate.'

'Well, you don't want the bull to get out, maybe.'

'Someone locked the gate from the outside,' said DS Mycroft and she opened a file. 'Unexplained circumstances according to the inquest report, and intoxicated, now why deal with a dangerous bull after a few drinks?'

'Dutch courage.'

DS Mycroft shook her head and said, 'Something must have aggravated the animal.' She turned over the pages in her file. 'Ah here, his mother apparently went into a state of severe depression.'

'Yes, a terrible time for her. What are you suggesting that years later she leapt off the waterfall?'

'It's a possibility.'

'Mary Dawson saw Mrs Wilcox at the Mill Pool on the day of the murder.' MJ flipped his file open.

'I've read that a few times. There is no mention of Mrs Wilcox or any other names.'

'No, but she told her husband it was Wilcox, before she died.'

'Can you substantiate that?'

'Mr Ferguson told Laura.'

'I see and you believe her. Just her word, then. I wonder what Laura Dawson has got against Wilcox.' She walked behind DC Davis's desk and studied the incident boards. 'Looks like Diane Wilcox visited Mary on the afternoon before she died. Odd.'

'Odd?' said MJ, and he came over to the board. 'What's wrong with visiting a sick and dying relative?'

'It was only the once in six months, and the day after her mother-in-law visited.'

MJ took a red marker and wrote in large letters: Wilcox–bull accident, then added Mary at the hospital–Wilcox. He wrote Mill Pool–Wilcox and drew lines and arrows to link each incident.

DS Mycroft grabbed the marker from him. 'Okay, enough, what's the motive?'

MJ flipped through the case files on the desk. 'Look, they identified no one from the third blood sample. During the investigation, the DNA samples collected were only from men. Maybe we should look for a woman.'

'You mean, Diane Wilcox.' DS Mycroft consulted a notepad and her list of names. 'Oakwood Farm. I'll get help from the uniform section and a car. At least we can eliminate her if nothing else.'

MJ picked up his briefcase and the folder. He started to put it away when DS Mycroft grabbed it and placed it with the others. She wagged her finger at him.

'I'll come with you,' he said.

'No, I think not.'

'Come on, Fiona, it's my case.'

'It was your case. Okay, come on, you can be an observer. Just say nothing. We'll bring her in to the station and get a DNA sample.'

It took forty-five minutes to organise a car and the help from the uniformed section. In the meantime, MJ grabbed a Cornish pastry and a coffee from the canteen. He added extra sugar and a pinch of salt to dilute the stale bitterness. The free coffee was a perk he did not miss since retirement or the noisy scrape of chairs on the hardwood floor or the loud banter across the tables. He would have preferred a Marston beer than suffer this awful gut destroying canteen coffee. He did not enjoy drinking it, but it was hot, wet, and addictive.

§

DS Mycroft drove the unmarked Mondeo and followed the police Vauxhall Vector out of Marston and through Kirkindale.

MJ sat in the passenger seat and shifted his briefcase from his lap to the floor and then back again.

'For goodness' sake! What's the matter?' said DS Mycroft. 'What do you keep in there anyhow? You better not have any of my files.'

'It's empty,' he said. 'I don't know why I brought it along.' On an impulse, he had taken his old notebook from the main file as a keepsake. No one should notice. He would frame it and hang it in his toilet at home. He should have left them in the main folder until the case was closed, too late.

They had found the skeleton of Mrs Irene Dawson and had a suspect for the murder of Sophia Dawson. He punched the air and felt like cheering.

DS Mycroft laughed at his exuberant gesture. 'Too soon, you were wrong before.'

The police car turned off the road, past a cottage, and onto a side lane leading up towards Oakwood Farm.

A woman ran around the bend in the track towards them, and a Land Rover raced behind her. Its driver saw the police vehicle and swerved to avoid a collision but was too late. It scraped along the Vauxhall's side, crashed through the hedge, and rolled over into the field.

'That's Laura Dawson,' said MJ.

Mycroft braked hard and stopped her car inches from the police vehicle in front.

MJ got out and shouted, 'Laura over here. What the hell is going on?'

Laura ignored him and went to the gap in the hedge. The policeman from the Vauxhall was already running into the field and was being followed by a policewoman. They both sprinted towards the upturned vehicle.

Edward crawled out through the driver's door and stood up. He shook off the broken glass and turned towards the police officers. Blood covered his face and his nose appeared broken. He staggered and then attempted to run towards the farm. The policeman caught hold of his arm and led him back to the lane. The policewoman called for an ambulance on the vehicle radio.

'What's going on, Laura?' said MJ.

Laura was gasping for breath. 'Look it's my teddy. Diane found it at the pool. She was there. She saw what happened. She said it was an accident. She stole my diary look, but I don't—'

'Whoa! Wait a minute, slow down. One thing at a time,' interrupted MJ.

'No MJ,' said DS Mycroft. 'Miss Dawson, it's best if you come to the station.' She took hold of Laura's arm and led her to the Mondeo. 'You can tell us all about it there.' She opened the car door. 'Please miss, in you go.' She waved to the policewoman who came and got into the rear of the car with Laura.

'McNally,' shouted DS Mycroft to the police officer. 'You wait with the gentleman for the ambulance, we are going up to the farm.' She got into the car and lowered the driver's side window. 'Oh, McNally make sure you get a statement, who, what, why and all that stuff.'

'John knows what to do, mam,' said the policewoman from the rear seat.

Mycroft ignored her and drove the Mondeo around the police vehicle and up the lane to Oakwood Farm.

'Bag that teddy and the book,' Mycroft said to MJ. 'There are evidence bags in the glove box.'

They drove into the farmyard and saw Margaret by the kitchen door; the dog sat by her side.

'Miss Dawson, please wait in the car,' said Mycroft, and she nodded to the policewoman. 'You come with me.' She opened her door.

MJ got out of the car and DS Mycroft shook her hand towards him.

'MJ, you stay in the car with Miss Dawson,' Mycroft said. She walked towards the farmhouse and looked back over her shoulder to make sure MJ was not following.

'Well, what's happening, Laura?' said MJ. He turned in the front seat to face her. 'I told you to stay away.'

'Diane wouldn't admit she was there, but Edward said it was an accident.'

'Edward?'

'Her husband, he knows. You should ask him.'

'What do you think happened?'

'I think Diane was there, I think she knows who killed my grandmother.'

'Did she say why?' MJ passed a tissue to Laura.

'Me, I am a lie.' She wiped her nose.

There was a gunshot from inside the house.

'Laura, you stay here!' MJ shouted. He got out the car and ran towards the kitchen door.

DS Mycroft came out the house with the shotgun. 'It's okay, it's okay,' she said and went to the rear of the car. She put the shotgun into the boot. 'Damn woman.'

'What's going on?' said MJ. 'Is anyone injured?'

'That bloody woman threatened to kill me.' She closed the car boot. 'Stay here with Miss Dawson. We won't be long. I've already telephoned for another car.'

'Is anyone hurt?'

'No. The younger woman is upstairs, fast asleep. Drunk or medicated or both.' DS Mycroft pointed towards Laura. 'What has she said? No, forget that. I'll get a formal statement from her at the station.'

Chapter Thirty-six

Daphne tapped her paintbrush on the garden table, and in her other hand she held a cup of mint and nettle tea. She looked at Laura. 'I'm waiting,' she said.

Laura shrugged. What could she say? She yawned, it had been a long night in the police station.

In the interview room, DC Davis had asked her if she knew why someone murdered Mr Scott Ferguson. She panicked and dropped her plastic cup; the water spilled over the table and dripped onto the floor. DC Davis had smirked at her reaction.

'Here,' said Daphne as she passed a tissue. 'It'll work itself out, you'll see, you have done nothing wrong.' She reached over and held Laura's hand. 'Have you?'

'No.'

'I have never been so angry in my life. Bloody police tramping through my garden,' said Daphne.

The police had spent the morning searching through Weir Cottage with particular attention to Daphne's collection of dried herbs and the fresh varieties growing in the garden.

She poured her tea onto the grass. 'I need a proper drink.' She went into the house and returned with a bottle of blackberry wine and two glasses.

'Not for me,' said Laura.

Daphne sat at the table and filled both glasses with wine. 'What have you done?' She drank back and finished the dark liquid from one glass. 'Come on Laura, what have you done? Police don't come searching for nothing.'

'Daphne, I'm sorry, but it has nothing to do with me.'

'Oh, they come banging on the door every day then.' She snorted. 'Yes, it has something to do with you.'

'Someone murdered my mum. What do you expect?'

'Yes. Oh, Laura, I'm sorry,' she said and grabbed Laura's hand. 'I'm just all wound up.'

'They suggested I might have poisoned Scott.'

'Bloody idiots. So that's what they were looking for, poison. They should have asked.' She laughed. 'The woods are full of Satan's angels, if you know what you're doing.'

Laura stared at Daphne. 'Satan's angels?' she said.

'Oh, don't worry.' She refilled her empty glass. 'This is lovely, sure you don't want to try it?'

They watched a car stop by the garden gate and MJ got out. He waved.

'What now,' said Daphne. 'Do you know him?'

'Yes,' said Laura, 'he's been helping me. He's a retired policeman.'

'Police, I've had enough,' she said. 'I'll be in my studio. Let me know when he's gone.' She picked up the bottle and strolled into the house.

MJ sauntered across the garden and sat on the bench next to Laura. He looked at the full glass of blackberry wine.

'It's Daphne's,' said Laura.

'How are you?' he said and lifted his briefcase onto the table. 'I've news.'

'Does that detective think I poisoned Scott?'

'DC Davis. No, I don't think so. He was being thorough.' He smiled. 'He is meticulous to a point of being annoying.'

'I'll make tea, or coffee?'

'Yes, a coffee would be nice.'

They sat discussing the case for over an hour, and MJ promised to update her before she left Marston.

Her knees shook as she watched him drive away. She came to Kirkindale to find her mum and family. What a mess.

MJ's involvement in the murder investigation was over and it satisfied him that the case, the one he had never solved, was near its conclusion. It was a cloud of professional incompetence that had tormented him and, at last, he could clear the shame from his mind. MJ had said that he planned to leave Marston. There was no reason to stay since the murder case was resolved; he had done his duty.

He had been itching for years to move south to Dorset, where his father had left him a cottage on the coast. It required renovation, and he looked forward to the challenge. Also, he had convinced Christine to take early retirement, and she looked forward to walking along the Jurassic beaches. He had suggested Laura should come for a visit and stay for a few days next summer.

The bitter taste of the blackberry wine lingered in her mouth; it was a flavour she would never get used to.

Did Mrs McLean know the truth and over the years was she protecting her from this terrible lie? What a mess.

She went into the kitchen and made a fresh pot of tea, which she took to the studio. Daphne sat by her easel and listened as Laura told her the details.

From the stains on Numpty, the forensics laboratory extracted DNA samples which matched those of Diane Wilcox, and both Irene and Sophia Dawson. The third blood sample identified that Diane Wilcox was present at the Mill Pool when Sophia Dawson was murdered. However, she denied any involvement.

The analysis of dried blood and skin flakes from under the fingernails of Irene Dawson's skeleton matched Diane Wilcox's DNA. The forensic team sent those samples to a specialist laboratory in Abingdon for confirmation. DS Mycroft was certain the results would verify that Mrs Wilcox was present at the Mill Pool.

The forensic team tested a bottle of liquid found in Mrs Margaret Wilcox's kitchen. It contained the identical toxin identified in both Mrs Mary and Mr Scott Ferguson's post-mortem reports. The forensic team substantiated the source of the poison was the hemlock plants grown in the garden at the Oakwood Farm cottage. DS Mycroft had charged Mrs Margaret Wilcox with murder.

Laura had felt a cold sweat run down her back when MJ went through these details. She had been in Great Aunt Margaret's kitchen. Had she poisoned the tea?

The forensic investigation and DNA analysis of the genotype from the samples from the relatives, Daphne Lister, Laura Dawson, and those received from the records of Jean Stewart confirmed the skeleton taken from the Mill Pool cavity was the remains of Irene Dawson.

She had cried as MJ spoke. If only he would stop repeating her mum's name, it was Mum.

Before he left, he had given her an envelope and asked her to prepare for a shock. The laboratory had been thorough in their analysis of all the samples in relation to the case. She read the information on the sheet from the envelope and felt the blood drain down her neck. Was this true? It can't be true. She read the results again. MJ helped her to recover from her semi-faint by pushing her head down below the level of her knees. She had grabbed the glass of wine and took a large gulp.

MJ was sorry, but she had to know, and yes, the results were genuine.

She wanted to scream; she had thrown the glass across the lawn. This was awful. Her grandfather, Mr Charles Dawson, was her biological father!

Chapter Thirty-seven

Laura sat by the Mill Pool. This was the last place she saw her mother but cannot remember what her last words were.

'Goodbye Mum, I am leaving today,' she said. 'I forgive you.'

She saw a fox on the far bank of the river; it sniffed the air and searched along the water's edge. It stopped for a moment and stared at her and gave a long yawn. It turned and wandered into the woods between the trees until Laura's glimpses of its red fur gradually disappeared from view as it pushed through the thicket of undergrowth.

'What happened, Mum?' she said. 'Was it my fault?'

She knew Old Charlie thought it was for the best to send her away to a foster family. Still, they abandoned her as if she didn't matter; that was not true, her mum loved her. She was Laura Dawson, and her mother was a gifted artist and a wonderful person.

Last night, she had telephoned Jenny, who dramatically giggled with frantic delight at her news; she would be home by the end of the week. Gertrude had snatched the handset and sounded tearful. She promised to come with the car to bring her home.

She picked a daisy and counted off the petals; he loves me not. She wandered around the large rock a few times, brushing it with her hand. By the wall, she climbed over the stile and took the path to the top of the falls and the memorial site.

She had organised a stonemason to engrave a granite stone with her mother's details and had it placed beside her grandmother's. She brushed off the leaves from the fresh flower bed and tied up a loose rose branch.

The bench felt warm where she sat, and she squinted in the sunlight to look down into the valley. This was the exact spot where her mother came and had painted her landscapes, and where the backdrop of fir trees provided shelter from the westerly wind. This is where Mum now rests; so peaceful at last.

In the far distance in the valley, she saw a man with his dog rounding up a herd of sheep, and she recognised the outline of a Pickup parked nearby.

Why had it come to this? Her grandfather had sent her away as an act of kindness, but he wanted only to remove his responsibility and guilt. He was her biological father, and he knew she was his daughter. She tensed her body and a sense of numbness engulfed her mind; she had been a horrible mistake.

Her birth showed without a doubt that her mother had been impregnated, as the justice system called it, either with or without consent. The crown prosecution services determined there was insufficient evidence to confirm without a doubt that Mr Charles Dawson raped Irene Dawson. They advised against bringing the case to court. Therefore, she would confront Old Charlie before she left Kirkindale to resolve the truth and understand why. Could she really have the mental strength to go through with her plan?

Her mother had not abandoned her. It was a revelation that brought a flood of emotional relief shuddering through her body.

Mum was a kind and beautiful person, with a forgiving nature. She was not the brutal murderer as portrayed by everyone in Kirkindale. How could they believe this artistic and cheerful person would kill her child's grandmother? Perhaps, they accepted the suppositions of her guilt and preferred the myth of a fugitive than accept the possibility of the evil perpetrator living among them in their respected, trusted, and close community.

Margaret and Edward had lived with the horror of knowing what Diane had done, but for how long could they have kept the secret? Poor Diane, yes, she felt sorry for her and she hated her. Diane will get help after the psychiatric assessment and before the prosecution services will charge her with murder. Was it really an accident or was it uncontrollable demented rage that drove Diane to kill?

They charged Great Aunt Margaret with various offences, obstruction of justice and the manufacture and supply of a poisonous substance being two among others. They considered Edward as a key witness for the prosecution and did not hold him in custody. He had admitted obstructing the course of justice and burying the body of Irene Dawson in the sluice. Laura wanted them sent to prison for their part in the cover up and support for Diane. Are family loyalties stronger than justice among the people you love?

During the last few weeks, the weather had warmed and a dry spell had reduced the river flow to a trickle over the waterfall. She heard something splash in the pool below and some laughter. She stood and looked over the edge and saw Anne and Tommy throwing skipping stones across the water. They bumped into each other and walked away hand in hand down the path towards the village. Life looked as if it was back to normal, whatever that was. Will Joe be fast asleep on the riverbank while the fish nibbled the bait off his angling hooks?

MJ and Christine will be on their way to Dorset to retirement in his cottage by the coast. His connection to Marston and a guilty sense of failure was over. He had finally seen the murder at the Mill Pool resolved. She had laughed when they said goodbye. No, he had said, he won't miss the Farmers' Jug with its Marston beer, instead he was looking forward to a decent pint of Badger's Bitter.

'Hello, Laura.'

She turned and saw Old Charlie with a shotgun over his arm, and his collie by his side. His flat cap sat on the back on his head. He was smiling. He was smiling! The same man she saw stumbling in the mist on her first morning at Russet House.

'You came.'

'Aye,' he said. 'I don't think we have much to say.' He lifted his Beretta shotgun and pointed it in the air. His collie dog shuffled on the ground beside him.

'I suspect not.' She touched the Bowie knife tucked in her waistband beneath her T-shirt. 'There is only one thing I need to know. The truth.' She tapped the bench with her hand.

Old Charlie opened the Beretta, removed the cartridges, and pushed them into the pocket of his dungarees. He laid the gun on the grass and sat on the bench.

'Crows are pulling up the barley down in the meadow,' he said. 'There must be some beetle grubs, and I'll check later.'

She stood up and strode around in front of the bench. She took deep breaths and struggled to find a composed way to broach the subject. What did she want? Make him admit what he did, to say sorry, to make amends. She hated him.

'Did you rape my mother?'

'Your mother was a beautiful person.' He leaned forward with his elbows on his knees and head in his hands. 'I'm sorry you believe—'

'Sorry! Is that it?'

'Yes, I am sorry that I believed Irene had killed Sophia.' He looked up. 'You must let the past rest. There is enough damage, justice has been done.'

She dashed over to him and punched him and kept up a torrent of blows. He rolled off the bench, got up and pushed her away.

The dog leapt in between them and barked.

She tripped and fell over. She scrambled to her feet and drew the Bowie knife from her waistband. She pointed the blade towards him. She snarled, tears streamed down her face. Her knuckles turned white as her fingers tightened around the hilt of the knife.

'Laura, don't.' He stepped forward, kicked out at her legs, slapped her face, grabbed her arm. She dropped the knife.

'Now sit down,' he shouted and pushed her onto the bench. 'Sorry, do you want me to say sorry? Sorry that Sophia lost baby Robert. Sorry that I was in love with your mum, yes I am sorry.' He picked up the Bowie knife and stabbed it into the ground next to his shotgun.

'I don't believe you,' she said through gritted teeth. She wiped the blood from her nose with the back of her hand.

'I was wrong, you must understand. She came here almost every day and I would come by. We talked, we laughed. She was wonderful.'

'Not true, you tried to steal the house.'

'Not then, no. I went too far, we promised never again. Then you came along.'

'What about William, did he know?'

'No. He would believe Irene, it was for the best.' He walked over to the memorial stones. 'To think a baby would end their lives.'

Laura took a bottle of water from her daypack and washed her face with a paper tissue. 'You raped my mother, I don't care what you say.'

He turned to face her. 'What do you want?'

'Oh, rot in hell,' she shouted.

'You are a snivelling little bitch. You are nothing like your mother.'

She jerked back on the bench and stared at him, at the face from her nightmares.

'Life goes on Laura, you have the house—'

'I am not living here,' she interrupted. 'No, no, I am not living here.'

'No, you're not wanted here,' he said and retrieved his hat. 'It will sell and when I am finished, the farm will sell. Can you accept that as amends?'

'So, you admit it, you raped my mother.'

Old Charlie picked up his shotgun and loaded it with cartridges.

'I'll keep this.' He pulled the knife out of the ground. 'There will be no more killing. Enough is enough, Laura. You have a chance of a wonderful life.' He pointed at her. 'Don't waste your life,' he shouted. 'Because stupidity is full of regrets.'

He strode along the path to the wall and climbed over into the field where he walked on to Springfield Farm. The collie ran in front of him.

She stood by the wall and watched him. She came to Kirkindale to find Mum and her family. She had found her father, but she would never call him Dad. She hated him.

The sky larks were singing, and she searched the sky but couldn't see them against the rolling puffs of cumulus clouds. She closed her eyes and lifted her face to the sun's warmth.

It was over. She walked across the dry riverbed to where the water trickled down the cliff into the pool fifty feet below. She stared at the valley, the same view in Mum's landscape paintings. With a tissue, she wiped away the tears and blew her nose. This should have been her home. What sort of life would it have been?

The wretched feeling of not knowing, of being unwanted and abandoned by her mother and why she had never contacted her, pulsated through her mind.

Now she knew, but the pain of the truth was worse than she had expected. Tears tumbled and trickled down her cheeks, and she stared at the inky surface of the Mill Pool. How could such a beautiful place be associated with evil?

A cloud veiled the sun; a breeze rustled through the wood and around the pool. She saw two women in the bull-reeds; their faces were bread white, and on their coal black hair they wore rings of daisy flowers.

'Hello,' shouted Laura and a chill rippled down her spine. The strangers smiled and turned away through the reeds. 'Wait, who are you?' she called and leaned forward. The women held the hands of a small boy who looked back at her and grinned. They pushed into the thick of the reeds and out of sight.

Laura leaned forward and slipped on a wet rock. She grabbed at a jutted piece of sandstone and stopped herself from falling over the cliff. Her feet dangled over the precipice. She clung onto the rock as adrenaline pumped through her veins; she hugged the cliff edge and took a deep breath. She waited a moment, then she crawled up onto the safety of the sand and gravel.

She had to leave, Jenny and Gertrude promised to be at the Weir Cottage by late afternoon.

Yes, it was time to go; the past had been expunged, and she had found Mum.

She followed the old path back to Russet House and wandered around the garden to the chestnut trees. One day she will push her children on a swing, but not here, and they will sing along, just as she had done with Aunt Mary.

Swinging high and swinging low.
Up in the tree, away we go.
Here the birdies nest.
And play all day.
And their world is bright and gay.
Swinging high and swinging low.

She would spend time with her children, one day, sitting on a rug in a garden, and they would enjoy strawberries and ice cream.

She walked around to the front of the house and kicked the porcelain sign by the door; Orchard House. She took a stone and smashed at the sign until it lay in pieces. No, she would never live here.

Strands of a police incident tape hung on the garage door and flapped in the wind, and the crunch of the gravel echoed as she lingered up the drive to the lane. She walked towards the road to catch the bus to Marston. She slowed, hesitated, and then stopped. She looked back up the track to the farmhouse. A faint column of smoke drifted from its chimney.

She could not leave like this. She hated him for what he had done and hated him more for what he had not done.

He was the origin of her identity, and she was somebody.

The years of anguish and bitterness could not continue; she was not a fraud. She had a history; she was somebody and wanted peace.

She adjusted the straps of her daypack and strode up the rutted farm track to Springfield Farm.

www.ingramcontent.com/pod-product-compliance
Ingram Content Group UK Ltd.
Pitfield, Milton Keynes, MK11 3LW, UK
UKHW021036270726
13967UKWH00013B/2695

9 781913 202002